Carla Kelly started writing Regency romances because of her interest in the Napoleonic Wars. She enjoys writing about warfare at sea and the ordinary people of the British Isles rather than lords and ladies. In her spare time she reads British crime fiction and history—particularly books about the US Indian Wars. Carla lives in Utah and is a former park ranger and double RITA® Award and Spur Award winner. She has five children and four grandchildren.

Louise Allen loves immersing herself in history. She finds landscapes and places evoke the past powerfully. Venice, Burgundy and the Greek islands are favourite destinations. Louise lives on the Norfolk coast and spends her spare time gardening, researching family history or travelling in search of inspiration. Visit her at louiseallenregency.co.uk, @LouiseRegency and janeaustenslondon.com.

Laurie Benson is an award-winning Regency romance author, whose book *An Unexpected Countess* was voted Harlequin's 2017 'Hero of the Year' by readers. She began her writing career as an advertising copywriter. When she isn't at her laptop, avoiding laundry, Laurie can be found browsing antiques shops and going on long hikes with her husband and two sons. Learn more about Laurie by visiting her website at lauriebenson.net. You can also find her on Twitter and Facebook.

CONVENIENT CHRISTMAS BRIDES

Carla Kelly
Louise Allen
Laurie Benson

MIX
Paper from
responsible sources
FSC
FSC C007454

This book is produced from independently certified FSC™ paper
to ensure responsible forest management.

For more information visit www.harpercollins.co.uk/green

MILLS & BOON

First Published in Great Britain 2018
by Mills & Boon, an imprint of HarperCollins*Publishers*
1 London Bridge Street, London, SE1 9GF

CONVENIENT CHRISTMAS BRIDES

© 2018 Harlequin Books S.A.

ISBN: 978-0-263-93317-8

by CPI, Barcelona

CONTENTS

THE CAPTAIN'S CHRISTMAS JOURNEY   7
Carla Kelly

THE VISCOUNT'S YULETIDE BETROTHAL   143
Louise Allen

ONE NIGHT UNDER THE MISTLETOE   257
Laurie Benson

THE CAPTAIN'S
CHRISTMAS JOURNEY

Carla Kelly

To my parents.

Chapter One

'Buck up, Captain Everard,' he told his reflection in the mirror. 'You promised you would do this, so to Kent you will go.'

Joseph Everard, post captain, Royal Navy, turned around to stare hard at Lieutenant David Newsome's paltry heap of personal effects on his desk, wishing he could make it go away. It remained there unmovable, another sad testament to the fleet action now called Trafalgar. That one word was enough to convey all the horror, the pounding and the fire, which combined to create the most bittersweet of victories, with the well-nigh inconceivable loss of Vice Admiral Sir Horatio Nelson.

Had anyone been interested, Joe could have explained his reluctance to deliver David's effects in person. It wasn't because his second luff had done anything amiss, or behaved in any way unbecoming an officer and a gentleman. True, he was young, but weren't we all, at some point?

Joe had done this sad duty many times before, whenever possible. He should have been inured to the tears, the sadness and the resentment, even, when a mother, father or wife had stared daggers at him, as if he was the author of their misery, and not Napoleon. Left to his own devices, Joe Everard would happily have served King and country patrolling the seven seas and engaging in no fleet actions whatsoever. He had never required a major, lengthy war to prove his manhood.

They were all puppets in the hands of Napoleon. Now that war had resumed, after the brief Peace of Amiens, Joe saw no shortcut to victory for years.

Something worse explained his reluctance for this distasteful duty, something Lord St Vincent, or as he had been then, Captain John Jervis, had described one night.

They had come off victorious in some fleet action or other—they tended to blur together—and Captain Jervis and his men were moping about in the wardroom. The wounded were tended and quiet, and the pumps in the bowels of the ship had finished their noisy job.

'Look at us,' Captain Jervis had remarked to his first lieutenant, an unfortunate fellow who died the following year at Camperdown. 'There is nothing quite as daunting as the lethargy that victory brings.'

No doubt. Trafalgar, a victory as huge as anyone in the Royal Navy could ask for, dumped a full load of melancholy on Joe Everard's usually capable shoulders. Why one man should die and another should not was a mystery for the ages, and not a trifling question for a mere post captain who had done his duty, as had every man aboard the HMS *Ulysses*, a forty-eight-gun frigate. He and his crew of well-trained stalwarts had babied the *Ulysses* through the storm the next day, limped into Torbay and remained there waiting a final diagnosis from the overworked shipwrights.

He and his officers had travelled from Torbay to Plymouth to sit in the Drake and drink. They talked, played whist and cursed the French until they were silent, spent and remarkably hung over. Joe couldn't release anyone to return home to wives, but the wives could come to Plymouth.

More power to you, he thought, as he had listened to bedsprings creaking rhythmically and wished he had found the leisure, or perhaps the courage, to marry.

After a week, the verdict was a month to refurbish and repair in the Torquay docks. He released his officers to their homes for three weeks and cautiously gave his crew the glad tidings, wary that some might not return and truth to tell, hardly blaming them if they did not. His sailing master, a widower with children in Canada, had no objection to staying in Torquay for the repairs. Such a kindness gave Captain Joseph Everard no excuse to avoid the condolence visit to Weltby, Kent, where Second Lieutenant Newsome's parents and one spinster sister resided.

Since England apparently still expected every

man to do his duty, Joe sent a note to Augustus Newsome, explaining the reason for his visit and hoping he would not upset the family by returning their son's belongings in person. He added a postscript stating when he could be expected in Weltby.

He chose to take the mail coach from Plymouth to Weltby, mainly because he enjoyed the sight of ordinary folk going about their business, almost as if the war raging at sea was happening on Mars. He could listen to idle chat and observe people not poised on the edge of danger possessed with that peculiar thin-faced, sharp-featured look that all men at war seemed to wear as a badge of office.

He hadn't reckoned on the power of Trafalgar. Joe never thought of himself as a forbidding fellow, but truth to tell, an ordinary ride on the mail coach would have been a silent one. Maybe he did look like a man who had no wish to talk. God knows he had frightened a decade's worth of midshipmen.

But Trafalgar had loosened people's tongues and heightened their curiosity. If the spirits of the deceased hung around for a while, as Shakespeare claimed they did in *Romeo and Juliet*, Joe had to imagine Admiral Nelson would have enjoyed the praise heaped on him by England's ordinary citizens.

Joe thought he might be troubled to talk about the battle recently waged that was still giving him sweating nightmares in December, but he wasn't. The other wayfarers were genuinely interested in the contest of the British fleet against the combined forces of France and Spain.

They even wanted him to explain his ship's role, which also surprised him, because the newspapers had sung the praises—well deserved—of *Mars*, *Victory*, *Agamemnon* and *Ajax*, ships of the line with stunning firepower.

But, no, they had questions about the service of the battle's four frigates and *he* was flattered enough to explain the frigates' role as repeaters on such a roiling scene, with smoke obscuring battle signals. 'We read the flags and passed on the messages, where we could,' he said. 'It meant moving about and coming in close so other ships of war could read Nelson's flags.'

It sounded simple enough, but the reality was timing movements and darting about to avoid obliteration, which nearly came when the French *Achilles*'s powder magazine exploded and rained fire on the deck of the much smaller *Ulysses*. That was when David Newsome died, struck by a flaming mast. Joe paused in his narration and bowed his head, which gave the old lady next to him silent permission to hold his hand, the first such gesture he had felt in years. No one ever touched the captain.

'It was a battle never to be forgotten,' he said, when he could speak. 'Our foe fought valiantly, especially the Spanish, but I do not think Boney will beat us now.'

The old lady still held his hand and Joe didn't

mind. 'Then hurrah, Captain,' she said quietly. The other travellers nodded.

When she did release his hand, she looked with sympathy at his face. 'Does it hurt?' she asked.

Joe touched the plaster on his cheek that covered black stitches from a splinter that missed his eye by a quarter-inch. 'A little,' he said. 'My Trafalgar souvenir.'

She rummaged in the bag at her feet and drew out a ceramic jar. 'Goose grease,' she said. 'Rub it in at night. Won't scar so bad.' She smiled at him. 'A handsome fellow like you doesn't need a reminder of battle, does he?'

He took it with thanks and turned predictably red, grateful none of his officers was there to chuckle at their captain. 'It's not as though I could forget, ma'am, but if you say it will prevent scarring, I believe you.'

He wondered if a traveller would comment upon his mail-coach journey, since they seemed to be settling into a certain camaraderie he found endearing. Sure enough, a little boy posed the question, curious why he was in a mail coach. Didn't the Royal Navy pay better than that?

The child's embarrassed mother tried to shush her son, but Joe laughed. Since they were all so plain spoken and kind, he felt no distance from them.

'It's this way…your name…'

'Tommy Ledbetter,' the boy announced. 'I am five.'

'Tommy, I like to travel by mail coach,' he

said. 'I like to sit here and watch people like you going about your business in an England I hardly ever am privileged to see, as I serve on the ocean.'

Tommy looked around. 'We're not much,' he said, which made the vicar sitting next to the boy smile and the old lady chuckle.

'You're England,' Joe said. 'That's enough for me.'

Chapter Two

'**W**hen will the mail coach arrive, Verity?' Mama asked for the tenth time since luncheon. 'I hope he does not expect too much from us.'

'Mama, I am certain he will do what is proper, in such circumstances,' Verity soothed.

'Does he have any idea how much we are suffering?' Mama asked in a voice close to a whine, but not quite.

Verity knew herself to be practical, a trait she had acquired from her father. Still, it was a good question and she knew her mother was in pain from the loss of Davey; they all were.

'I expect Captain Everard has a considerable idea of suffering, Mama,' she replied. 'Quite possibly he does this sad duty often. I imagine it takes a toll on him, too.'

She could tell her mother had never considered this angle of mourning, so consumed had she been with her own loss of a beloved son in October. Perhaps the workings of time on even the most tragic of events would spread its unique balm. Verity could hope, anyway, because she suffered, too.

Verity had suffered another loss not long after Trafalgar, one that ranked low, compared to Davey's death, but which caused her anxiety of another sort. Barely had they digested the news of his death when Lord Blankenship, the marquis who employed her father as his estate manager, had informed her that her services were no longer required as teacher in the entirely satisfactory school where she had educated tenant children, much to her delight and their gain.

Lord Blankenship, a kind enough fellow, had hurried to assure her that he did not question her abilities. The issue was a personal one. He informed her that an impoverished relative had petitioned him for employment, because the creditors were circling his wounded finances like wolves and all was not well.

'He claims he can teach and blood is still thicker than water,' Lord Blankenship said. 'I had my secretary write this morning that I will employ him in your position, starting after Yuletide. I will give you a small supplement and any sort of reference you could wish, Miss Newsome. I trust you will understand.'

What could she do but assure him she understood? Because he seemed to expect it, she also pasted a pleasant smile on her lips and told him not to worry about her. He left her classroom relieved and justified; she seethed inside, angry because the world was not a fair place for ladies.

Her father had taken her dismissal with remarkable calm; her mother, in agony over Davey's death, heard her not at all. Mama did question her two weeks later, when Verity stayed home from what would have been a school day. When Verity told her again, Mama patted her hand. 'You can mourn here with me, Daughter,' she said. 'Besides, you do not need to earn your bread. Papa is able to provide, as long as he is alive.'

After then, what? she wanted to ask her parents. Papa earned a modest living that had sufficed, probably because for all of Mama's flyaway airs, she had a remarkable ability to rein in expenses. The Newsome household probably even resembled the taut ship that Davey, in letters home, said Captain Everard ran.

Now Davey was dead, a promising career gone. In the course of things, he likely would have married and set up his own household, which, he had assured her, would always have room for his only sibling, should she never marry, as seemed the case now.

As she waited for Captain Everard's arrival on that late December day, Verity chafed on several accounts. The death of her brother had rendered her as sorrowful as her parents, who mourned their son and comforted each other. She mourned her brother feeling much more alone, sorry for his passing above all, but sad that his death had diminished her own future.

The matter seemed dismal beyond belief, but for her parents' sake, she stifled her emotion; they had enough to worry about. David Newsome, as bright and promising a lad as anyone in Weltby had known, had been consigned to the deep off the coast of Spain, fish food and out of reach. She also stifled her unreasonable anger that Admiral Nelson's body had been returned to England in a keg of spirits, to be buried in the coming January with high honours in St Paul's Cathedral. Everyone else was slid off a board into the sea. There was no grave where Mama could plant flowers.

I want what I cannot have, Verity thought, as she went to the sitting room, the better for her to spot a post chaise pull up and deposit a captain with a box of all that remained of David Newsome, Second Lieutenant, late of the HMS *Ulysses*.

Papa had said they could offer the captain a bed for the night and so they would. Perhaps he could tell them something of Davey at sea, before her dear brother faded from everyone's memory except the memories of the three people who had loved him best.

She forced her unproductive thoughts to the sitting room, which had been decorated for Christmas with only a modest wreath over the fireplace. Mama had decided that ivy garlands on the banister in the hall were too much this year. Verity *had* waged a polite battle with her mother that resulted in the removal of the black wreath from the front door. The thing had grown more distasteful by the hour to Verity.

Braced for Mama's tears, she had removed the odious wreath and thrown it in the compost heap. To her relief Mama only nodded, sniffed into her ever-present handkerchief, and let the matter rest. Verity wondered if she dared search for ivy, because the banister cried out for it.

Any day now, she knew she had to take some interest in her wardrobe, considering that, following Christmas, she was to show herself at Hipworth Hall near Sudbury in Norfolk. Relief expressed on his homely face, Lord Blankenship had announced that he had found her employment as an educationist to Sir Percy Hipworth's children. Lord B. had informed her that Sir Percy was a baronet of some pretension, but nevertheless a 'good fellow, once his bluster is stripped away'. His offhand remark that the Hipworth children were no better or worse than you might expect did not ease Verity's mind.

The promised salary was adequate, but only just, and Sir Percy's letter had also included passage on the mail coach. 'He says he will have a dogcart there in Sudbury for you, which I consider a good beginning,' Lord Blankenship had told her.

To Verity it seemed like the barest of courtesies. Had her future employer expected her to walk with her baggage to wherever Hipworth Hall found itself? Suppose it was raining or sleeting?

Verity Newsome, you are feeling sorry for yourself, she scolded. Positions of any kind for ladies of a certain age—*hang it all, you are nearly thirty*—didn't spring forth unbidden from the brow of Zeus. True, she could remain at home in idleness, but that had even less appeal to a capable woman. To Norfolk she would go.

Dusk was fast approaching. She told her worries to go on holiday until she felt more inclined to deal with them and returned her attention to the window.

And there he was. Not for ordinary mortals was the bicorn of a post captain, which made the man walking up the lane with a swinging stride appear considerably taller than he likely was. He wore a dark cloak and had slung a duffel on his shoulder. She smiled because he looked like a man home from the sea and maybe not too happy about it.

The smile left her face. He carried a smaller grip, one she recognised. Davey Newsome had come home, too.

Chapter Three

Joseph Everard raised his hand to knock, but the door opened before he needed to. He found himself looking at an older female version of his second luff, down to lively eyes and curly black hair.

'You bear a remarkable resemblance to your brother,' were the first words out of his mouth. He could have smacked his forehead for his idiocy when those brown eyes, so like Davey's, filled with tears.

'I'm sorry. That was clumsy of me,' he said. 'I am Captain Everard of the White Fleet, your late brother's commanding officer. May I come inside?'

'Of course you may,' the woman said quickly. 'How clumsy of me! You'll think we never have visitors.'

'Not at all, Miss… Miss Newsome, is it?' he asked. 'I didn't actually arrive in a coach and four with post boys, did I? I like to take the mail coach and so I walked from Weltby.'

She ushered him inside, let him unsling his duffel like the common seaman he suddenly felt himself to be, then helped him from his boat cloak. With a start, he realised he was being organised by a woman used to management and, by God, it felt surprisingly good. With the heavy cloak slung over her arm, she handed it to a maid who had stopped at the sight of so much naval splendour, here in quiet Kent.

Or maybe it was the crosshatch of black stitches that still ruined whatever looks he had imagined were his. He had taken off the blamed plaster in hope that the air might prove more useful to its healing. He might even apply goose grease tonight as he prepared for bed back at the inn.

'Your hat, Captain?' Miss Newsome said and held out her hand.

He doffed it and gave it to her, hoping that his hair wasn't sticking up on the side. He had never given his wretched cowlick much thought before, but for some reason, it mattered, standing in the hall of David Newsome's childhood home. At least he had the good sense not to lick his fingers and try to tame the thing. Certainly there were worse physical afflictions.

His bicorn overwhelmed the maid, who gave him a plaintive look. 'Just rest it on its side,' he told her. 'It won't bite.'

The girl grinned at him and darted away, in spite of the fact that his boat cloak threatened to trip her.

'I…er…assume you don't see too many navy

men in Weltby,' he said, wishing he knew more about polite conversation. 'At least the servants don't.'

'No, indeed, Captain Everard,' Miss Newsome said, her eyes on his stitches. 'A Trafalgar souvenir?'

Joe knew better than to say that the same flaming mast that crashed to the deck and killed her brother managed to shoot a splinter through his cheek. 'Aye, it was. Should've healed by now, but for several weeks the surgeon couldn't decide whether to suture it or leave it alone. He finally decided to stitch me up. Consequently, I am not as far along the path of recovery as I could wish.'

He couldn't think of anything else to say. Miss Newsome gestured towards the hall. 'My parents are in my father's book room. Y-you could bring Davey's effects to them, if you please.'

'I will.'

He walked beside her down the hall, pleased not to have to shorten his stride to accommodate her. He was on the tallish side, but so was Miss Newsome.

She was dressed in black, a daunting colour for most females, except that it became her, with her pink cheeks, pale face and black hair. She was by no means thin, but he found her pleasant shape more to his liking, anyway. She looked practical and kind, which he found soothing.

'My father is an accountant and estate manager for Lord Blankenship, who owns numerous properties in Kent and East Sussex,' she said. 'I have lived on this estate all my life.'

'It must be a fair property in the springtime,' he said, wincing inwardly at his paltry supply of conversation.

Either it passed muster, or Miss Newsome was even kinder than he suspected. 'It's glorious in April, when the lambs are new,' she said. 'Here we are.'

They stopped before a closed door and she tapped lightly. He heard no reply—years of bombarding could do that to ears—but she opened the door and gestured him inside.

He knew a book room when he saw one. His own chart room aboard the *Ulysses* was tidier, mainly because space was more of a premium on a frigate and demanded economy.

His eyes went immediately to the map of the world, where the Newsomes had traced his lieutenant's travels with pins and thread. With a pang, he saw how few pins there were and how the enterprise ended at the coast off Spain known as Trafalgar. His own world map in his cabin crisscrossed the oceans many times, and touched on all the continents except Antarctica, proof of nearly thirty years at sea. Where had the time gone?

After Miss Newsome's introductions, he executed a workaday bow, which was the only kind he knew, and sat in the chair Mr Newsome indicated. In double-quick time a servant arrived with afternoon sherry and almond-flavoured tea cakes.

The sherry was dry the way he liked it and the

tea cakes moist and flavourful, two adjectives that his steward had never thought to associate with ship's fare. Joe could have eaten them all.

Instead, he held out the handsome leather case that Second Lieutenant Newsome had brought on board the *Ulysses* a bare eight months ago. He could have told the Newsomes that the other officers had chuckled over the unscratched leather and working clasps, perhaps trying to remember when they had been that young and green. He chose to say nothing.

'I put your son's second-best uniform in my own duffel,' he said, 'as well as his sword. I will leave those with you.'

'Where is his best uniform?' Mrs Newsome demanded.

Surprised, Joe wondered if she thought he had sold it, or given it away. Might as well tell her, even though he knew it would hurt.

'He wore it on deck for the battle, ma'am,' he told her, dreading the way her face paled. 'We all dress for battle on my ship.' He swallowed the lump in his throat. 'He is wearing it still, a credit to King and country.'

Mrs Newsome burst into tears and threw herself into her husband's arms. *Oh, Lord, I made a mess of that*, Joe thought, as Mr Newsome began to weep. Alarmed, Joe looked at Miss Newsome's expressive face as she dissolved in tears, too.

There they sat, Mr and Mrs Newsome locked in a tight and tearful embrace, with Miss Newsome suffering alone, no one's arms around her.

Captain Everard knew he was famed throughout the White Fleet for his unflappable demeanour in battle and the deliberate way he went about plotting courses and thinking through all possible outcomes of a fleet action. Not an impulsive man, he was also noted for the ability to move with real speed when events dictated.

He did so now, moving close to Miss Newsome as she sat in solitary sorrow on the loveseat. He pulled her close and wrapped his arms around her as she sobbed into his uniform, convinced that had there been another family member present, his action would not have been necessary.

Recent years had acquainted him with too much suffering, too much sorrow, too much pain. To say that holding Miss Newsome close was the least he could do was a regrettable statement of fact. He wanted to do more. He wanted to bring back the son, brother and second lieutenant who had showed such promise. He could do nothing but hold Davey Newsome's sister and let her cry.

He would have managed well enough, if her arms hadn't gone around him and if she hadn't begun to pat his back, and then hold him close until he cried, too. He was sick of war and death and knew in his soul that Trafalgar was not the end of the struggle for world domination, but merely one step along the way. Damn Boney anyway.

Chapter Four

‿‿‿◆‿‿‿

Her parents still wept. Miss Newsome pulled away first, but did not leave the circle of his embrace. She sniffed back more tears and he gave her his handkerchief, hoping he had not committed some massive social blunder. He had visited many bereaved families—too many—but this was the first time he had cried, too, and held a grieving sister close. Perhaps an explanation was in order.

'Miss Newsome, I do not generally… Well, I do not…' *That is pathetic, Joe*, he thought. 'No one should be alone in sorrow.'

She blew her nose, then endeared herself to him for ever by resting her forehead against his arm for the smallest moment. 'Begging your pardon, Captain, but you were alone, too,' she said softly. 'Let us go into the hall and leave my parents to their grief.'

She picked up her brother's leather case and took it with her. In the hall, she motioned towards a door that opened into a small but charming breakfast room. She set the case on the table, took several deep breaths and opened it. Her lips trembled as she took out David Newsome's few possessions. She held up the strip of rolled cloth that held his scissors, some thread, a thimble and needles, and managed a smile that touched Joe's heart.

'I gave my little brother a brief tutorial on how to sew on a button,' she said, before replacing it in the case.

She seemed to be in control of herself again, so Joe knew he could do no less, himself. God, how he hated to deliver bad news.

'I must inform you that he was terrible at sewing,' Joe said, which brought what appeared to be a genuine smile to her face. 'He showed up in the wardroom one evening for dinner with a button sewn on with black thread on his white shirt. I told him to do better, in no uncertain terms.'

'Did he look at you with those big puppy-brown eyes and appear wounded beyond belief? Sort of like this?' she said and turned the expression on him.

'Aye, he did,' Joe said, astounded again at the resemblance between brother and sister, although he had to admit that the expression was vastly more appealing on Miss Newsome's face. 'I told him not to toy with me, but resew that button.'

Should he say more? He knew he should not, but there she was. 'All joking aside, Miss Newsome, if *you* had practised such an expression in my wardroom, I would have let the matter slide.'

She laughed, seeing right through his mildest of flirtations in perhaps the most unsuitable moment imaginable. 'Captain Everard, could it be that you have a softer heart than even Davey described in his letters?'

Good God, had he been served up to the family as a martinet with the heart of pudding in Lieutenant Newsome's letters home? 'I hardly know what to say to that,' he managed.

'Davey wrote how you never could quite inflict the lash beyond a stroke or two, when probably more was needed,' Miss Newsome said. 'Personally, I thank you for that and so did Davey.'

He mumbled something about the idiocy of getting men to follow, when their captain made life unbearable aboard ship. 'I've never been afraid to err on the side of leniency, Miss Newsome, but I do know when discipline is necessary,' he said in his own defence. 'I'd rather have a sailor swab an already white deck than suffer the lash.'

He could have added that his ship was known to be a well-disciplined war machine where few men deserted, but it wasn't necessary to praise himself. He was only going to be here a few more minutes. His Quaker mother, long dead, would have scolded him for puffing up his consequence, had he said more.

But there she was, looking at him with admiration. He did his job as he saw fit and nothing more. He knew it was time to move this conversation along.

'Let me give you your brother's uniform and I'll be on my way,' he said.

Before she could speak, he went into the hall and retrieved his duffel bag. He had carefully folded the uniform on top, so it came out easily. He set it on the table and Miss Newsome broke his heart into even more pieces by smoothing down the wrinkled wool.

'I tucked his bicorn beside him before my steward sewed him into his hammock for burial,' he said. 'Miss Newsome, I am so sorry.'

She cried again and he patted her shoulder until she drew a shuddering breath and applied his handkerchief to her eyes. 'See here,' she said, 'I have quite ruined your handkerchief.'

'I have plenty more,' he told her.

'I would imagine other families have cried into them.'

'Aye, they have.'

With a resolution that touched his heart, she returned her attention to her brother's leather case, which held his shaving equipment, pen and nibs, ink, the Bible, two works of fiction he had passed around for others to enjoy and his private journal.

She picked up the journal and flipped through the pages. 'Interesting how a life can move along and then it is over and the pages are empty,' she murmured, more to herself than to him. 'I will give this to my parents. I don't have the heart to read it. Maybe later.'

She looked at him in surprise when he unbuckled the sword at his waist and placed it on the table next to the uniform.

'I left mine back in Plymouth,' he explained. 'This is Davey's sword. And now I had better be on my way.'

'We had expected you to stay the night,' she said.

He doubted the Newsomes wanted any such thing. The usual bereaved family was only too happy to see him off, as if his continued presence only made death more real and he was somehow to blame. True, most of his visits had taken place in daylight hours. He glanced out the window, dismayed to see full dark. No matter. Weltby was no more than a mile away and he never minded a walk, he who was usually confined to pacing back and forth on a quarterdeck.

'Thank you, but, no,' he said. 'Your mother will rather have me gone. I understand that.'

Throwing caution to the winds, he stood up and held out his hand, because he already could tell Miss Newsome was a practical sort of female. 'Shake hands with me, Miss Newsome,' he said. 'Please know it was a pleasure to have Lieutenant Newsome serve on the *Ulysses*. He was a brother to be proud of.'

They shook hands. He appreciated her firm grip.

'Good luck to you, Captain Everard,' she said as she opened the door and stepped back. 'And best of the season to you.'

Season? What season? he almost asked, until

he remembered that Christmas was a mere week away. 'And to you and yours,' he replied. He had been so long away that he could not recall his last Christmas on land.

It might have been awkward then to stand there, waiting for the maid to return with his cloak and hat, except that carollers stood outside the front door. His exit from the house seemed to signal a burst of music, almost as if they were celebrating his departure from a house of mourning that he had disturbed.

They sounded quite good, harmonising on 'God Rest Ye Merry Gentlemen', as he walked down the steps and stood beside them, digging out a few coins to give the collection. He saw many children and likely parents among that number, supplying volume where needed. He could tell from their sturdy but practical clothing that they were of the same social sphere as his friends from the mail coach. He looked at the boys, seeing them in the fleet in a few years, or marching with Sir John Moore in Spain and Portugal. He averted his gaze; it was not a pretty thought.

He shouldered his duffel again and started back the way he had come. Too bad there were no intelligent men in Kent who should have courted and married such a pretty lady as Verity Newsome.

He shook off the thought, reminding himself that he had fully discharged his duty to his second luff and bore no more responsibility for a young man gone too soon. In Plymouth he had discharged a similar duty to the widow of his carpenter's mate. He had given her a small sum that he lied and said was Nahum Mattern's share of prize money gone astray from a mythical fleet action in the Pacific. He had sent two letters to more remote families of able seamen, along with more prize money of a mythical source. He had done what he could.

He counted his blessings that his frigate had only lost four men at Trafalgar. He knew the butcher's bill was much higher on the ships of the line that did the actual fighting. He didn't envy *those* captains.

He stood in the shadow of trees a short distance from the Newsome house until the last strains of 'We Wish You a Merry Christmas' died away in the cold air. He knew he had two weeks before reporting to London for Admiral Nelson's funeral, without a single clue how to spend leisure time. It was a foreign concept. Perhaps he could catch up on his reading.

Chapter Five

Joe enjoyed a good dinner at the Gentleman Johnny, propping a book on navigation against the water jug while he ate shepherd's pie—two dishes—brown bread with butter—not rancid—and rice pudding with sultanas and figs. He decided against coffee.

He slept well enough, thanks entirely to a bed-warmer with just the right amount of coals in it, well wrapped in flannel. He dreamed, but of nothing more strenuous than hauling down and raising signal flags with amazing speed. Some-how—how curious was the overactive brain—the final signal was 'brown eyes'. He woke up with a smile on his face.

Late breakfast was another pleasure: all the bacon he wanted, eggs fried so carefully that the yolks quivered, but remained intact, and toasted brown bread with plum jam. Coffee suited him, well sugared and with fresh cream, another novelty.

His scar hurt less. Too bad he did not have the name and direction of the kind lady who had pressed that jar of goose grease into his palm on the mail coach. He would have sent her a letter of thanks. Maybe in a week he could work up the nerve to clip the sutures.

He sat by the window, looking out at a slight drizzle that seemed certain to dissipate any moment. He wondered whether to stay another night to read and continue eating well, or return to Torquay and bother the shipwright about repairs.

His gaze focused on a young person, head down, cloak-enveloped, pushing towards the Gentleman Johnny. When she looked up, he recognised the young maid from the Newsomes' home. He poured himself another half-cup of coffee and looked around when the same child approached his table and peered at him, too shy to say anything.

'Aye, miss?'

She stepped closer, looked at the ceiling and recited, 'I am to give you this, Captain Everest, and they will not take no for an answer.' She held out a note.

So he was Captain Everest to a Kentish maid? Hiding a smile, he took it from her and nodded to the innkeeper. 'Can you find some more toast and jam for this little lady?'

'I can and will, sir. Come along to the kitchen, Susan.'

He read the note. 'So you won't take no for an

answer?' he asked out loud, since the inn's dining room was empty. 'What can have happened?'

Dear Captain Everard,
We were remiss in our hospitality to you last night. Would you return and spend a few days here? We'd like to hear stories about our son on your ship. We hope you have time to humour us.
Sincerely,
Mr and Mrs Augustus Newsome

I suppose there is a first time for everything, Joe thought, as he pocketed the note, drained the coffee cup and stood up.

To go or not to go? He had faithfully discharged his last duty to a crew member. He owed the Newsomes nothing more. He shook his head. They owed him nothing, either. Better to let the dog of duty turn around a few times, settle down and go to sleep. They would get on with their lives and he with his.

All the same, he knew he owed the Newsomes a response and it was easy enough to write one because it was the truth. While Susan ate her toast and jam, Joe procured a piece of paper and a pencil from the keep and wrote a reply there in the kitchen. He folded it and held it out to the child. 'Take this back to the Newsomes, if you please,' he said and took out a coin. 'And this is for your troubles.'

His heart sank when her face fell. 'Sir, I was supposed to bring *you* back,' she said.

'Oh, I can't…' he started to say, but stopped when she put down her toast and folded her arms, refusing to take the note or the coin. She was almost as tough as the men he commanded, looking him in the eyes, her gaze not wavering.

He reconsidered. What was a few days, in the larger scheme of things? 'Very well, miss. Let me get my duffel and pay the keep, since you insist.'

She had a winning smile. 'Finish your toast,' he said. 'I'll be back.'

Upstairs, he spent one cowardly moment wondering what would happen if he refused to come downstairs. How long would she wait? Deciding such chicken-heartedness was not worthy of an officer and gentleman who had prevailed at Camperdown, the Battle of the Nile and, for God's sake, Trafalgar, Joe bowed to the inevitable and packed his duffel. He paid the grinning landlord and joined Susan in the dining room.

'We'd better go now, Susan,' he told her. 'Though we're going to get wet.'

They did, but it wasn't a trial, because Susan proved to be a charming companion. She had a tongue on wheels and knew something about the occupants of every cottage they passed. By the time they arrived at Chez Newsome, he knew that Mrs Buttars was due to be confined any day, Paddy Bennett liked his rum a little too well, the vicar's sermons were so boring that several of his parishioners wagered each Sunday on whether they would exceed thirty minutes. And Millicent Overby had got herself into trouble of some sort that Miss Newsome refused to divulge.

'I want to know what sort of trouble she is in,' Susan concluded as the house came in sight. 'Perhaps Miss Newsome would tell you.'

'I'm not that brave,' he admitted, even though he wanted to wander out of the maid's hearing and have a good laugh.

'But you're Royal Navy, sir,' the irrepressible Susan reminded him. 'You must be a hero because you have stitches.'

He decided that logic was not her strong suit and assured her that anyone could come by stitches in the navy.

She seemed ready to argue, except that the front door opened and Miss Newsome stood there to usher them in. He still hoped that an afternoon of discussion would be enough to satisfy their curiosity about their son and brother. Long acquaintance with grief had informed him that most people needed time to turn catastrophe into acceptance.

He tried to explain this to Miss Newsome as they stood together in the hall, but she wasn't buying it.

'Captain Everard, my mother wants you to stay a few days,' she explained again in her kindly way. 'I confess she surprised me with her request, but I assure you that Mama, once set on a course, does not usually deviate from it.'

He felt some disappointment at her answer.

Somewhere in his brain in a corner not occupied by the alarms of war, he hoped the request had come from Miss Newsome, as well.

'Please, sir.'

'I don't wish to upset her further,' he hedged. He noticed that Miss Newsome had raised her hand as if to rest it on his sleeve, then lowered it. She smelled divinely of roses.

'She will be more disappointed if you choose *not* to stay,' Miss Newsome told him, then smiled. 'Let me show you to your room, Captain.'

'I am being managed by females,' he protested, but mildly, as she indicated the stairs. 'First Susan bullies me into walking here and now I must stay on pain of disappointing a lady who I was certain yesterday wished to see me no more. And here you are, looking at me with…'

Good God, someone stop me, he thought, as his neckcloth felt tighter and somehow hot. *One just doesn't blurt out 'big brown eyes' to an acquaintance of scarcely twenty-four hours.*

To his relief, Miss Newsome laughed at his feeble diatribe. 'You told us yesterday that you have no pressing engagements of a nautical nature, since your ship is in dry dock,' she reminded him.

He had the good grace to know when he was defeated and capitulated, thinking of moments when it was better to salute as the ship went down. What did a few days matter?

So there he was, following a managing female up a flight of stairs and admiring her hips in motion under her dress.

I need a holiday far from here, he thought. *Perhaps Constantinople or Madagascar.*

She opened a door on a room that Joe knew at once must have been her brother's. 'Make yourself comfortable, Captain Everard,' Miss Newsome said. 'If you would come downstairs in a half hour, Mama would like to pour tea and hear about Davey.'

He managed some pleasantry which must have satisfied Miss Newsome, because she smiled and closed the door after saying, 'One half-hour, if you please.'

He took off his shoes and set them by the grate, where coal glowed. His stockings came off next, the soggy things. Barefoot, he padded to the window and looked upon Kent in winter, with fields fallow. He saw an oast house in the distance with its distinctive two spires that looked like witch's hats, where farmers dried hops, in preparation for making beer.

A good dark beer sounded appealing, but he doubted the Newsomes indulged themselves. The bed appealed even more. Taking off his uniform coat, he lay down with a sigh, unbuttoned his trousers and waistcoat and stretched out. Just a minute or two would be enough, he had no doubt. He closed his eyes.

Chapter Six

'Verity, it is one hour since you directed Captain Everard upstairs,' Mama said. 'I am past ready to pour tea and listen to stories about Davey. You are certain you told him one half-hour?'

'Positive, Mama,' Miss Newsome said. 'I'll knock on his door.'

Verity went upstairs and stood outside the door a moment before she worked up the nerve to knock. She tapped and listened. Nothing. A second knock yielded the same result, so she turned the handle quietly and peered inside.

Captain Everard lay spread out on the bed, trousers and waistcoat unbuttoned and neckcloth askew. He was barefoot. He had somehow tacked his stockings to the fireplace, hung there to dry. He looked completely relaxed, flat on his back, hands spread out, snoring softly.

She had seen Davey sleep a time or two, but never a full-grown man with whom she could claim no relation. He intrigued her because he was handsome in a rugged sort of way, not like a solicitor or country gentleman who did nothing more strenuous than tend to other people's genteel business.

This was a man of the sea; she could tell by the fine lines around his eyes caused by exposure to scouring winds and salt water. His hair was ordinary brown, but with flecks of grey in it. One of Davey's letters had referred to Captain Everard as the Old Man, but she doubted him much over forty. When she remarked on it to her father, Augustus Newsome had told her that was the common navy term for captain. 'And that, dear daughter, exhausts my entire knowledge of the maritime profession,' Papa added.

She had no business to stand there gawking. Strange how he could look capable, even as he looked vulnerable. She watched his expression, which seemed to change as he lay there. He frowned, he sighed audibly, spoke as though he were giving an order, then settled back into deeper slumber. She hadn't the heart to wake him.

Before she left the room, she quietly put a few more lumps of coal in the grate, then covered him with a light throw from the chair by the fireplace. Perhaps she shouldn't have tucked the coverlet by his side, because as she straightened up, he opened his eyes, hazel ones, and looked at her as if he wondered where he was.

'Captain, I didn't mean to…'

''Pon my word, Miss Newsome, I never oversleep.'

They spoke at the same time, stopped, laughed, then spoke again. 'Beg your...'

'Such rag manners, 'pon my word.'

He put up his hand finally, but beyond that, remained as he was, stretched out and comfortable. Verity thought that singularly charming, for some reason.

'I obviously overslept, Miss Newsome,' he said, not moving. 'Please extend my apologies to your mother and tell her I will be down directly.'

Verity made an executive decision. 'Stay where you are, Captain. You look comfortable and would probably go back to sleep if I left you alone.' She went to the door, grateful she had not closed it. 'We keep country hours, so dinner is at six.'

He laughed softly, turned over and went back to sleep as she stood there.

Awake, alert and with his hair combed—he did have an amusing cowlick—Captain Everard presented himself downstairs at six o'clock. With a bow, he greeted them and said, 'Now, where was I?', which made Mama laugh, a sound Verity had not heard since news of Davey's death.

Dinner was sheer delight, somewhat to Verity's surprise. Captain Everard's first impression as a cut-and-dried, strictly business sort of man was perhaps not accurate. Had oversleeping in a soft bed rendered him more casual? He asked a few questions about Papa's business and even seemed interested when her father launched into detailed description of his duties as chief steward of Lord Blankenship's various holdings in this part of Kent.

'I noticed oast houses,' Captain Everard said, as he passed the beef roast to Verity. 'Do you make your own beer on the property?'

'We call them hop kilns here in Kent,' Papa corrected. 'And, yes, we do. If you have time tomorrow, I could take you to our brewery.'

'I will go gladly,' Captain Everard said. 'Please tell me it is a good, dark beer with a woody taste.'

'I can do that, sir,' Papa said and beamed at Verity. 'You could come, too, my dear, even though I know your opinion of beer.'

'I might,' she replied, surprising herself.

The ease with which Captain Everard inserted himself into their house impressed Verity, because he made it simple to include her brother into the dinner-table discussion in a way that caused her mother no pain. After a few well-placed questions, Mama started talking about Davey's early education at the hands of the local vicar and the way he wore them down with his patient but firm insistence that the seafaring life was the career for him.

'When he came aboard *Ulysses*, his excellent scores on his lieutenancy exams and good references from his captain convinced me that we were lucky to have David Newsome,' the Captain said over the final course of fruit and nuts. 'And so it proved to be. He was an apt student of the sea.'

They adjourned to the sitting room, since no one in the Newsome household had enough puffed-up consequence to leave the gentlemen with cigars in the dining room and the ladies engaged in idle chat elsewhere. Verity watched Mama, pleased with her eagerness to learn more of Davey's short life on the water and hoping she would not overexert herself.

She shouldn't have worried. Captain Everard had no trouble in reading the signals either, telling her worlds about his care of his own crew.

'Please, Captain Everard, tell me everything you remember about my son,' Mama said, once they were seated and she had taken out her mending.

Verity watched as the Captain's demeanour turned thoughtful, and then amused. 'I have such a story for you,' he said.

Mama and Papa both leaned forward, eager as young children prepared for a treat of epic dimensions.

'If you looked in David's leather case, Miss Newsome, you found volumes one and four of *The Mysteries of Udolpho*,' he said, settling back.

'But no two and three,' Verity said.

'Nowhere in sight. We were suffering through months of blockade duty off the coast of Spain.' He passed his hand in front of his face. 'It's beyond me to describe the tedium of the blockade so I will not attempt it. Morale was lower than a dungeon cell in the Tower of London. David tapped on my door one night and asked for a moment's time.' He chuckled at that. 'Hell's bells—beg pardon, ma'am—I'd have given him all the time he wanted, anything for a diversion.'

And we here in England take your efforts and our safety for granted, Verity thought, as she picked up her knitting.

'He said he wanted to write a play for the crew to perform, based on *Udolpho,*' Captain Everard continued. 'I asked him what he planned to do about the two missing volumes, and he just waved his hand and said, "That's a mere trifle."'

Mama pressed her handkerchief to her eyes. 'He said that often enough at home. Nothing daunted him.'

Verity watched the captain observe her mother, as if assessing her and not wanting to cause her undue anxiety. He must have liked what he saw, because he continued. 'The scamp called it *The Mystery of Udolpho on Short Rations, or Better Two Volumes Than None.* Signor Montoni, the villain of the piece, looked and behaved remarkably like Bonaparte.'

'Who played our hero, Sue Valancourt Brown?' Verity asked.

'Can you doubt?' the Captain teased. 'Your irrepressible brother.' He sighed. 'I was asked to play Emily St Aubert's father, so was mercifully allowed to die early in this masterwork. Perhaps he assumed that, as captain, I had more important things to do, although I did not.'

Mama and Papa chuckled at that. Verity's eyes filled with tears as they held hands, something she had not seen in months. It was as if Davey's death had stifled all normal emotions. But here they were, holding hands as she remembered from earlier, happier times.

Captain Everard was looking at her parents, too. He smiled, but she saw no joy in his eyes. She wondered what a man like him thought of settled lives and domestic hearths, and the everyday sameness of a routine life. Did he envy it? Would it bore him? Heaven knew nothing appeared likely to ever change her ordered, quiet life.

'Miss Newsome? Are you on a distant planet?'

Startled, she glanced at the captain. 'I don't know where I was,' she said honestly, then knew she must exert herself. 'Er…well, I would like to know who was convinced or coerced into playing the heroine, Emily St Aubert.'

'What do you think my second luff would do?' he asked in turn. 'You knew him better than I did.'

That took no imagination. She only wished she could have witnessed the diplomacy required. 'He probably found the biggest, ugliest, hairiest man on the *Ulysses* to play that dainty French creature,' she teased in turn.

'Precisely, my dear,' he said. 'The Ulysses happens to rejoice in a cook with a peg leg and a patch over one eye. He hawks continually and we only pray he does not do it over the porridge. You'd have thought he was born for the role. I dare even Mrs Radcliffe herself to find a better Emily.'

Mama burst into laughter, which made Papa tighten his grip on her hand and carry it to his lips for a kiss.

You are a master, Verity thought, as she allowed herself to relax and let Captain Everard carry them all aboard a wartime frigate presenting a comedic version of the first novel she ever stayed up all night to finish, suffering along with Emily and Madame Cheron, and a host of characters transformed somewhat in the HMS *Ulysses* version because the middle two volumes were missing.

'And that was that,' the captain concluded. 'All the ships in our vicinity on the blockade took turns rowing over for an evening of entertainment, courtesy of your remarkable son, Mrs Newsome. Lord St Vincent himself took me aside and told me how lucky we were to have such a lovely Emily.'

He looked around the sitting room and she saw it through his eyes. A shabby, cosy room—a better word than small—with outdated wallpaper and old furniture. She wondered what he was thinking.

She knew soon enough and it warmed her heart. 'By God, Mr and Mrs Newsome, you are kind to let me visit for a day or two,' he said. 'I can't recall the last time I was in an actual home.'

Mama's eyes filled with tears, but Verity felt only relief. She wasn't crying for Davey this time, but a solitary frigate captain sitting in her parlour and sipping sherry.

'Davey would want you here,' Mama said.

And so do I, Verity thought.

Chapter Seven

'I'm not certain I have ever met braver people than your parents,' Joe said, after Miss Newsome's parents said goodnight. 'I cannot recall a time when grieving parents have invited me back to talk about their son.'

'I'll admit I was surprised, as well,' she said. She handed him a candle. 'Goodnight, Captain Everard, and thank you again for agreeing to stay a few days with us.'

She waited for him to go up the stairs before her. When he stood there, she headed towards the kitchen. To his own surprise, he decided to follow her.

'Wait up, if you please,' he said. 'Are there any of those tea cakes left?'

He wasn't hungry; he wanted to spend more time in Miss Newsome's orbit. The odd lethargy troubling him since Trafalgar was starting to lift. In telling the Newsomes about Davey's life instead of his death, he felt more energised, more optimistic. Once the *Ulysses* was repaired and back to blockade duty, maybe things wouldn't be so dreary.

'I confess it,' he told her as they headed to the kitchen. 'I love cake. Cake in any form, even stale cake. Cake.'

She smiled as Joe had hoped she would, throwing off some years and cares of her own. 'Is that the first thing you ask for, when you reach port?' she asked and, to his ears, she sounded interested.

'Water first, a big pitcher of it. Clean water that came out of a well and not a wooden keg,' he said.

'And then cake?' she prompted, when he wondered why he was rattling on, at least, rattling on for *him*.

'Aye, cake, two or three layers if it is available, with lots of icing, the gooier the better,' he said and followed her into the pantry. 'I swear there were times in the South Pacific as a midshipman that I would have killed for cake.'

Miss Newsome laughed and reached for a breadbox. 'No need for carnage,' she said as she took out a plate of tea cakes. 'Will these do?'

'Aye, they will.'

'Come then, Captain. The pantry is a little crowded.'

True, it was, but he hadn't minded proximity to Miss Newsome. He followed her into the servants' dining room and sat down where she indicated.

Miss Newsome put a plate in front of him and set a place for herself, too. 'Eat as many as you want, sir, but save one for me. I like the plain icing.'

Since they were small, he set four on his plate, careful to leave several plain cakes for his late-night hostess. She ate with relish and made no comment when he finished his four, eyed the plate and appropriated the remaining four.

She seemed to look for signs he was ready to retire, but saw none. She must have been wondering how to entertain him.

He had the same thought, because he gave a self-conscious laugh and shook his head. 'Here we are,' he said. 'I am depriving you of sleep just because I enjoy the novelty of sitting somewhere with no demands on my time: no emergencies brewing, no bosun grousing about shiny new sailors who won't stop puking every time the ship yaws and no surgeon fretting because we have run low on medicinal spirits and who in God's name is drinking it?'

Verity laughed at the picture he painted. 'Now, sir,' she teased, 'you come ashore wearing a glamorous cape and a magnificent, intimidating fore-and-aft hat, and expect mere mortals to think your exalted position can be as mundane as our lives are on shore?'

'Guilty as charged,' he replied, with considerable aplomb. 'You cannot imagine the boredom of life on the blockade.'

'No, I cannot.'

'Damn me if I didn't leap with joy when we were pulled out of formation to follow Admiral

Nelson to Trafalgar,' he said, his eyes full of sympathy. 'Meeting you and your parents, I wish to God he had summoned someone else.'

What could she say to that? He sat before her, feeling tired. Suddenly she picked up a napkin and brushed off the icing, which could have embarrassed him, but didn't.

He smiled at her. 'I never was a tidy eater.'

'Fiddle,' she said. 'Icing is ungovernable at times. You had to obey the Admiral. You had no choice, did you?'

'None.'

'I assume Admiral Nelson had his pick of frigates and captains and he chose you and the *Ulysses* because he knew you would not fail him,' she said.

'What a battle it was.'

'One to tell your children some day,' she said.

'Or yours,' he replied. 'Your brother was valiant to the end.'

He startled himself by leaning across the table that separated them and kissing her forehead.

'With that, I am off to bed,' he told her. 'I certainly won't burden your parents with much of a visit, in spite of their kind entreaty. I do think that before I leave, you and I should gather some ivy. Your sitting room looks a bit bare, don't you think?'

Verity stared at him. He gave her a wink, then

touched his dessert plate and planted some icing on *her* nose.

'I'm an early riser and ivy awaits, Miss Newsome. Goodnight.'

Chapter Eight

'I am starting to remind myself of every stereotype about the Royal Navy that I ever heard of,' Joe told his shaving mirror before breakfast. 'You dog, you.'

He tried to let dismay at his casual behaviour last night exact its obvious toll, but all he felt was pleasantly tuned up. He had slept well for the first night in ages. He knew tackling ivy and chatting with Miss Newsome would not be onerous.

She waited for him in the breakfast room, still dressed in sombre black, but with high colour to her face. 'Good morning, Captain Everard. I trust you slept well?'

'Better than any night in recent memory,' he replied as he eyed the bacon all lined up like good soldiers on the sideboard. 'I am about to embarrass myself here.'

'I asked Cook to fry extra bacon. Have all you want.'

He took her at her word and finished by overburdening his plate with enough eggs to maintain proper balance. Two slices of toast continued the symmetry. He sat down and eyed her single baked egg and one slice of bacon.

'Miss Newsome, you will dry up and blow away with that short ration,' he commented.

'Hasn't happened yet,' she said, placing a napkin in her lap. She got up and added two more slices of bacon. 'You're right. I don't want to blow away.'

Joe tried to be proper and cut his bacon. A glance at Miss Newsome picking up her bacon gave him leave to follow suit and made her laugh.

'I'll tell you a story on me, Captain,' she said, wiping her lips. 'A mild-mannered fellow, Weltby's solicitor, started visiting me. Papa assured me he was interested, so I humoured him. Here is the odd part: For two years he showed up Tuesdays, ate breakfast with us, of all things, and sat silent in the sitting room until he left for work. He stared at me; it was unnerving. Breakfast?'

Two years? What is wrong with the men of Kent? he thought as he happily dispatched a fried egg.

'After two years, I decided there would never be an offer of marriage, which, truth to tell, I found reassuring,' she said. 'Perhaps he liked the food. One morning I picked up my bowl of porridge and said, "Sir, I am taking our peculiar courtship to an entirely new level."' She laughed out loud. 'I drank the milk from the bowl. He ran out of the house and was never seen again.'

Joe leaned back in his chair and joined her laughter. 'Miss Newsome, you two would never have suited.'

'Precisely. Answer me this: Captain, would *you* cry off if the lady you had been courting for two years suddenly drank from the porridge bowl?'

'In the first place, I cannot imagine such a scenario,' he said. 'In the second place, two *years*? You can drink from that vase of mums over there, if you wish. I am indifferent to the matter.'

It was her turn to laugh and promise him she had no such plans. 'Mama did lament that I would probably never have another such opportunity,' Miss Newsome told him. 'Opportunity for *what*, I should have asked her.'

He finished breakfast with Miss Newsome, pleased with her easy manner and good humour. There she sat in full mourning, vibrantly alive.

'Mama has been resisting my hints that the house needed more greenery to properly celebrate the season,' she told him as they started to walk down the fence row to the nearest copse. 'When I suggested you and I might go hunt the wild ivy before you left, she practically leaped about in agreement. I swear I do not know what has got into her.'

'I'm grateful she let me tell her about her son,' he said, transferring the basket to his other arm so he could steady her on an icy patch. Well, it looked icy to him.

'We have all been too silent since your letter.' She stopped. 'How many of those do you write, sir?'

He considered, knowing the butcher's bill would startle her. 'Let me think: I have been a post captain for eight years. Before that I was a captain. Before that, first lieutenant for a captain who never could bring himself to write such missives. Probably more than two hundred, Miss Newsome. Fleet actions are a nasty business, but so are accidents and illnesses.'

'You poor man. And we only had to receive one.'

'It's not the same,' He knew the personal loss he suffered with each death, whether the sailor was a second lieutenant like David Newsome, or an able seaman. Joe was the man in charge, until a battle or disease reminded him he was no such thing. 'It's not the same.'

He looked into her eyes and doubted she believed a word of it.

'Thank you for your sacrifice.' She hurried on ahead, either giving him a moment to grieve, or her such a moment. Perhaps it was both.

He joined Miss Newsome at a stone wall which had once formed the back of a crofter's cottage, from the looks of it. She simply stood there, staring at the ivy.

'Miss Newsome?' he said cautiously. 'I'd offer you a penny for your thoughts, but I suspect I know them.'

She turned around, startled, then relaxed. 'Perhaps not. This is the time of day when class begins in the school for tenants' children that I used to teach.'

'I had no idea,' he said. 'I assumed you lived quietly at home.'

'I educated children for five years,' she said and he watched her eyes soften. 'Lovely children.'

'May I ask...?'

Her eyes hardened then. 'Lord Blankenship, who employs my father, informed me that he had a poor relation needing work. I was released and another put in my place.'

She pursed her lips together and frowned. Joe knew if this were his misfortune, he would be swearing and throwing things about. Obviously Miss Newsome was better equipped for ill fortune than he was.

'But, sir, here is holly, with berries properly red. You cut there and I will hold this end.'

He did as she asked, struck by the fact that a woman of Miss Newsome's obvious calibre would even consider work. When he finished, she deftly wound the length of ivy into the basket he had set down.

'Lord Blankenship has found me similar employment in Norfolk,' she said. 'I am to go there on the mail coach after Christmas.'

'I confess I do not understand why you need employment,' he said, then knew he owed her an immediate apology for inserting himself in family matters that were none of his business. 'Beg pa—'

'Oh, please, not that,' she interrupted. 'Perhaps we Newsomes appear more genteel than you think.'

'I never thought…'

Shut up, Joe, he told himself. *Admit your interest, at least to yourself.*

She indicated a rustic bench and sat down, giving him leave to do the same.

'Papa is an estate manager of several large properties,' she said, 'but we fall far short of gentry. What is your background, sir, if I may ask?'

'You may. My father was a solicitor in Cornwall,' he said. 'My mother was of the friendly persuasion.'

'My goodness, a Quaker,' Miss Newsome said. 'What did she think of your profession, if I may be so bold?'

'She died before I went to sea. My father remarried and his new wife was happy to see me gone. She brought several hopeful offspring to the connection', he said, leaving it at that.

Miss Newsome gave him a sympathetic look, which took him aback. No one had ever looked at him that way. 'No fears, there, Miss Newsome,' he hurried to explain. 'Her indifference moved me quickly into a career for which I am entirely suited.'

'And I am suited to education,' Miss Newsome said. 'Lord Blankenship was kind enough to find me that position. I considered a bolt to Boston, United States of America. My uncle there said he would help me.'

'But why…?'

'Must I earn my bread?' she finished. 'Sir, David was supposed to make the family fortune as an officer with prize money. He promised me on his last visit home that I need not worry about my spinster state, because he would always support me. Trafalgar changed that and here I am, heading to Norfolk when Christmas is over.'

'You have no other relations?'

'None, Captain Everard, except that Boston uncle. How fortuitous that I enjoy teaching.'

What could he say to that? If Miss Newsome had only until after Christmas to celebrate with her parents, he had no business intruding on family intimacy. He stood up and reached for the basket of coiled ivy.

'I will take my leave, since you have so little family time remaining,' he said. 'I wish you well in your future plans.'

Good God, that sounded stiff. Life was simpler at sea.

'Sir, have you never in your life met a practical female before?' she asked.

'Not one as resourceful as you, perhaps,' he hedged. 'Botheration, Miss Newsome, but I must know: Why are you not repining that you are a single lady of…of…?'

'Nearly thirty,' she said, with that lurking smile of hers he was beginning to enjoy, if the truth were told.

'Very well, nearly thirty,' he said, as he floundered in deep water. 'Davey was to have been your saviour. You are heading to godforsaken Norfolk and...'

He stopped, because she was laughing. 'Captain Everard, *why* do men think women cannot be resourceful?'

'Why indeed? I stand corrected,' he told her promptly and offered his arm, which she took. 'All the same, I will leave this afternoon.'

They walked to the house in silence. He stopped at the door before she could open it. 'I have to tell you: I was thinking that you would have made an excellent lieutenant on any ship I have commanded.'

Miss Newsome had a hearty laugh. He felt a mixture of pleasure and ease, just listening to her. The other sensation startled him: what a pity he hadn't time to pursue an interest with Miss Verity Newsome.

Chapter Nine

Verity reached for the doorknob, but it was pulled from her grasp.

'Daughter! We are at sixes and sevens!' her mother declared, taking her by the arm as if to haul her inside. 'Come along. There is this letter to you from Sir Percy of Hipworth Hall.'

'Perhaps he is wishing us good tidings,' Verity said, too pleased with present company to wish to bother with her future employer right now.

'No. Read this,' Mama said as she thrust the letter into Verity's hand.

'Surely it can wait until we get inside the house,' she said, wishing her mother could show a little more countenance around company. Mama had already opened the letter. What must Captain Everard think of them?

'Very well,' she grumbled. 'My, what poor hand-writing.'

Mama snatched it back. 'Daughter, it says quite

plainly that he wants you to arrive *before* Christmas. He wants you in three days!'

Verity took it back, squinting at the spidery handwriting, blotched as if the writer never put pen to paper, or had less patience even than Mama. 'Such poor handwriting. I can't read it.'

'Hand it to me,' Captain Everard said. 'I have some proficiency with illegible handwriting, as found in various logs.'

Verity gave him the letter gladly. For a moment in her heretofore self-reliant life, she wanted someone to solve her problem for her. It was a new sensation and not unwelcome.

'That's it. He wants you in three days.' He handed the letter back to her. He looked over her shoulder at the letter he had just returned. 'And look here: Either this reads, "My life is in peril", which I cannot credit, even in Norfolk, or "My wife is nonpareil".' He shrugged as she laughed.

'Perhaps he wrote, "My wife is feral",' Verity quipped and they laughed together, which seemed to her ears a most delightful sound.

Mama would have none of it. 'Verity. Captain Everard. Do be serious!'

Captain Everard seemed disinclined towards soberness. 'My mother once declared me a feral child when I slurped soup from a spoon, or, heaven forbid, picked up my cereal bowl and drank the milk.'

Another slow wink and Verity laughed some more, which did not please Mama. 'Verity, this is a house of mourning,' she reminded her daughter.

'I know.' Verity felt some contrition, until she remembered how much Davey would have enjoyed this exchange. 'Davey would have tossed in his tuppence-worth, too, Mama, you cannot deny.'

'No, I cannot,' Mama said after a moment's reflection. The notion seemed to calm her. 'My dear daughter, you must be on your way tomorrow.' She looked at Captain Everard with apology in her expression. 'We so wanted to keep you here with us for a few days, sir.'

So did I, Verity thought, hopeful her disappointment didn't show on her face. She was too old to moon about over a possibility that no one had offered.

Mama wasn't done. 'And now I must send my child on the mail coach through stormy weather and deep snow by herself to a remote location and a questionable set of strangers.'

Verity couldn't help noticing the interesting way Captain Everard's dimple in his cheek could disappear and reappear when he was amused. Once those distressing black sutures were a thing of the past, he could almost be considered a handsome fellow. She saw before her a solid man, probably not inclined to flights of fancy, which made her wish for another day in his company, before he returned to war and she to her less sanguine future.

There stood Mama, her lip quivering. Verity put her arm around her mother. 'Dearest, you know I have no qualms about solitary travel on the mail coach.'

Me, oh, my. It wasn't going to be enough. Verity tried again, unwilling for their brief guest to see Mama in hysterics. 'You know as well as I do that people are at their best during Christmastide.'

She held her breath, hoping Mama would proceed no further than with tear-filled eyes. Where *was* Papa?

Her help came from an unexpected source, considering. As she watched in big-eyed amazement, Captain Everard took her mother's hand in his.

'Mrs Newsome, would you feel more comfortable if I agreed to escort your daughter to Norfolk? It's not that far and I am at leisure for nearly two complete weeks.'

'Sir, I really don't want to—' she began to say, but Mama overruled Verity's sensible reminder on the tip of her tongue that the mail coach *any* time of year was not generally regarded as a gypsy caravan ready to steal away unwary children or oblivious spinsters.

'Captain Everard, that would relieve me greatly.'

'Oh, but…'

Captain Everard clinched the matter with a single, inarguable sentence. 'Mrs Newsome, Miss Newsome: I would be honoured to perform one last service for my second lieutenant.'

What could she say to that, especially when Mama threw herself into the captain's arms? And here was Papa now, coming out of the book room, ledger in hand, only to look up in surprise when

Mama explained that Davey's captain had kindly agreed to escort their sole remaining child to the wilds of wintry Norfolk.

Papa astounded her by putting a spoke in the wheel of Mama's enthusiasm.

'I am not convinced of the propriety of this,' he said.

'Papa, I am perfectly safe on a mail coach,' Verity reminded him. 'Only last summer I went from here to Brighton to see my aunt. Alone.' She bowed to necessity. 'If I *must* have an escort, I cannot think of a better one than a post captain in the Royal Navy.'

'I don't think it is proper,' Papa insisted, which made Verity want to sink through the floor with embarrassment. To her further dismay, Captain Everard's stunned expression changed to one verging on amusement. What must he think of them?

'What would you suggest that we do?' the captain asked. 'I feel inclined to agree with you that she should not travel alone and…'

'Captain Everard, I will be thirty years old in March,' she said. 'Thirty. Older than some bottles of wine.'

'You look considerably younger,' he replied, then addressed her father. 'Sir, what would *you* do if a pretty lady who barely looks four and twenty argues that she is safe on the mail coach?'

'Overrule her, naturally,' Papa replied.

'Papa!' Verity exclaimed, at a loss.

There they stood. Mama whispered in Papa's

ear. He brightened, nodded, avoided Verity's glance and spoke to the captain.

'Captain Everard, would you consider something a little radical?'

'As long as it does not involve mayhem.'

'You are all hopeless,' Verity said.

'Just careful, daughter,' Papa replied. Verity saw the love and concern on his kind face. 'Captain, would you agree to… Augusta, what does one call such an ad hoc proposition?'

'An Engagement of Convenience,' Mama said, as calmly as if she had suggested a turn about the garden to look at roses in July.

'What?'

Silence reigned supreme in the Newsomes' hall, Verity too stunned to say more, Mama and Papa nodding at each other in evident satisfaction and Captain Everard… She could not define his expression.

Papa recovered first. 'I would have no objection to that,' he said. 'What say you, sir?'

Verity tried again. 'But…but… Papa, besides being unheard of, this isn't necessary.'

Drat Captain Everard. Why did he have to lean close enough to whisper in her ear?

'Beg pardon, Miss Newsome,' he whispered. 'Too many years around big guns have made me slightly hard of hearing. Could it be that you do not wish an engagement that would be temporary in nature?'

'Oh, I…' Hands on her hips, she glared at him. 'See here, sir, this is unnecessary.'

'I think it would please your parents,' he said.

The captain turned to her father. 'As I see it, such an engagement would suffice for the trip to Norfolk. I can escort your daughter to Hipworth Hall, assure Sir What's-His-Name that this is my fiancée and I am headed back to sea. Perfect.'

'Have you all lost your senses?' Verity asked, which meant the three of them started to laugh.

Captain Everard made it worse by taking her hands in his. 'It's completely unexceptional. You'll get to Norfolk, your parents won't worry and…'

'Captain!'

Then he delivered the statement she had no argument against.

He squeezed her fingers gently. '…and I can do a final service for an excellent officer gone too soon.'

'Oh, but—' she said, even though she knew the matter was now closed.

'Perhaps you had better…er…pack.'

He smiled then, a huge smile that transformed his face. If she hadn't been so irritated with him, she would have enjoyed the sight.

'Or rather I should say, go and pack, my dearest love.'

Chapter Ten

They left at the ungodly hour of six in the morning. Joe had no difficulty with early times. From the looks of his soon-to-be travelling companion and sudden fiancée, the matter was thornier. Miss Newsome was obviously not a cheerful riser.

'I gather you are not a lark,' he said and regretted his good cheer the moment the words tripped off his lips like happy sprites and crashed to the floor, victims of a frown and a pout.

She did have lovely lips, full and nicely chiselled. Wiser now, he knew better than to venture another comment, positive or negative. Some people needed an hour or two to accustom themselves to a new day. On the other hand, he felt like a wrung-out rag after eleven in the evening. Make that ten. She would find out soon enough.

Over breakfast, the Newsomes and Joe discussed the matter of an engagement ring while Verity ignored the three of them. She turned her attention to her baked egg, but soon gave up.

Breakfast might be her favourite meal, but this morning it was gall and wormwood.

'I don't have anything even for short loan,' Joe confessed.

'You can tell anyone who asks that this is a quite recent engagement and you haven't a ring yet,' Mama said.

Verity raised her eyebrows. Obviously she was not one to indulge in prevarication.

He couldn't disagree with her reluctance. 'Perhaps, Mrs Newsome, but too many lies require extreme vigilance in keeping a story straight.'

'And you know this *how*, Captain?' Verity asked, all sweetness.

'Miss Newsome, my darling, affianced dear, I was eight years old once, as hard as that is to credit. I recall a painful spanking from my mother.'

Good God, where was his conversation coming from? Not a single member of his crew would recognise him.

Miss Newsome seemed to take pity on him then. 'Very well. We can say it is an engagement of recent origin,' she conceded, after a sigh of theatrical proportion.

'Which is precisely true,' Captain Everard said, keeping his expression bland. 'Only a mere ten hours ago I was a free, unencumbered man.'

Miss Newsome burst out laughing. She looked in the captain's eyes and he gazed back, perfectly calm. This was no fleet action, but he was beginning to enjoy himself.

'Oh, for goodness sake. We'll be late,' she said.
'Eat your eggs, Captain.'

'I'd better be Joe to you, Verity,' he told her.

It appeared that a fair number of Weltby's citizens were either travelling this morning, too, or liked to see people off on a journey. To Joe's eyes, most seemed to have no specific purpose at all.

'Does everyone in Weltby bail out at Christmastime?' he asked, genuinely puzzled. 'What do you make of this, Mr Newsome?'

Augustus Newsome regarded the crowd and turned back to Joe with a bland expression containing the hint of apology to it, which roused Joe's suspicions.

'I mentioned to a few people in the village yesterday that you were a genuine Trafalgar hero, come to offer personal condolences to us about Davey,' he said.

'No hero. I was merely attending to my duty.'

Mr Newsome continued to beam at him, so Joe tried another tack. 'We weren't doing anything glamorous,' he said, as the crowd gathered closer. 'Frigates serve as repeaters in a large ship-to-ship engagement as Trafalgar was. We were just doing our job.'

He didn't mean to raise his voice, but there was Verity's hand on his arm. Her touch calmed his heart, something he needed at that exact moment, because Trafalgar felt too real again.

He dug deep and thank God the coachman was climbing into his box. 'The real heroes are those of you who give us your sons,' he said quietly. 'I mean that with all my heart.' He touched his chest. 'Thank you from the bottom of mine.'

Goodness gracious, now his audience was sniffing.

'Are ye bound back to war, sir?' someone in the crowd asked.

'Aye, but first I have agreed to escort Miss Newsome to Norfolk,' he said, happy to change the subject.

Knowing looks passed from one to another, which made his face feel warm. He knew small villages because he came from one, where people shared all news because nothing important ever happened. He looked for kindness and charity in those eyes, and did not look in vain. They could imagine all they wanted over someone who was obviously a village favourite, from the kind looks coming Miss Newsome's way. No need for him to explain himself further.

'It is one last service I could perform for my second lieutenant,' he said. 'I do it with pleasure. Good day. I believe the coachman would like to keep to his time.'

He held out his hand for Verity and helped her up, where four travellers already on the coach looked back at them. One rotund little fellow moved as close as he could to the window, but the space remaining was scarcely adequate.

Miss Newsome seated herself next to the window and he squeezed in beside her.

'I wish I didn't have to keep explaining myself,'

he whispered to her. 'I didn't reckon it would be this hard.'

'Easily dealt with,' she whispered back. 'Put your bicorn in my lap and your head against my shoulder and go to sleep.'

'I'm not tired,' he whispered back.

'I am. Be quiet and pretend.'

'There's no room for my arm,' he said, feeling like a pouty child.

'Put it around my shoulders,' Miss Newsome replied. Was the woman never at a loss?

She was right. He eased his arm around her shoulders and gained enough space to wedge himself into the tight space. But his head on her shoulder? They were much the same height, so the theory was sound enough. He tested cautiously, and actually found himself relaxing. Maybe he hadn't slept as soundly last night as he had imagined. Maybe he hadn't slept well in weeks.

He woke up several hours later, looking around in surprise because he had actually relaxed. Miss Newsome was knitting and chatting with a woman about her age seated across from her, from the looks of her about ready to give birth.

Without raising his head from its admittedly comfortable resting place—thank goodness Miss Newsome wasn't a skinny thing with bones everywhere—he managed a sideways glance at the little man crowding him, also asleep and leaning against him.

Such a dilemma: if he sat up, the porky fellow

would likely wake up, too. Joe doubted too many men had leaned against Miss Newsome, which he privately discovered was a pleasant thing to do.

'I could sit up, but I would wake up the man leaning against me,' he whispered to Miss Newsome.

'Let him be, then,' she said. 'I'm having no trouble knitting and you are not a burden,' she replied. 'In fact, if I may speak plain, I like the fragrance of your cologne. So does Mrs Black. Mrs Black, let me introduce Captain Everard. Joe, Mrs Black is the wife of a joiner and headed home after a week visiting her sister.'

'Pleased to make your acquaintance,' he said, ready to laugh at the incongruity of the situation, but happy to have his notion confirmed about the interesting people one could meet on the mail coach.

'Same here,' Mrs Black said. She shifted a little and winced, obviously finding not a single bit of comfort in her gravid state. 'We've been wondering, your wife and I, where you got that fragrance. She said you're newly back from Trafalgar.'

'Oh, but...' Miss Newsome began saying. 'I should explain...'

Oh, worse and worse. Mrs Black was labouring under a not surprising misapprehension, since he had made himself at home against Miss Newsome, with his arm around her shoulder and his fingers drooping perilously close to her bosom. Joe didn't know a great deal about social niceties, but he strongly suspected that even a fiancé would not sit this way. Mrs Black had made the logical connection. If he said anything, fiancé or not, she would probably be aghast.

'I *was* at Trafalgar and newly back,' he said quickly. 'I haven't had enough time to tell Verity all my stories.'

He could explain to Verity later why he was continuing an understandable error. 'My crew had an opportunity to relieve the officers of the captured *Ildefonzo* of some personal possessions. I am the dubious beneficiary, but I like lemon, too.'

'Poor, deluded men,' the joiner's wife said in sympathy. 'Couldn't you stop the looting?'

'Joe… Captain Everard…was unaware of it,' Miss Newsome said, as smoothly as if she lied every day. 'You can see that he had a dreadful wound to his face.'

'That's the whole story,' Joe said, well aware that it was fiction—calling it a story was no stretch. He had bought the cologne at Gibraltar, where they docked for enough repairs to limp them home. 'Spoils of war, Mrs Black, and nothing more.'

Apparently satisfied, Mrs Black continued her own knitting and Verity returned to the sock in her lap. Considering discretion the better part of valour, Joe pretended to be asleep.

When they arrived in Whistler, he happily escorted Mrs Black from the mail coach and wished her well with her upcoming blessed event. She touched his heart by kissing his cheek and thanking him for his role at Trafalgar.

'Please tell Mrs Everard how mindful England is of her family's sacrifice,' she said.

'I will,' he said and that was no lie.

He helped Verity down next because the coachman had announced a noon stop. He laughed inside at the contrition on her face and waited for her apology, which wasn't long in coming.

'Captain, I had no idea she would assume we were married,' she whispered. 'I never had a chance to mention our engagement and I didn't want to embarrass her.'

Her lips nearly tickled his ear and he found the sensation beguiling and far from unpleasant. 'No fears, Verity,' he said. 'If the others on the coach continue their journey, we have no choice but to continue the charade.'

'It's perhaps regrettable, but no hardship,' Miss Newsome said. 'We looked even more casual than an engaged couple, didn't we?'

'Decidedly ramshackle on my part, but I have to say that your shoulder is comfortable.'

'And your arm around me equally so,' she said quietly. 'But that is travel on the mail coach, eh?'

Chapter Eleven

The charade continued, because the round man remained aboard.

'There is one problem with lying,' Verity whispered as they tried to make themselves comfortable for the continuation of the journey.

'Only one?' he teased.

'Wretched man,' she said with some feeling. 'We have to remember our lies so we do not misspeak.'

'Heaven forbid,' Joe said, enjoying this journey more by the minute. Blockade life bored him so badly that even this gentle misdemeanour amused him excessively. Still, a man should explain himself.

'When we followed Villeneuve and the *Bucentaure* from Toulon, and thence to Trafalgar, you could have sliced our enthusiasm with a sharp knife and made a sandwich of it,' he whispered. 'Every one of us happily traded the boredom of the blockade for sea action.'

'Even my brother?' she asked without a falter.

'Especially Davey. He was eager for action. That is life at war.'

Her tears did not surprise him. He put his arm around her and touched her head until she rested it on his shoulder this time. Her bonnet poked his eye so he removed it and placed it in her lap. Nothing was easier than inclining his head against hers and giving her his handkerchief.

He met the sympathetic looks of the new riders on the mail coach with honesty, or as near as. 'I am Captain Everard. I served at Trafalgar and my dear…wife's brother died under my command,' he said. 'Forgive us, please.'

He would have told the simpler lie, but the silent little man had not quitted the coach. What else could he do? The engagement of convenience that had seemed so plausible and foolproof in the Newsomes' sitting room had not lasted for the smallest portion of the journey.

The other riders nodded in sympathy and spoke quietly among themselves, content, apparently, to leave the Everards alone. The round fellow gave them a benign glance and settled back with his book again.

'Dear wife?' his incorrigible helpmeet whispered after she blew her nose.

'Only the best for me, my heart,' he whispered back, wondering where this gleeful streak was coming from. This earned him a little dig in his ribs, which further strengthened the reality that not one single midshipman on the *Ulysses* would recognise this side of their Captain. He would have to tell that to Verity when they had a moment alone.

Verity had relaxed against his shoulder, which touched his heart for some strange reason. Maybe she trusted him; more likely she was simply tired.

As the afternoon wore on, he became aware that the mail coach was travelling slower and slower. A glance out the window explained the matter. The rain that had started falling after their noon stop had turned into sleet and then slush.

Slower and slower, and then a stop. He looked out again, surprised at the gloom, then realised that he had returned to sleep as well, Verity tucked close to him and his head against hers.

He sat up carefully, not wanting to wake her. He heard the relief in the coachman's voice when he announced they had arrived at Chittering Corner, where they would stop for the night. The other riders left the coach quickly, leaving them alone, which bothered Joe not a bit. With any luck, the silent rider had found his destination, which would simplify the rest of the trip. He gave his head a mental slap. What about the others who had heard his 'dear wife' remark?

Please, Lord, let them be from Chittering Corner and walking home now, he thought. It wasn't too much to ask.

Joe touched Verity's shoulder, feeling shy even though they had spent most of the after-

noon cuddled close in sleep. She woke up and
looked around, but stayed in his loose embrace.

'Where are we?'

'Chittering Corner,' he said. 'This is our stop
for the night.'

'Somehow I thought we would travel through
to Norfolk.'

'Unlikely, even in good weather,' he told her.
'Your strength does not lie in geography or navigation. I should have found that out before we became, ahem, engaged.'

She smiled at that, a sleepy smile that touched
his heart again. Her eyes were heavy-lidded anyway, a feature he had not thought to find so attractive.

'Let us venture inside and seek a couple of
rooms,' he said. 'I can make arrangements.'

Joe stepped from the mail coach and felt the
mud ooze over his shoes. Whoever cleaned shoes
in this inn would be busy tonight, he decided.
Luckily it was but a few steps to the inn, somehow appropriately named the Noah's Ark. He held
out his arms for Verity.

'I'll carry you,' he said hopefully in his captain's tone of voice.

It worked. She took one look and didn't argue.
She put her arms about his neck and let him carry
her the short distance to the Ark. The coachman's
assistant slogged behind with luggage.

The inn was crowded with other travellers from
early coaches and he wondered if there would be
a room for Verity. He knew he could sleep any-

where. Oh, no. He saw familiar faces smiling at him, even leading him to the desk where the innkeeper waited.

'Captain, these riders tell me that you fought at Trafalgar.'

'Aye, sir, as did many others in the fleet. Is there possibly a room left?' he asked.

The keep leaned over the desk. 'There would not have been, but for the generosity of these,' he said. He gestured to the little traveller and the clergyman Joe recognised. 'This man and this man said they would make themselves comfortable in the public room so you and your wife could have the last room. It's the least we can do for a hero and his wife, who probably seldom sees him.'

The older fellow nodded. So did the round, silent gentleman. Caught and trapped.

Joe looked around at Verity, who gave the slightest shrug of her shoulders, indicating she had no idea how to get out of this mess, either.

He could try. 'Perhaps my…wife, uh, my wife could share this room with another lady who would otherwise be discommoded.'

'Look around, Captain. It's just us men tonight.' The keep chuckled. 'Between you and me, sir, the ladies are always smarter about these things.' He held up that single key. 'You have a room at the inn,' he said with a laugh. 'Matthew, Mark, Luke and John could tell you how hard that is to come by at this season! Cost you three shillings, and that includes dinner. Come, sir, and take it.' He added a leer to the laugh. 'How often

are you ever on land long enough to get reac-
quainted with this little lady you married? Three
cheers for the Navy!'

What have I done? Joe asked himself as he
pocketed the key in the middle of enthusiastic
applause.

Chapter Twelve

I daren't laugh, Verity thought. She wanted to in the worst way. She had not a single doubt that Captain Everard would treat her with the greatest respect, no matter what others imagined would be happening behind that door, but she couldn't help smiling, which only encouraged the innkeeper.

'See there, Captain? Mrs Everard is smiling!'

Soon everyone was at least grinning, except for the captain, who had a stricken look on his face, as if wondering how what had begun as a simple plan had turned into this.

The innkeeper didn't know when to stop, apparently. 'Cheer up, Captain Everard,' he said. 'I imagine it has been a long time since you have been ashore, to say the least.'

'You cannot imagine how long it has been,' the captain said. 'I scarcely can.'

Verity had to give the captain his due. He took a deep breath and crooked out his arm. 'Come, my dear.'

'Shall I send my wife upstairs directly with a dinner menu?' the keep asked.

'Please do,' the Captain replied. 'We would like to eat at six.'

The innkeeper bowed. Verity let Joe lead her out of the lobby, but not before she heard one of the wags from the public room make some not-so-silent comment about Captain Ever-hard. The captain sighed and tightened his grip on her arm.

I'll pretend I didn't hear that, she thought, even as she wanted to sink into the floor.

He was utterly silent on the stairs and down the hall to the sole remaining empty room in the inn. She had to give him credit for a steady hand with the key in the lock. A glance at his face showed her a man with high colour on his face and grim, tight lips.

He opened the door, ushered her inside and stood there, looking as uncertain as the most callow youth to be found anywhere civilised society existed.

'Captain Everard, you probably thought it would be a simple matter to escort me to Norfolk, didn't you?' Verity said as she removed her bonnet, fluffed her hair and looked around.

The Noah's Ark was true to the sign creaking in the wind outside: no more than two at a time would fit in this room. The bed occupied most of the space, with a begrudging amount of room left over for a small table, two chairs and a fireplace. She opened the door on a tiny closet. A washbasin and stand filled the rest of the room. There wasn't even room for a three-legged dog to turn around and lie down.

And there stood Captain Everard, looking positively stricken. *Now what?* Verity thought. As she stood there, bonnet in hand, all she wanted to do was laugh.

She sat down carefully on the bed, then leaped up when it squeaked. It more than squeaked; it seemed to shriek, as though every wooden peg was protesting years of abuse ranging from overweight occupants to amorous lovers.

She didn't want to look at Captain Everard, but the room was too small to ignore a fairly tall, sturdy fellow wincing at the sound and probably wondering how far it would carry. She couldn't help herself; she started to laugh.

She sat down in what she hoped was a quieter chair, leaned forward to let her forehead touch the table and gave herself over to mirth. She laughed as quietly as she could, too old at nearly thirty to care what anyone thought.

She suddenly heard a massive squeak from the bed and turned around to see Captain Everard lying there, his legs hanging over the edge, laughing along with her. He finally pressed his hand to his stomach and declared, 'Oh, stop! One of us has to stop or neither of us will.'

It took a moment. Every time she thought of the humour of the situation, Verity laughed a little longer. At last her good humour dwindled down to a hiccup, which set off the Captain again, for some reason. When he was finally silent, Verity looked at him lying there relaxed and felt her heart grow oddly tender.

She knew next to nothing about Captain Eve-rard's life, except that it had to be an exceptionally difficult one, with constant war and deprivation. Impulsively she reached out and touched his leg, which she instantly regretted. What a forward thing to do.

He only opened his eyes and smiled. 'This is nice,' was all he said.

'We should tell amazing lies more often, I sup-pose you will say,' she teased.

'I'm no liar and neither are you.' He started to sit up, then rethought the matter. 'I suppose I am fair amazed how people assume this or that. Ev-eryone assumes we are married. Tell me, Miss Newsome, do we *look* married?'

His question set her off again and she laughed. 'We rather do,' she said when she could speak. 'Look at you, flopped there!'

'No, no, I mean before now,' he said. 'I suppose we are of roughly the same age and there we were on the mail coach, sleeping like puppies in a pile.'

'I suppose,' she agreed, deciding to stop fret-ting over their situation. They would be in Norfolk tomorrow and he would have finished his obliga-tion to his late second lieutenant.

She noticed a slip of paper under the door and picked it up. 'Here we have the dinner bill of fare,' she told the Captain, whose eyes were closed now.

Heavens, whoever put this here must have heard a lot of laughter, she thought, which made her smile instead of worry what anyone thought. *We are only one night in Chittering.*

'Read it aloud,' he said, without opening his eyes. 'If anything contains beets, that is an automatic nay from me.'

'They're good for you,' she said, which earned her one open eye and a sour expression. She read the bill of fare. They debated a moment over shepherd's pie or roast beef and decided on the pie, with barley-broth soup first and custard last.

His eyes closed. In a moment he was snoring softly, which touched Verity's heart; he evidently felt comfortable. His arms were stretched out, his hands open. She saw no tension in him.

Feeling shy but hungry, Verity covered him with a light blanket and went downstairs with the menu. She reminded herself that she had always been forthright and no-nonsense and nothing had changed. Still, she had to steel herself to approach the innkeeper and hand him the menu.

'We would like these items,' she said.

'At six o'clock?' he asked, smiling at her, which told her all she wanted to know about who had put the menu under the door and heard their laughter.

'Yes, please,' she replied, ready to be formal, but governed by an imp of her own. 'You're probably wondering what was so funny.'

'Not at all, Mrs Everard,' he told her and she saw something wistful in his eyes now. 'War is war. Sometimes you need to laugh.'

His artless comment brought tears to her eyes, but they weren't tears of sorrow, for a change. She felt a kinship she had not anticipated and good will, which reminded her forcefully of the season, which sorrow had dismissed as too much to manage this Christmas.

Happy Christmas to me, she thought, *and Happy Christmas to Captain Everard.*

Chapter Thirteen

With a gentle hand on his arm, Verity woke him when dinner arrived. She had covered him with a blanket, and must have removed his muddy shoes and pulled his legs up on to the bed. Under cover of the blanket he touched his trouser buttons, relieved she had not gone so far as to unbutton him. He thought a moment, almost wishing she had.

Hands behind his head, comfortable as seldom before, he watched from the bed as the maid arranged the food on the table and stepped back, proud of herself. It was that kind of an inn, apparently. Verity gave her a coin and sent her on her way. Joe was struck how gracefully Verity performed that small service.

'You'll have to pry yourself out of bed for dinner,' she said.

He got up, excused himself for a visit down the hall—no sense in humming and hawing about nature—and returned to see the table set, wine poured and Verity with her finger in the soup, tasting it.

'Good enough?' he asked.

'Delicious,' she said, not in the least embarrassed. He had never met anyone like her.

They sat down to eat. What could have been a strained experience proved to be delightful in the extreme. Verity kept up a pleasant commentary on their fellow travellers, a funny story about David that made her tear up and smile at the same time, and what he suspected was the gentle talk of people at an English dinner table.

She even got him talking about the blockade and shook her head over the boredom of it. 'How do you keep from going stark raving mad?' she asked over custard.

Should he say? He put down his spoon and looked into her eyes. 'This may sound contrived, but I think about people like you who depend upon people like me.'

Her eyes were brown. With tears in them, they seemed truly like the limpid pools that poets spoke of.

Before the moment became maudlin, he had a question for her. 'What are your future plans?' he asked. 'They must go beyond teaching a few children on a Norfolk estate.'

'Do you mean, am I ambitious?'

'I suppose I do,' he replied. 'I always tell my subordinates to have one or two plans for every possible outcome.'

'Wise of you,' she said. 'If this new position

proves useful, I would like to apply myself towards a female academy. I know of one in Bath.'

'What would you teach?' he asked, intrigued and a little embarrassed at himself because he had never thought of women having ambitions beyond husbands and children.

'Perhaps English and diction.'

'What, no embroidery?' he teased.

'Never,' she said firmly. 'I am dreadful with needle and thread at the despair of my mother. I am also opinionated.'

He smiled at that. 'Not a bad thing.' He pushed back his empty bowl. 'You're quite prepared to move through life on your own.'

'I hope to be,' she said quietly. 'One takes the hand dealt and plays it, or so Davey used to tell me.'

'Good for you,' he said and never meant anything more.

He touched his sutures, wishing they did not itch, but she noticed the gesture.

'You know, I could remove those,' she said. 'You look like you want to scratch them, which suggests that they have pulled tight and done their job. Or you could do it yourself. I have a pair of small scissors.'

'I'm squeamish,' Joe said and couldn't help a laugh. 'Good God, I've seen men cut in two by cannon fire and I don't want to take scissors to a simple stitch.'

She took a deep breath at his clumsy comment and he could have slapped his forehead.

'Beg pardon. That was indelicate.'

'No, it was honest,' Verity replied. She reached out and turned his cheek to one side. 'I need some tweezers. Perhaps I can find a pair downstairs. I'll send the maid up for the dishes, too.'

She left the room before he could protest or agree. He listened for footsteps, but heard none. She must be standing there, perhaps gathering herself together after his stupid comment. He wanted to fling open the door, apologise and hold her close.

In a moment he heard her steps on the stairs. A few minutes later the maid came to retrieve the dishes. After she left with a shy smile at the additional coin he gave her, Verity returned. She held up the tweezers.

'Your fate is in my hands, Captain,' she said. 'Sit down.'

He sat, slightly apprehensive, which must have showed in his eyes because she chuckled.

'Coward,' she remarked. She bent over and then straightened up. 'Will you think me unbearably forward if I ask you to lie down on the bed?'

'Heavens, no,' he said. 'We've discussed politics and custard and laughed about that silent fellow in the coach. Do with me what you will.'

She laughed, as Joe hoped she would, even as he wondered deep down in that place no one had ever touched before, if he didn't mean it.

Chapter Fourteen

He lay down and slid over to accommodate her. There was no denying her high colour. He knew she had never done anything like this before with a man nearly a stranger, except he did not feel like a stranger.

It was more than that. Certainly in his lengthy naval career he had stretched out on a bed with a woman nearby, but never like this. It touched him, mainly because her care seemed so homely, almost as if she truly were his wife. He knew he was in good hands.

He closed his eyes when she started to snip through the centre of each suture. Six snips. He opened one eye.

'See here, I am being brave.'

'You are marvellous,' she replied. She set down the scissors. 'Hopefully this won't curl your toes.'

She carefully teased out each suture, a frown of concentration on her face. The knot required a little tug, which made him wince, because the whole matter did terrify him.

'I have a scar on my neck from a Barbary pirate who thought to remove my head.'

'I see it. We have lived different lives, Captain Everard. Hold still.'

She gave another tug and nodded in satisfaction. 'Done.' She sat back. 'Have you any ointment?'

'Look in the drawstring bag inside my duffel. Jar right on top.'

Obviously embarrassed to be fumbling in his duffel, she found the jar, returned to the bed and applied a dab of goose grease. 'It's an honourable scar.'

Joe sat up and touched his cheek gingerly. 'I won't frighten babies, will I?' he asked, thinking it was in jest, but not entirely certain. Suppose, just suppose, he ever married and returned to port after a voyage to a new baby in his theoretical wife's arms? Would he frighten babies seemed like a good question.

Well, damn him if she didn't take him seriously. 'Neither yours nor anyone else's,' she said.

And damn him again if she didn't go right to the meat of their next problem. She looked around the room elaborately—which reminded him forcefully of her brother, about to announce some misdeed—and plainly stated, 'There is no room for one of us to be gallant and sleep anywhere but on this bed.'

He returned some vapid remark, which earned

him a frown—my God, but the woman had a way about her!—and the comment, 'The issue remains, sir: how are we going to accomplish this?'

There she stood, hands folded so ladylike, face charming, but not a woman to be bamboozled, gulled or otherwise suckered into anything not of her choice. She radiated independence in a manner that he found more than admirable. Verity Newsome was an utter original, a woman who could stand her ground.

'How, indeed?' he teased. 'I like you a lot, Verity Newsome, but I would never dream of shenanigans.'

Her eyes lively, she dipped a little curtsy that made him laugh. 'I like you, too, Captain Everard, but your virtue is safe with me.'

They both laughed at that and suddenly, improbably, maybe against his own personal counsel, he loved her.

The idea jolted him and he immediately thought of all manner of reasons why it was foolish: the war, the times, the tides, the mere logistics. He brushed them all aside and decided on the spot to see what he could engineer in Hipworth Hall to change matters in his favour. As for right now, he was and would remain a gentleman, especially since he had no idea how Verity felt and knew better than to enquire.

But he was used to solving everyone's problems. He had a solution for the current dilemma. 'Simple. I will lie down on top of the coverlets, wrapped in a blanket, and you will get between the sheets. We will line up back to back. We will probably pretend all night that we are sleeping.'

She laughed and agreed. She went first to the necessary on the bottom floor and did whatever it was ladies did to prepare for bed. He left the room when she returned. When he came back after a decent interval, she was under the covers, her eyes resolutely closed.

So far, so good. He went into the tiny closet, struggled into his nightshirt and wrapped a blanket around himself.

She had taken the side of the bed near the door, which he took exception to.

'It will not do, Verity,' he said, after he doused the lamp. 'I realise this is a temporary arrangement, but I insist on being closest to the door.'

'Why?' she asked, even as she obligingly moved over to the side of the bed closer to the window.

'God rest his soul, my father told me once, "Lad, if you ever marry, always keep yourself in bed between your wife and the door."'

'But we're not married,' Verity pointed out.

'He was still right. Hush now and let us pretend to be asleep.'

She was close enough that he could feel as well as hear her chuckle.

He had to test the waters, simply because he knew they would be in Hipworth tomorrow and his own intentions had changed. 'Do we look married?' he asked into the darkness.

'We're of that age,' she said. 'I'm not going to see twenty again…'

'Horrors,' he teased and she thumped him.

'You are somewhat older,' she said, getting her dig in and making him smile.

'I am not a day over forty,' he told her.

'Maybe not a day, but how about a thousand or so days?' she asked.

He rose up on one elbow, ready to turn around, then thought better of it. 'I really *am* forty. War tends to age one. Imagine.' He thought of fleet actions and young men dead, and sighed.

When she spoke, she seemed subdued. 'I should have thought of that, sir. We are of an age to fool anyone on a mail coach, without even meaning to.'

He could tell she briefly rose up on one elbow and thought better of it. 'We do have a certain camaraderie, do we not?'

He smiled in the dark. 'I believe we do. I've enjoyed it. Go to sleep.'

'Not yet,' she said, surprising him. 'I have to tell you that Davey spoke highly of you in his letters.'

'He got his fair share of scolds and dressings down from me, I assure you,' Joe replied .

'He wrote about those, too,' she said. 'In his last letter, he mentioned a regular fierce jobation from you about letting a midshipman get away with some minor misdeed.'

'I remember it well,' Joe said as he turned on to his back and put his hands behind his head, forgetting the rules they had established. 'I told him in no uncertain terms never to slack off with a midshipman, else how would they learn the rigour of life in a warship? Lives depend on it, Verity.' He smiled at the memory. 'Davey stood there and took it like a champion.'

'Do you know what else? At the end of his letter he added a postscript.'

'About how he could barely wait to transfer to a different frigate?'

'No. He wrote, "Some day, I want to be the commander Captain Everard is right now."'

She was in tears. Joe pulled her close as she wept.

'I wish to God he could have done precisely that,' Joe said softly as he held her close. 'I hate war.'

When her tears subsided, she turned from him, which hurt his heart. She must have been looking for a handkerchief, because soon enough he heard her blow her nose.

What should he do? He wanted to hold her close until she fell asleep. He imagined lonely nights as she lay in bed at home and cried for a beloved brother. He also knew he needed to turn his back. It was the sensible thing.

He didn't care. 'Come close, Verity. Don't be sad by yourself. I'll hold you.'

She went into his arms. He held her close until she felt heavy against him and slept. He never wanted to move again, even as he knew dawn would come, as it always did. Thank goodness they both had plans for their futures that did not involve each other.

Easy to think; harder to believe. He lay there in silence, cradling Verity Newsome to his chest as she slept. When the strangeness of the experience turned into ineffable sweetness, he slept, too.

Chapter Fifteen

When Verity woke, the captain was gone. She hoped she hadn't snored or drooled in her sleep, and then laughed at herself, imagining what her mother would think of this admittedly odd situation.

That was the virtue of being nearly thirty: no one in the Newsome family need ever know.

She dressed quickly, but took longer with her hair than usual. She thought of all the years when she hadn't cared about her hair. It mattered now, because someone she more than admired had seen it spread out on a pillow.

More than admired. Could last night have been any more awkward? As she brushed and combed, Verity realised it had been anything but that.

She had always been the family member to decorate for Christmas. This year of Trafalgar had proved too difficult, except for the ivy she and Captain Everard had gathered and which she had strung on the banister, her tardy gift to the season.

But as she stood there, brush in hand, she felt the peace of the season nestle into her heart, much as she had nestled so close to a man generous enough to let her mourn a little longer. She knew she would never forget Davey. She hoped she was not being a traitor to want to remember him less relentlessly. Time would work on the raw spots.

She took heart, knowing soon the mail coach would let her off in Hipworth, and she could continue doing what she loved so well, teaching children. If she made a creditable showing, perhaps there would be good letters of reference to move her into a position at a young ladies' school, as she had told Captain Everard.

Verity stuffed a few hairpins here and there to complete her efforts. She would have managed quite well, if she hadn't stood there one moment too long, looking into her reflection and deep into her eyes.

Don't leave me in Hipworth, Captain Everard, she told her reflection. *I don't care how dangerous your life is. Let me share it with you.*

Where that little revelation had come from, she couldn't have said. Hadn't she told the man only last night of her ambitions and seen his smile of approval? He was kindness itself and she knew he wished her well, but probably nothing more.

Ah well. Maybe it was enough to wander into his orbit, much as Davey had done. In her brother's eight months aboard the *Ulysses*, his letters had shown her a new maturity, the kind that comes from hard work and good leadership. If only there had been more time.

Knowing what everyone in the Noah's Ark supposed about their night together at the inn, she should have felt more reluctant to go downstairs. She didn't because she decided to embrace the falsehood, honestly devised, for a few more hours, and resolve to remember it forever. It was harmless enough, and she needed to store up memories against the winter of her spinsterhood.

Joe had been working his magic below stairs. When she came into the public room, the captain was holding his small audience of the innkeeper and his wife and two daughters captive with a tale of sea life on the far side of the world. She stood in the hall and listened, wanting to hear his stories, too.

A person can only stand in a hall and eavesdrop so long. She entered the room and was waved in by her supposed husband. His gesture was so informal and probably precisely something a husband would do. He didn't rise; he generously allowed her into his seafaring world, too.

'Everyone thinks my life is glamorous, Verity,' he told her as she sat down beside him. 'You know it is not.'

'We still think it is glamorous, Mrs Everard,' the keep's wife said. 'Eggs and bacon, dear?'

As she ate—he had already eaten, but made her smile by filching a piece of bacon from her plate—he continued his narrative. The scattering of guests in the dining room also listened, in-

cluding the round little fellow who had been their
coach companion for much of yesterday.

The arrival of the mail coach ended the lop-
sided conversation. As the travellers prepared to
leave, Joe took her aside in the hall and helped
her into her cloak.

'You are quite the entertainer,' she said.

'I did it for you,' he told her quietly. 'How else
could I let you know of Davey's life, those inci-
dents that never made it into letters home? Was
it enough?'

Touched to her heart's core, she leaned forward
and rested her forehead against his chest. 'Thank
you,' seemed fearsomely inadequate, but it was
all she could manage.

The snow had lessoned and they continued
their journey. This time, the silent man sat across
from them. Feeling remarkably forward, Verity
caught his attention.

'I do beg your pardon, sir, but you've been so
silent on this journey.'

The fellow nodded to her and permitted himself a tiny smile. 'I come from a large, noisy and
vulgar family,' he said. 'Imagine my delight to
be able to ride and read in silence.' With that, he
returned to his book.

They arrived at Sudbury in late afternoon, everyone in the crowded mail coach ready for the
journey to end, if frowns and exasperated sighs
were any indication. The trip should have ended

closer to noon, but snow began to fall more heavily with every hour.

The greatest relief Verity felt came when they were the only two travellers who disembarked. The silent man stayed on the coach.

'I intend to consider that a Christmas miracle,' she told Joe as they stood with their baggage by the entrance to the inn. She couldn't help a laugh. 'After his comments, do you suppose he is one of those men who contrives travel so he can read in blissful silence?'

'Who could blame him?' the captain joked. 'I am relieved, too. Think of our imaginary dirty linen he could have waved about, were you to be introduced to the probably censorious citizens of Sudbury as Miss Newsome.'

She rolled her eyes. 'It doesn't bear thinking about and you know it!'

She took his arm as they walked towards the inn. 'All's well that ends well, I suppose. I will advise Mama never to create an engagement of convenience again.'

'Wise of you.'

The innkeeper inside only shrugged when she enquired if a conveyance had arrived earlier in the day from Hipworth Hall.

'Nothing's stirring, m'um,' he said.

'I'm the new teacher for Sir Percy Hipworth,' she told the man. 'I know he is expecting me.'

'That may be, m'um, but 'tween you and me, Sir Tight Pursey never much concerns himself about the comforts of others.'

Oh, dear. 'Perhaps he forgot,' she said, wishing the best of her new employer because she had to.

He shrugged again and leaned closer in a conspiratorial manner. 'A teacher, you say? That'll be a first for Hip-worthless Hall.'

He would have said more, but Captain Everard had fixed him with a scowl she suspected as coin of the realm for a naval officer demanding silence.

'Then acquaint us with someone who can convey us to Hipworth Hall, if you will,' Joe said. 'I am Miss Verity's escort and this is my last duty to discharge.'

The innkeeper hurried into the gathering darkness, likely in search of a carter. The words 'my last duty' sounded in her ears and she felt lower than at any point in the journey.

'"A first for Hipworth Hall"?' the captain said. 'What kind of port are you headed into? It's starting to sound like a lee shore to me, Verity.'

This was no time to bare her own uncertainties. 'When he made this arrangement, Lord Blankenship assured me I would be teaching,' she said. 'I have to trust he knows Sir Percy well.'

Her disquiet increased when the keep returned with a carter in tow, a cheerful fellow who assured them that if they didn't mind a little weather, he could get them to Hipworth Hall, which wasn't far.

'A little weather?' was Joe's comment as he helped her into the narrow seat directly behind the carter and saw to the arrangements of her luggage and his solitary duffel before he climbed in.

Cold inside and out, Verity bowed her head against the pelting snow. Without a word, Joe wrapped her inside his own boat cloak. 'No sense in having you arrive frozen and half-dead on your future employer's doorstep,' was his only comment.

There was no need for conversation, because the carter supplied the text as he hunched inside himself and urged on his horse.

'A teacher for Hipworth Hall? That's a good plan, says I. Hipworth's scamps have had free rein too long, from what I hear at the estate from my cousin the gardener,' he said.

She returned some remark, wishing herself anywhere but here, and yet enjoying Captain Everard's comforting presence.

'Get along now, my beauty,' the man continued, addressing his struggling horse first. 'If he's hiring you, miss, things must be perking up. Rumour says t'man has debts everywhere.'

'Really?' was Joe's only comment. It was enough to keep the flow of words coming from their driver, who seemed to relish others' misfortunes.

'They say he's trying to marry off his daughter for money and to that *I* say fiddlesticks. She's a mousey piece and I doubt any man of sense would have her.' He chuckled at his own wit. 'They'd only inherit Sir Percy and Lady Hipworth, too, and I wouldn't wish that on my enemies, had I any.'

'Perhaps you have said enough,' Joe told him. 'Miss Newsome is soon to be his employee.'

'P'raps I have,' he agreed, ever cheerful. 'You'll do fine, missy. Here we are.'

She thought Captain Everard would see her inside and then leave, ready to retrace his steps towards Devon. Instead, he paid off the carter and sent him on his way.

'Captain Everard, I have encroached on your time long enough,' she said, even as she felt huge relief to find herself still with an ally.

'I'm not leaving you here alone,' he said. 'I'm concerned.'

'I am, too,' Verity admitted.

Captain Everard knocked. After a lengthy wait that only let her misgivings multiply, the door was opened by what must be the butler, but who looked more like a man tried to the end of his patience.

'Miss Verity Newsome is here at Sir Percy's request,' Captain Everard said. 'She is the new educationist.'

'Oh, my word,' he said as he ushered them inside.

Cold and snow-covered, she stood with Captain Everard and stared at the sight of what must be all the Hipworths bickering at the end of the hall.

The captain had obviously had enough. He cleared his throat and shouted, 'Merry Christmas!' in what she supposed was his voice used in gale-force winds.

As one, the quarrelling family turned and stared at them. What must be Sir Percy detached himself from the group and came towards them. He looked from her to the captain.

''Pon my word, sir, you needn't raise your voice,' he said. He turned to Verity and peered closer, looking her up and down until the captain beside her stirred and opened his mouth. She put a hand on his arm to stop him.

'I am your new educationist, Sir Percy and Lady…' she said and waited for an introduction.

'Lady Hipworth,' Sir Percy said. 'The governess.'

'The educationist,' Verity repeated.

'The governess. What on earth did Lord Blankenship tell you?'

'Oh, God,' Captain Everard said under his breath for her ears alone. 'We've fallen among thieves.'

Chapter Sixteen

Verity gave him a grateful glance, as if relieved he had said *we* instead of *you*. He looked over the shorter man's head to see a wife, the mousey daughter the carter had mentioned and two boys of roughly three and four years. The lads were kicking each other and the daughter looked like she wanted to disappear. He could scarcely blame her.

Someone had to take charge. Since this was his usual duty, Joe sized up the situation and did precisely that.

'Sir Percy, I assume?' he asked and didn't bother with the engagement-of-convenience nonsense. 'I am Captain Everard. I volunteered to escort Miss Newsome here, as a final service to my late second lieutenant, her brother. Perhaps you could invite us in and…'

'I didn't hire *you*,' Sir Percy said, which made Verity stir beside him and open her mouth to speak. It was Joe's turn to put a hand on *her* arm.

'No, you didn't,' Joe agreed. 'Her parents and I agreed it would be a kind gesture, considering the distance and the weather.'

'She's a spinster rising thirty, or so Lord Blankenship told me,' the man said, as if Verity weren't even there. 'Wouldn't think she'd require an escort.'

You, sir, are an abomination, Joe thought, as he bit back every word he wanted to utter, the kind of words that had quailed midshipmen and sufficiently chastened lieutenants on all seven seas.

'I suppose you are expecting us to put you up tonight?'

'It would be a kindness, Sir Percy,' Joe replied, wanting to grab the man's scrawny neck and wring it until he squawked. 'Once Miss Newsome is settled here, I will take my leave.'

'That will be tomorrow,' Sir Percy said. 'I'm not running an inn. Very well, come inside. Fowler, take their bags upstairs somewhere.'

Captain Everard removed his cloak and took off his hat and held them until it became obvious no one was going to relieve them from him. He draped them over a chair in the hall and helped Miss Newsome from her cloak. She could barely look at him, so great was her humiliation.

'Say the word, Verity, and we're out of here,' he muttered under his breath.

'Where would I go?'

'Home with me,' he said without thinking, he who had no home except his frigate. 'I mean, well, Kent.'

'Not without an attempt here, sir,' she whispered back. 'I need to earn my living.'

Not with these nincompoops, he wanted to say. Maybe he did say it, because Verity's eyes opened wide.

'And you need to be at Lord Nelson's funeral in less than two weeks,' she reminded him. 'Perhaps they're having a bad day. That happens around Christmas, I am told.'

He looked at the Hipworths, who had drawn themselves together, as if closing ranks against the enemy. He had seen that sort of behaviour aboard ships, when the fo'c'sle crew sniped at each other and promised all manner of bodily harm, only to draw into a unit when confronted by an officer. He doubted supremely that the Hipworths ever had a good day. A cursory glance suggested they enjoyed making themselves uncomfortable and, by extension, all others nearby. It was a quick assessment, but he was good at those.

Standing close to Verity, he waited as the elder Hipworths whispered to each other. The result was Lady Hipworth extending her hand in a gesture as theatrical as it was phony.

'Do join us for dinner, unless you have already eaten,' she said, then negated whatever hospitality she had attempted by adding. 'We weren't informed of your early arrival.'

Verity took up the gauntlet then and Joe had to give her credit for remarkable forbearance. 'Sir Percy sent a letter requesting that I arrive before rather than after Christmas, which is why I am here now,' she said, all the while keeping a firm grip on his arm.

'Yes, I did,' Sir Percy told his wife when she gave him a fishy stare. 'Didn't want us to be discommoded if the weather turned foul.'

Joe couldn't help himself. 'Sir Percy, wouldn't it have been a kindness to allow Miss Newsome one more holiday with her parents, after the recent loss of their son and her brother at Trafalgar?' he said.

His question met with blank stares.

A great silence seemed to settle over all of them until the lady of the house renewed her invitation to dinner. 'We are going in now, Captain. Join us, please,' she said, with a sigh of resignation. 'You may come, too, this time, Miss Newsome, but ordinarily the governess eats below stairs with the servants.'

'Governess? I had thought I was to be a teacher to these sons and your daughter,' Verity said. 'Lord Blankenship told me....'

'He was mistaken,' Lady Hipworth said. 'You will be paid twenty pounds a year for your service tending to our darling sons.'

The darling sons had resumed kicking each other. Captain Everard had to hand Verity the palm. He was ready to kick everyone.

'Your daughter, then? I will teach her.'

'She knows enough,' Sir Percy said. 'We're planning an advantageous marriage soon.'

'My congratulations,' Captain Everard said smoothly.

'As soon as we find a juicy match for her,' Lady Hipworth told him. 'Let's eat. The food is getting cold.'

The food was cold, but Captain Everard couldn't blame the staff. He had seen sullen looks aboard any number of ships as he made his way up the seniority ladder. On ships of war where the captain was a martinet and heartily disliked by one and all, he had noticed that those serving had ways of making life miserable for those served. He doubted it was any different on land, if he was correctly interpreting the surly expressions on the faces of the domestics probably working at Hipworth Hall because there was no other employment nearby.

The two boys, one Edward and the other Hector—which seemed an appropriate name for the one doing the bullying—kept up their sniping throughout the meal. The daughter, who mumbled that her name was Clarinda, mostly stared at her plate and kept her own counsel.

They were joined mid-meal by a youth who slouched in, looked around and seated himself next to Verity. It wasn't lost on Joe that there was a chair next to the lad's father where he could have sat.

'My son Gerald,' Sir Percy said, 'back from Gonville and Caius.' He laughed. 'Sent down a bit early for the holidays two weeks ago, eh, lad?'

The boy grunted.

'This here is Miss Newsome, who is going to

organise your little brothers,' Sir Percy said. 'And this is Captain Everard, Royal Navy.'

Gerald seemed to take an interest. He leaned across Verity, who leaned back, trying to keep her expression neutral. 'Taken lots of prize ships, sir?' he asked.

What did a man say to that? He heard Verity's gasp at such impertinence, even as Joe wondered how it was possible to raise feral children in the nineteenth century. He had heard stories of little ones found in the woods and supposedly raised by wolves, but as a natural sceptic he had discounted them. Maybe it *was* possible.

'I've done well enough,' was all Joe offered. His finances were his business alone.

Gerald wasn't done with him, apparently, which made Verity stiffen and set her lips in a tight line when the imposing mushroom leaned closer to her. Under cover of the table, Joe touched her hand, which made the high set of her shoulders relax, to his relief.

'I hear there's money to be made in the fleet,' Gerald said. 'Could you put in a good word for me? There must be lots of openings for officers, after Trafalgar.'

That was his limit. Joe pushed back his chair and rose to his feet, taking Verity with him. He thought she might object, but she stood beside him. In that moment, confronted by awful people, he knew his course.

'Miss Newsome and I will leave at daylight,' he snapped. 'This is no place for humans.'

Sir Percy gave his son a filthy glance. 'Sit ye down, Captain Everard! We are men of the world, are we not? I'll pay Miss Newsome thirty pounds a year, which she seems to think I promised. Maybe she can pound some wisdom into Edward and Hector. Calm yourself, sir.' He glanced out the window. 'Besides, it is snowing and I doubt you can go anywhere tomorrow.'

I can try, Joe thought grimly. 'Only if there will be no more hurtful comments,' he said, turning his fiercest quarterdeck stare upon Gerald, who shrank back and starting playing with his table knife.

'I was only teasing,' the lad whined. 'Didn't mean nothing.'

'Keep your remarks to yourself,' Joe said. 'Did no one ever tell you it is rag manners to lean across someone?'

Gerald left the room. Joe did not mistake the sigh of relief that seemed to rise from everyone. *Good God, does this frippery bunch of mushrooms fear that little weasel?* he asked himself, aghast. He was going to advise Verity to push a chair underneath the doorknob in her room tonight.

He exchanged glances with Verity. Her face, normally rosy, which provided such a lovely contrast to her black mourning, had gone chalk white, her eyes huge in her face.

What else could possibly go wrong? he thought, feeling helpless, an unusual emotion for him. *Can tomorrow come soon enough?*

Chapter Seventeen

It was easy to plead exhaustion from travel and ask directions to her room. Verity sank down on the bed, appalled at the situation she found herself in. Joe was ready to take her home tomorrow, or she could dig in and stay.

She knew she was a good educationist and she knew she had plans for herself. She knew Captain Everard had far too much responsibility to concern himself too long about the welfare of someone he had met only a week ago. The world was at war and he was needed by his nation. He had been kind to stand up for her, but she knew she needed to stand up for herself.

'You can do this, Verity,' she told herself. The odious Gerald would be returning to Gonville and Caius College, once the holiday was over, although how he managed to gain admittance in the first place to one of Cambridge's premier colleges she could not fathom. Obviously the family had plans for…for…what was her name? The quiet, cowed little thing had done nothing more than stare at the food on her plate during the entire, agonising meal. No matter what her parents arranged for her, it couldn't be worse than remaining one moment longer than necessary in such a household.

As for Edward and Hector, she knew little boys. She had taught more than a few who were high-spirited when they came to her in Lord Blankenship's estate school and who learned and matured. She had no doubt she could manage them, provided their parents let her.

I have to weather it, Verity thought. *Why would any academy of note hire me to teach if I could not prove myself?*

She looked around the room and was not disappointed. She could unpack in the morning. If she could weather a few years here and keep alert for better positions, she could manage.

She looked towards the door when she heard steps and voices. Loudest was Sir Percy, apologising for his gormless offspring, almost as if he wanted to placate the captain, heaven only knew why.

She settled the matter in her mind. When the door closed and the single set of footsteps faded, she had convinced herself to make the best of a bad business. Her resolve lasted until someone tapped on her door.

Cautious, not wanting to see the dreadful Gerald leaning in and leering at her, she asked, 'Who is it?'

'Joe. Let me in,' came back the whisper she wanted to hear, if she was honest with herself.

She opened the door. He had removed his shoes, which made her smile and wonder how much practice he had sneaking about in manors. Little, she imagined.

He closed the door quietly, leaned against it and folded his arms. 'What's it to be, Verity?'

'I will stay,' she told him quietly. 'If I am to advance, I need this position.'

'You can find another. Let me ask among my brothers in the fleet.'

You have no idea how tempted I am, she thought, even as she shook her head. He was too busy for this.

'Joe, you have fulfilled all obligations to my family,' she reminded him. 'I can manage two little boys.'

She didn't think she could look him in the eye and stared at the carpet. He put his finger under her chin and made her look at him.

'Come with me tomorrow,' he said and kissed her forehead.

He put his arms around her and she only hesitated a moment before doing the same to him. She tried to tell herself it was a brotherly embrace, but even she could not stretch that little fable. If only he wouldn't rub his thumb against the nape up her neck, which felt soothing and electric at the same time.

This would never do. 'Captain, you have done so much for me and I know there is a great deal on your mind,' she said as she disengaged herself from his embrace. He had never held her tight, so it was not difficult. 'I will manage here. Thank you from the bottom of my heart for your concern.'

He smiled at that and backed away. 'Miss Newsome, you are an independent lady, able to function on your own without a man's protection, aren't you?'

'I need to be, considering my spinster state,' she said, wishing he would go away, but enjoying, as always, his mild banter. She could pay him in the same coin. 'I enjoyed being Mrs Everard to all and sundry on the mail coach, but you have duties and so do I.'

He took it in good grace, making her promise to stick a chair back under her doorknob. 'I wouldn't trust anyone in this house.'

'You shouldn't either,' she teased, on safer ground. 'Did you see how Sir Percy's eyes lit up when his horrid son mentioned prize money? Be careful or he will try to foist his poor daughter on you.'

'When pigs fly, mum,' he teased back. 'Goodnight.'

She laughed and closed the door, grateful he could tease and thankful he would not be troubled much longer by worries which must seem trivial to him in the extreme. Someone who commanded a frigate had more on his mind than defending a spinster from toadies.

No one had bothered to put any coal in the

grate in her room, which surprised her not a bit. In the morning she would have to make the acquaintance of the cook and housekeeper, if there was one, and figure out her place in this decidedly ramshackle household.

She changed and crawled into bed, drawing herself into a little ball, already wishing for spring when it was still two days to Christmas.

She had closed her eyes and must have slept, but not soundly, because a small tap on the door across the hall woke her immediately. She cocked her head and listened, wondering what she was hearing. There it was again, a distinct tap.

She got out of bed quietly and padded to the door. She removed the chair she had propped there and opened it a crack.

Good heavens, there was mousey Miss Hipworth, tapping on Captain Everard's door. Verity's indignation gave way almost immediately to pity. Sir Percy must have ordered his daughter to do such a shocking thing, in the hopes that the captain would open the door so Miss Mouse could compromise the man and demand marriage.

She knew she would not put anything past Sir Percy. She hoped Captain Everard had the good sense she suspected, as long as he didn't think it was her and open the door.

The moment called for action and she did not hesitate, considering all Joe had done for her. She crossed the hall quietly and touched Clarinda Hipworth on the shoulder. The girl jumped, then ran down the stairs.

'Verity?' she heard at the closed door. 'Is that you?'

'It was Clarinda Hipworth before it was me,' she whispered back. 'I just saved you from a monumentally compromising situation.'

'So my virtue is intact?' she heard next, which made her laugh.

'I suppose as intact as it is ever going to be, considering you claim to be forty and have been a man of the world for a voyage or two,' she said when she could talk without giggling.

'Verity, remind me to put all of my funds in your name when I return to Plymouth,' he teased. 'Goodnight. Do consider leaving with me in the morning.'

Chapter Eighteen

No one was going anywhere in the morning. One glance out the window assured Joe of that. After negotiating with a servant girl to bring him enough hot water to shave, Joe managed to scrape his face and wonder if he could find his way back to Sudbury through mounds of snow.

Thank you, Verity Newsome, he thought again.

He had been about to open the door last night, thinking, perhaps wishfully, that the person on the other side was Verity. Her warning had probably saved him from utter ruin. He wondered if Papa Hipworth had planted himself somewhere close by in the dark to register shock and dismay at finding his only daughter in a room with an unmarried man wealthy enough to make everyone rejoice, then demand marriage and overlook such evil.

Joe looked out the window again, certain he could shoulder his duffel and escape, if the snow let up even a little. Getting Verity to come along might require more effort, but he had to try. It was a dilemma. He knew he loved her, but she seemed determined to make her own way in the world.

'You have no idea, Verity,' he told his shaving mirror. 'You are independent, stubborn and eminently qualified to make your own way without a man nearby. You are the perfect wife for a captain in the fleet.'

She was. She was also lovely to look at and kind. He had no doubt that he could return from sea a battered man, be resuscitated by her love and goodness, and return to the fight a better captain than he left it. If they were fortunate enough to make babies when he was briefly on land, their children would be independent and strong, too. What more could a seafaring man want?

It would help if she loved him. Such wooing, delivered mainly through correspondence, might require patience, but he was not afraid of the attempt. He was also something he had rarely been of late: he was hopeful.

So it was with a spring in his step that he went downstairs in search of something for breakfast. The dining room was precisely where he had left it and there sat the horrible Hipworths and someone else, who looked equally surprised to see him.

It was the little man from the mail coach, the chap who had hunched himself into the corner, slept and read, and kept entirely to himself. It was the man he had hoped only yesterday never to see again, when he wanted to shelter Verity from rumour and falsehood.

But Joe was a fast thinker. The man's presence made Joe realise he had an ally in Father Christmas, who governed the holiday, up to and including doing a kindness to folk who didn't expect it.

He gave a short prayer of gratitude consisting of a mere, *Thank You, Lord*, and said, 'What a surprise, sir.'

'You *know* Captain Everard?' Sir Percy said.

'A brief acquaintance on the mail coach,' the man said. 'How is your wife, Captain?'

'I have no wife,' Joe replied. 'You made an assumption that I suppose was logical. Who, sir, are you?'

The mail coach companion stared. Joe looked from the little man to Sir Percy and had his answer. 'Ah, you two must be brothers. And here I had assumed you were travelling on, after we were dropped off at Sudbury.'

'I did travel on, but only to Quarle,' the man said, sputtering scrambled eggs around the table, which confirmed him as a Hipworth, to Joe's amusement. 'It's nearer to my residence. What do you possibly mean, you have no wife? You two were cosy enough sharing a room at Chittering Corner.'

Lady Hipworth leaped to her feet and clapped her hands over her daughter's ears, which made the poor thing wince. 'What is this outrage, sir? Have we been about to nourish a viper in our bosom?'

Joe wanted to point out that she was amazingly flat chested and no viper could possibly find nourishment, but he had more sense than that. He shrugged. 'I can obviously tell you the truth and you wouldn't believe it. An earlier traveller on the coach had assumed, for no particular reason, that Miss Newsome and I were married. Being a kind-hearted lady, and not wanting to embarrass the woman, Miss Newsome said nothing.'

'But the inn! The inn!' the man exclaimed.

'Same thing,' Joe said, enjoying himself hugely. 'There is something about the two of us that makes people assume we are married. We were offered the only remaining room. If you recall, I suggested that considering the circumstances, another lady could share the room with Miss Newsome and I would happily have managed in the commons with the rest of you. But no one would hear of that, would they? There you have it.'

He went to the sideboard and dished up some cold eggs and congealing bacon. He ate because he was hungry and used to bad food.

The silence around him felt like a veritable presence. Lady Hipworth removed her hands from her daughter's ears and fumed at him. Joe regarded the daughter and felt nothing but sorry for her, trapped with odious parents. And there was Sir Percy, ready to pounce.

Joe followed nautical tactics, knowing it was always wisest to attack first, if the wind was right. He pushed away his plate, ready to turn serious.

'Sir Percy, did you send your daughter upstairs to knock on my door last night?' he asked.

His unwilling host's guilty look was clearly

evident. Joe glanced at the brother and saw that open-mouthed stare again, but directed at Sir Percy, as if the man knew his brother was entirely capable of such devilment.

Lady Hipworth's gasp sounded theatrical in the extreme, but there was no denying the tears in her eyes. They looked genuine enough; so did the way she pulled her weeping daughter to her skinny chest.

'I would never do that,' Sir Percy declared after a moment, as if he had needed to consider all the other comments—precious few—available to him.

Coward to the bone, Sir Percy turned his attention to his defeated, terrified daughter. 'Tell them the truth, Clarinda.'

After an excruciating moment that made Joe cringe inside for her, the girl shook her head. 'The captain imagined it,' she mumbled.

'He was probably going across the hall to that woman's room, wasn't he?' Sir Percy demanded further.

She nodded. 'Miss Newsome was in the hall.'

'She was,' Joe agreed, even as he looked up and saw the lady in question standing in the door of the dining room, her eyes troubled. She must have heard the whole exchange and no one had noticed her. 'She heard your daughter tapping on my door and came to warn me not to open it.'

Tired of present company, Joe stood up. 'Assumptions and lies. Hurry up and fire Miss Newsome so we can shake the dust of this place off our feet.'

'You're fired!' Sir Percy exclaimed, pointing his finger at the love of Joe's life, even if she didn't know it.

'I was going to resign this morning,' she told him. 'Do not make your daughter suffer because she had to lie for you.'

'I would never do such a thing,' the baronet declared.

Sir Percy looked around the room. His wife couldn't meet his eyes. His daughter turned away. His brother shook his head.

'You're fired,' he repeated. 'If you attempt to seek another teaching position I will scotch you at every turn.'

Verity turned pale, but her attention went to Clarinda Hipworth. 'I wish I could take you with me,' she said, 'but I cannot. Perhaps your uncle might help you.'

'We don't need help,' Lady Hipworth said. Joe saw nothing but trouble ahead for this wife saddled with a supremely unscrupulous husband, a son about to become as useless as his father, a daughter who would always be victimised, with no relief in sight.

'Very well,' Joe said. He smiled at Verity, who looked nearly as troubled as Lady Hipworth, because he knew she had a soft heart. 'I'll return you to your home in Kent.'

'I think that best,' she said. 'I never unpacked.

I came down here to resign, before I heard any of this.'

'It's snowing to beat all hell outside,' Joe reminded her.

'The village is close and my baggage is not that heavy,' she said. 'If you can carry one valise, I can certainly manage the other. Now where is my cloak?'

Without another word, she turned on her heel. He followed her into the hall.

'I had no idea the little man was Sir Percy's brother,' he said by way of apology. 'He painted rather a lurid picture for everyone, as you can imagine.'

He saw no tears in her eyes, so he knew the whole sordid business had not ruined her. He saw sympathy instead.

'I would never treat my children that way, had I any,' she said as she took her cloak from the maid.

'I know you would not. Neither would I,' he replied, accepting his heavier cloak and bicorn and leaving a large coin. 'Let us see how tough we are in a Norfolk snowstorm.'

Chapter Nineteen

They were destined to travel no farther than Sudbury that night. The roads were closed and the inn full. Verity told the innkeeper's wife that she'd decided not to accept the position after all.

Verity had seen no more than a passing glance from the woman yesterday, but there was no mistaking the relief on her face. 'It's a terrible place,' the keep's wife told her. 'Any day now, I think Sir Percy's younger brother will own the manor and all the land. You're wise to go away.'

'I owe that to Captain Everard,' she said. 'He minced no words in finding a way to end my brief stay there.'

'He likes you, dearie,' the keep's wife said. 'I can see it in his eyes. Surely you can, too.'

'I never looked,' Verity said honestly. 'You must be mistaken. He has squandered far too much time helping me, when I know he has far more pressing matters on his mind.'

'I doubt it,' the keep's wife said. 'No man

is *that* busy and I know something about men. More'n you, anyway. Maybe you should look a little closer yourself.'

Verity was spared the spectacle of groping around for a suitable reply because the woman hurried off to the kitchen. She followed the woman, which seemed terribly forward of her, but she had a question.

Verity stopped her. 'I know you're busy, but answer me this: Do Captain Everard and I seem like a married couple to you?'

'Aye, you do,' she said. 'That's what I thought, anyway, until my husband said you were here about employment and the captain was your escort.' She laughed. 'You fooled us all!'

'But why? How?'

The woman set down the bowl, her expression thoughtful. 'It's the way he teased you and you laughed,' she said. 'I think you even argued a little about something. That's what married folk of some years do.'

Verity spent the afternoon sitting in the ladies' parlour with a clergyman's wife and a miss fretting over this delay in her return home from St Clare's Female Academy in Cambridge. It was a place Verity knew of, the sort of school where she wanted to teach some day. The girl's companion, a desiccated-looking lady, was a teacher there, if the conversations she overheard were accurate.

She listened on the sly, well aware as the afternoon advanced that perhaps she did not want to spend her holidays that way, escorting spoiled pupils home and living on the edge of everything. Better she stay at home. She could find some work on the estate or in the village—nothing exalted, but there might be an opportunity to flourish in a modest way that didn't leave her at the beck and call of others.

She wandered into the commons area once or twice. Captain Everard stood at the window, rocking back and forth, even pacing a bit, as she imagined he paced on his quarterdeck. He winked at her, but continued his pacing until she stopped him.

She watched his eyes. It began to dawn on her that perhaps an innkeeper's wife was right. She saw kindness and something else. Why not brazen it out? She put her hand on his arm. 'I hope you are not distressed that we're stuck in an inn, it is Christmas Eve and you're worried about me.'

'That's precisely what I am,' he said. 'You deserve better. I set out to do a good turn for Davey Newsome and I have muddled it.'

'How, exactly?'

She watched high colour arrive at his face, which would have made her smile, because she doubted that a post captain blushed overmuch.

'Do you really want to know?'

'I rather think I do.'

He looked around. 'This is not the right place,' he muttered. 'Oh, bother it, is anyone busy in the kitchen?'

'I'll look.'

Sure of herself now, she went into the kitchen, where the innkeeper's wife was chatting with her husband. The afternoon lull before dinner had turned the room quiet. Might as well continue brazening her way through, considering that her life and heart hung in the balance, whether Captain Everard knew it or not.

'Would you mind terribly if the Captain and I had a few moments of privacy in here?' she began. 'You're crowded and busy, but I believe he has something to say to me.'

The husband and wife exchanged glances. 'We can do better than a kitchen, if you don't mind bundling up a little,' the keep said. 'There's a wee summer porch this way.'

They showed her where, and she peeked into a pleasant room with tables and chairs that must be delightful in the summer. Perfect.

She returned to the commons, where the captain had resumed his solitary post at the window. She looked at his back, humbled by how many burdens he already bore. He had told her parents this was a nasty war that wasn't going to end any time soon.

She knew his first responsibility lay with the fleet. She also knew she would do nothing to ever change that: no tears, no demands, no ultimatums that would deter him from the service he had pledged to King and country. She knew he would likely be absent at times when she needed him. She also knew she loved him.

'Joe, come with me, will you?'

He turned around, his face troubled. As she watched and held her breath with the loveliness of it, his expression changed to one that suggested she was not wrong.

She had put on her cloak and held his out to him. He grinned like a little boy and put it on.

'Where away, Miss Newsome?' he asked in proper shipside fashion.

'There is a summer porch.'

He took her hand. 'Better than the kitchen, you think?'

'You can decide for yourself, Captain Everard.'

'Now *that* frightens me,' he teased.

They sat close together in the summer porch. She looked her man square in the eye. If she was wrong, then she was wrong, but she had to try.

'I love you, Captain,' she said, casting away all propriety because it mattered. 'Everyone at every stage of this bizarre journey has assumed that we are an old married couple. Why is that?'

He sat back in his chair, a silly grin on his face. He never took his eyes from hers, which would have unnerved her, had she not cared so deeply for him. How many moments would they have like this?

'Let me draw a decent breath,' he said finally. 'I've been stewing and second guessing and havering about, convinced that you were far too intelligent to bind yourself to a man who will not be around much.'

'I accept that.'

'I never knew what I needed until I met you,'

he said and took her hands. 'You are independent and perfectly able to function on your own. Have you any idea how intoxicating that is to a man who needs a wife with precisely those attributes?'

She laughed out loud. 'You don't mind curly hair and an ordinary face?'

'I think you are beautiful and I have discovered I like curly hair. Tall women are probably handier than short ones, since you'll need to reach top shelves when I am far away at sea. Who knew?'

They both laughed at that. She sobered first. 'It's a matter of pride, but I have no money.'

'Hardly matters,' he said, sliding closer. 'That odious Hipworth spawn hit the mark, which I am certain propelled his even more odious father to force that poor girl to attempt heaven knows what last night. I have a decent fortune percolating in a clever counting house. It's enough for both of us.'

'Well then, sir?'

'Marry me, if you dare,' he said. 'I love you and everyone seems to think we already look married.'

'That is not a very romantic proposal,' she said.

'How about this?'

He stood up, pulled her up with him, hauled her close and kissed her. She hadn't reached the ripe age of almost thirty without being kissed, but Verity Newsome knew she was in the hands of a master. Wherever he had learned to kiss—Spain, Portugal, England, Italy, the Antipodes, God help us, France—he had been an apt pupil. His lips were warm and searching and the only thing that made her finally pull away was the urgent need to breathe.

'Yes.'

'That's it? Yes?'

All those people had been right. How else was it possible to be so comfortable with a man of brief acquaintance, who had offered condolences and turned into a friend, an escort and quite soon a lover and a husband, and probably in that order?

'Oh, no,' she teased, even as he pulled her close again. 'I will want a house and servants, and a good library.'

He smacked his forehead. 'I was almost ready to change my mind until you mentioned library.' He turned serious immediately. 'Once we return to Weltby I will hurry to London for a special licence. Until then, well…'

'Captain, would you ever play me false?' she asked.

'Good God, never,' he said quickly.

What she was about to say went against everything she had been taught, but these were no ordinary times. 'I prefer not to sleep alone between here and Kent.'

'Nor do I,' he said softly. He looked around the summer porch. 'With a mattress and enough blankets, this will do.'

He was right. Verity had never spent a better Christmas Eve.

Chapter Twenty

꧁ ꧂

Four days later they arrived in Weltby, after weathering two glorious nights in a summer porch that had proved to be surprisingly adequate for their minimal needs. She was there, he was there and it was private. Verity Newsome-nearly-Everard was, as he suspected, not a woman to do anything by half-measures. They suited each other right down to the marrow of their bones.

On the return mail coach, Joe managed to secure a room in Chittering Corner again, with results similar to the one in Sudbury, except that he finally could throw off the blankets and admire his wife's lovely body without the addition of gooseflesh. True, the mattress was still noisy, but who cared?

Twilight came early as they walked up the lane to her parents' house on Lord Blankenship's estate. He wondered what her parents would think when they announced the need for an immediate wedding and hoped they would not be too distressed. After all, his good lady was well beyond the age requiring any consent.

They astounded him and, to his delight, Verity, too.

Mrs Newsome opened the door, stared at them both, immediately figured out what had happened, whooped like an Algonquin and ran to fetch her husband, leaving them there on the front steps to stare at each other in dumbfounded amazement.

They went inside. He helped Verity out of her cloak and handed it to the maid, who beamed from ear to ear. As he removed his own cloak, Verity went in search of her parents. He followed her down the hall to the book room where, as he recalled, this whole enterprise had begun. Gadfreys, he hoped they were not recoiling in terror or fury at how quickly things had progressed since they entrusted their sole remaining child to him.

'I pray they are not angry,' he whispered in Verity's ear. 'I am hoping to be the favourite son-in-law.'

'Their *only* son-in-law, you wretch,' she teased back. 'Let us face the music. Surely your quarterdeck at Trafalgar was more frightening.'

He wasn't certain about that, but a mere few days of Verity's generously given love had already taught him not to assume as much as everyone around them had assumed. The Newsomes could be genuinely upset.

The door was open and they went inside.

'Let me explain—' he said, only to be cut off

by the sight of Papa Newsome going off in a gale of mirth.

Verity knew her parents far better than he did, so he let her proceed. 'Mama and Papa, what are you up to?' she asked. 'Let me state first that Joe and I are heading at dawn to London to procure a special licence. We'll marry there.'

Mama stopped laughing first. She fished about on the desk and held out his second lieutenant's journal that he had taken great pains to return to them. Mystified, he reached for it, but she pulled it back.

'Tell me first, Captain: did you read it?' she asked.

'Good God, no, ma'am,' he assured her. 'I would never. I left the reading to you.'

With a smile, even though her eyes were bright with tears, she held out the journal to him. He took it from her as tenderly as she offered it, because David Newsome had been an officer of real promise, cut short in his prime.

'This is his last entry. Look what he wrote, second paragraph from the bottom. Read it out loud, because I want to hear it from *you*.'

With Verity resting her chin on his shoulder and looking on, he read. *'"He's a hard man, but a fair one. He is scrupulous in his duties and never flinches in battle."'* He looked up, embarrassed. 'This is difficult to read, ma'am. I do my duty, nothing more.'

'Keeping reading, son,' she said, which made him smile.

'Let's see. *"...scrupulous...never flinches... Between these journal pages and me, let me add that Captain Everard would be the perfect husband for my sister, who is equally fair, scrupulous and devoted."'*

He stopped and took a deep breath. His arm went around Verity and she clung to him. 'I had no idea,' she whispered. 'I never saw this.'

He kissed her cheek and continued. *"'I wish that fortune might place them together,"'* he read, his heart tender, *"'but I do not know how that can happen."'*

He closed the journal and returned it to Davey's mother. 'You read this the night I arrived, didn't you?' he asked. 'I wondered why you were so insistent that I escort your daughter to Norfolk, when she was obviously capable.'

'Tell us the whole story over dinner,' Augustus Newsome said.

'Aye-aye, sir,' Joe said. 'Then Verity and I must bolt to London for a wedding and Admiral Nelson's funeral. I must return to my ship in Torbay. There are inns aplenty in Torquay, Verity. You'll come, too.'

The four of them stood close together and he put his arms around them. 'I'll charge my wife with purchasing a home somewhere between Plymouth and Portsmouth. You might look hardest in Lyme Regis, dearest, but I trust your judgement.'

'My goodness, why does this not seem to startle you, Verity?' Mrs Newsome said. 'I could never buy a house without Papa there.'

Verity looked at Joe and smiled with her whole heart. 'You read the journal, Mama. Davey thinks I am scrupulous in my duties and so does Joe. I'll have a wonderful house ready for him, when next he returns from war.'

Her wise parents knew better than to insist upon separate rooms. Hours later, after exquisite lovemaking, Joe thought about what Verity had said. There would be someone waiting for him when he returned from the sea, someone he could rely upon utterly and who loved him to the exclusion of all others. With luck, she and their children would greet him, love him and let him return to war until the whole business was done and Bonaparte gone from the earth.

How odd was life. He had begun this Christmastide with nothing on his mind except doing his duty to a subordinate, who turned out to have a lasting effect on him far beyond what the shortness of their acquaintance would have suggested.

The New Year would be here soon, with all its promise, certain to be battered by war, but here all the same. Joe kissed his sleeping darling and closed his eyes, content, fulfilled and happy beyond measure.

* * * * *

THE VISCOUNT'S
YULETIDE BETROTHAL

Louise Allen

Chapter One

Albany, Piccadilly, London—
December 19, 1815

"'*The Vagabond Viscount, Captain A— P —S—*
is finally in London! The dashing Captain has re-
turned to claim the title after the death last year
of his cousin, the reclusive Viscount R—'"

Jack Harfield, Lord Burnham, strolled into the
room, nose in newssheet, and propped one shoulder against the doorframe as he read out loud.

From the depths of an armchair by the hearth
Captain Andrew Padgett Stanton bestirred himself to hurl a cushion at his host. 'Stop reading
that trash. *"Vagabond Viscount"*—what will they
think of next? *Absconding Aristocrat? Peregri-
nating Peer?* Just because I didn't abandon my
unit in the middle of Waterloo and rush back
doesn't make me a vagabond.'

'You must admit, it might have made claiming
the title smoother if you'd done something about

it immediately your ghastly relative shuffled off instead of re-joining your unit the moment Boney left Elba. And it didn't help being stuck like a pin-cushion by a French lancer, trampled underfoot, losing your kit and all identification and being returned to England four weeks after the battle, still feverish,' his friend pointed out with infuri-ating reasonableness.

'What would have made it *smoother* was that spiteful old lunatic my second cousin not doing everything in his power to ruin whoever had the misfortune to end up as his heir just because my great-grandfather cheated him out of two acres of land.' Drew hauled himself upright in the arm-chair. 'I don't know how the newspapers get hold of this stuff. All I wanted to do was sort out the paperwork and go to Suffolk to try and put things right.'

'And the paperwork involves the College of Heralds, the House of Lords, the Bank of Eng-land and four sets of lawyers. Of course someone sold the story to the gossip-hounds. How could they resist?' Jack wandered over and dropped the newssheet on to Drew's stomach.

'Damn good story, too,' he added as he sank into the chair on the other side of the hearth and picked up the pile of post his man had brought in. 'Family feud, the eccentric, reclusive and an-cient Viscount Ravencroft laying waste to his own lands to spite his family, cousins in line for the title dropping like flies from influenza, too much drink and hunting accidents leaving one man standing. You. Although you were hardly on your feet for long. Then the heroic Captain Stanton, gallant veteran of Waterloo, finally wanders back from the Continent to make his claim.'

'I didn't *wander*, I was carted back on a stretcher,' Drew pointed out. If he could keep his patience with a mob of paper-pushing heralds and lawyers, he could keep it with his best friend. 'This came with the post while you were out.' He prodded an impressive wedge of papers on the stool beside him. 'Finally, after four months, they've got it sorted out, or as sorted as one might expect given that they appear to have half their minds on a prolonged Christmas and New Year holiday away from London. The College of Heralds and the House of Lords say I'll be confirmed as Viscount Ravencroft in early January and the lawyers and the bankers agree that the property— and the money, such as it is—will be mine by then as well.'

And I won't have to sponge off you any longer.

He knew better than to say it. Jack had given him a room in his Albany chambers and fed him. He'd loaned him his shirts and his valet as well, saying that Drew would have done exactly the same for him if their situations had been reversed. Which was true, although that wasn't much salve for his pride. He had always lived on his pay— now half-pay—and it was hardly holding up under the onslaught of legal costs. He could have sold his commission, but caution told him to wait until he had the confirmation of his title and estates signed, sealed and delivered.

Jack was opening post, tossing bills aside. He stopped to read a single sheet. 'Mama's wanting to know when I'm coming down for Christmas. Why don't you come with me, stay until New Year? I promise, no dreary relatives. You'll enjoy it.'

'Thanks, but I'd best stay in London.' His sensitive pride wouldn't let him, was the truth of it. His dress uniform was shabby, he hadn't bought new shirts in an age and he certainly couldn't afford gifts for his hosts. It would be good to be able to tip Jack's valet and the Albany porters and to afford better food than chophouse fare while Jack was away.

'I've got a pile of reading.' Which was true. Somehow he must turn himself from a soldier into a landowner and there were books on estate management and agriculture, maps and paperwork in a daunting stack in his room.

Drew scanned the front page of the *Morning Post*. Young gentlemen with excellent references were advertising for posts as confidential secretaries, a governess was wanted in Perthshire, there was a highly dubious advertisement for shares in a Peruvian silver mine and—

'Something interesting?' Jack looked up from muttering over what, from the scent that was wafting across to Drew's nostrils, had to be a *billet doux* from his mistress.

'This. It sounds decidedly peculiar. *"A Lady requires the Services of a Gentleman of the Ut-*

most Discretion over the Christmas period. Full board and lodging for the Festive Season and Remuneration Fully Commensurate with the Delicacy of the Task and the Degree of Sensitivity required. Apply in person to Templeton, Ague and Ague, Old Mitre Court, Middle Temple, between the hours of ten and four."* Delicacy, sensitivity and discretion, indeed? I wonder what the lady in question requires and what payment is fully commensurate with that.'

Payment. He could do discretion. Sensitivity at a pinch. He wasn't too sure about delicacy.

Jack snorted. 'Easy enough. It can only be one of two things. A lady wants to present her husband with an heir because he isn't capable of fathering one, or a lady wants to experience the joys of the marriage bed without benefit of clergy.'

'And approaches it by advertising through a solicitor? Surely not.'

'You'd be surprised,' Jack said darkly. 'Those lawyers will do anything for a price. You aren't still fretting about money, are you? Damn it, if you'd only borrow what you need— All right, have it your own way, you stiff-rumped idiot,' he said with a grin when Drew shook his head. 'I'll bet twenty guineas against your Manton pocket pistol that you won't answer that advertisement, in person, tomorrow—and take the job if it is offered.'

Drew rolled up the newspaper, lifted it in mock threat, then lowered it again. What harm could a simple enquiry do? And, besides, he wasn't convinced by Jack's glib explanations. It was a mystery and he enjoyed a mystery. Twenty guineas won fair and square was a different matter entirely from a loan. 'Done, I'll take your wager.'

'I do not like to say *I told you so*, Miss Jordan, but every man—I will not say *gentleman*—who has passed through these doors in the past two days has come with the basest of motives.' Mr Ague Junior—Mr Templeton had long been gathered to his rest and Mr Ague Senior who was eighty-six and irascible with gout had refused to have anything to do with the matter—drew a line through the latest applicant. He pulled his spectacles off his nose and tossed them on to the desk with the air of a man throwing in his hand.

Ellie peered through the fine mesh of her veil at the list in front of the solicitor and shuddered faintly. She had thought she was unshockable, worldly-wise. It was clear that she was not, as the heat in her cheeks testified. 'I do not know how else I could have worded the advertisement, not without revealing the exact purpose and that would be self-defeating. Are there no more applicants?'

Mr Ague rang the bell on his desk and his clerk came through from the outer office. 'Just one more, sir. In uniform. A Captain Padgett.'

'Give us two minutes and show him in. The name has novelty, at least. Not one of the Smith or Jones clans.' Mr Ague gave a high-pitched titter as Ellie moved back to her chair in the shad-

owed corner. Her spirits were sinking along with
the light levels.

Outside it was barely two o'clock, but a smoggy
winter gloom was descending over the narrow
courts of the Middle Temple and all the light in
the room was concentrated around the desk, the
better to conceal her in the shadows. The only
bright spot was the incongruous sprig of holly
sitting in an empty inkwell on the desk, its berries glowing. And even that reminded her how
close Christmas was and how desperate she was
becoming.

'Captain Padgett, sir.'

Well. Goodness. Ellie blinked as the tall figure
moved into the pool of lamplight around the desk.
He seemed to bring cold air with him, a swirl of
fog. And, paradoxically, heat. Or perhaps intensity. Masculinity, certainly.

'Please sit down, Captain.' Mr Ague put on
his spectacles again. 'You are an army officer, I
see. Why do you wish to apply for this position?'

'I am a half-pay officer. The *fully commensurate remuneration* is, naturally, a consideration.
I also have to confess to curiosity.'

Mr Ague cleared his throat, stared at the Captain over the lenses and made a note.

Ellie felt like fanning herself. *That voice.* Deep
and amused and not remotely salacious as every
other applicant had sounded. He was a genuine
officer, she was sure. Anyone could buy a sec-
ond-hand uniform from some clothes stall, but
the one before her had become faded and patched

on the back of this man. The cuffs ended at the
right place above those capable hands, the shoulders of the jacket sat perfectly on shoulders that
were, themselves…perfect. It was a trifle loose,
to be sure, but he had lost weight recently, she
thought, striving to think with her brain and not
with parts of her that were normally well under
control. The parts that forgot she was not a responsible, ineligible spinster and had ridiculous
dreams and fantasies whenever she was foolish
enough to let them slip the leash.

'Curiosity?' Mr Ague probed.

'It is an unusual advertisement, you must agree.
A friend of mine placed interpretations upon it
that I will not mention in the presence of a lady.'
He gave no other indication that he had seen her
in her corner. 'I, however, thought it likely to be
more in the way of a cry for help. I am at a loose
end over Christmas and I would welcome the full
board and lodging, and the promised payment.'

'I see.'

It was more than Ellie did. *A cry for help?* It
was certainly that, because if this did not work
then she was in despair about what to do to save
Theo.

'And have you references?'

'I am staying at Albany with a friend, Lord
Burnham. He would provide you with a charac-
ter reference and you have my word that I will not
reveal any details of this matter to him, or anyone
else, come to that. If you require other assurances
I am afraid I can offer none. I am a serving of-

ficer and I have no desire to display the fact that
I am engaged in…in whatever this proves to be.'

'So the name you have given us is false?'

'In part.' He was very relaxed, very confident
in a reassuring way, as though if a group of armed
desperadoes or an escaped tiger burst into the
room he would deal with them without breaking
a sweat and without spilling too much blood on
the carpet in the process.

Really, my imagination!

It was that romantic, dreamy side of her again.
Probably all army officers were like this. Tough,
capable, confident. They couldn't all be this
darkly good-looking, though.

'If you could give me some idea of exactly what
is required?'

Mr Ague sent her a quick glance. Ellie nodded.

'The lady concerned needs a gentleman to act
as her betrothed for a week. He will reside in her
household along with the family and visiting relatives. He will need to be able to convince her
uncle that he is sincere and respectable and also
an excellent role model and mentor for a sixteen-
year-old youth in need of masculine guidance.'

That did make the Captain blink. 'A wild
young man?'

'Certainly not,' Ellie said before she could stop
herself. 'That is the problem.'

Captain Padgett shifted in his chair and stopped
the pretence that she was not in the room. He was
close enough, and the light on the desk was strong
enough, that she could see that his eyes were grey,

his lashes black, like his hair. He watched her from under levelled brows. There were pale circles under his eyes as though he had been ill and his cheekbones stood out, giving his face with its strong jawline a craggy look.

'My brother's guardian, our uncle, thinks my brother is subject to too much feminine influence, that he needs toughening up. He is arranging a midshipman's berth for Theo. That would be a disaster.'

'He is sickly?'

'Not at all. He is a perfectly healthy, active young man. He is also a brilliant mathematician, a scholar, and should be going to Cambridge, not into the Navy. In October, despite his age, he has a place at St John's, thanks to his godfather. It would be a tragedy if he cannot take it.'

'A good college for a mathematician.' When she made an interrogative sound he added, 'I am an artillery officer and we have to understand mathematics. So, you want a fiancé who will convince your uncle that he will be a strong masculine influence on your brother and that it will therefore be unnecessary to send him to sea to provide that. I can see a major flaw in this scheme—your fiancé is not going to be around for the wedding.'

'Neither is my uncle. He is leaving the country with his wife on a diplomatic mission for over a year, hence his anxiety to see my brother settled before he leaves on December the twenty-seventh. By the time he realises that the wedding has not taken place he will not be able to stop Theo from entering university. After that we are counting on it being a *fait accompli.*'

Captain Padgett studied his clasped hands. 'Who else will be at this gathering?'

'My two younger sisters, our widowed cousin who lives with us, my aunt and uncle and my brother's godfather, also an uncle.'

'There are two issues should you decide to trust me with this charade.' The Captain cocked an eyebrow at Mr Ague. 'We should both be protected by paperwork that will prevent a suit for breach of promise.'

'Really, Captain.' Ellie found she was on her feet. 'Are you suggesting that this is some ruse to gain a husband?'

'I do not know you from Eve, ma'am. You do not know me from Adam. What motives you may have I do not know and *you* certainly should not trust me blindly. I merely suggest doing the prudent thing.'

'It does seem a sensible precaution,' Mr Ague said, making a note.

'The very fact that you raise the issue should indicate that you—'

'It merely shows I have a suspicious mind. And as for my motives—if I was wanting to entrap you, then raising the issue in the hope you would react as you just have would be good tactics.'

'Oh.' She subsided back on to the chair. 'What is the other issue?'

'We are going to be living with a number of people who know you well and who will be watching us with close attention. Are you able to convince them that we are in love?'

Chapter Two

'In love?' If she was not very careful the fact that she was in *lust* would be all too clear, Ellie realised. Love, though, that was a different matter.

Captain Padgett had risen to his feet when she had jumped to hers. Now he approached her. 'May I see your face?'

Ellie hesitated, then put back her veil. Either she trusted him or she didn't.

'Will you take my hand?' He held out his and she put hers on it, palm down. The long fingers closed over it. 'Now may I kiss you?'

Yes. 'No!'

He waited, his grip light but strong on her hand. 'I meant, on the cheek.'

'Very well.' He was right. It would hardly be convincing that she had invited him to stay when she was too skittish to even allow a kiss on the cheek. Ellie managed a smile. There would be mistletoe...

The Captain's grey eyes seemed to darken as he

closed the distance between them. She smelt wool, damp from the outside mists, plain soap, the faintest hint of cologne. And man. His lips, when they touched her cheek, were warm, his skin, lightly brushing her own, was still chill. Then he stepped back and she swallowed hard. That was as harmless as any of the kisses her male relatives gave casually in greeting, so why did her pulse race?

A little voice in her head said, *Stop this now. You will regret it.*

'I believe we will manage,' Ellie found herself saying, with a coolness that startled her. 'My name is Eleanor. Miss Jordan.'

This was the man to help her, she was certain. *Almost certain. But there is hardly any time left,* almost *is going to have to do.*

'And there is something that you should know about me, before we go any further. I am illegitimate. My brother and sisters were born within wedlock, however. My uncle will wish to make this clear to you. He is ashamed of the fact, I am not.'

'Why should you be? It was hardly your fault.' The Captain still held her hand.

That was a novel reaction. Most people were embarrassed, or judgemental, in Ellie's experience. 'Our father was in the Navy. He should have been home long before I was born, but he was shipwrecked after a battle in the Baltic and arrived home a week after my birth.'

'If he should raise the subject, I will assure your uncle that my affection for you overrides such considerations.' His thumb was stroking back and forth across her knuckles. She should protest, but perhaps he was only intent on accustoming her to his touch. 'I am not pretending to be a marquess, concerned about impeccable, legitimate bloodlines.'

'Good, because my maternal grandfather was a coal merchant. You should also know, that in some compensation for my birth, my father left me with both a substantial trust fund and dower. My uncle sees that as useful in attracting a husband for me. I see it as bait for fortune hunters and have no intention of marrying such a man. I despise them. Uncle and I do not see eye to eye on this matter.'

Mr Ague cleared his throat. 'Er…yes. I am sure the Captain is now very clear on the situation, Miss Jordan. If you could wait outside, sir, while Miss Jordan and I consult?'

'Certainly.' He released her hand and went out, closing the door behind him.

'You appear to have made up your mind, Miss Jordan.' Mr Ague had the *Peerage* open on the desk and was flipping through it. 'Lord Burnham does give a London address in Albany and I seem to recall seeing in the society pages that he is in town at present.'

'I have decided, yes. I trust the Captain, which I am sure you will say is nothing more than unreliable feminine intuition, but he did not say any of the things someone trying too hard to convince me would say.'

*And he has laughing eyes and strong hands.
And those are no reason at all to trust a man.*
'What should we do now?'

'We should tell him to wait until I have a response from Lord Burnham and then I will discuss terms with him.'

'I cannot afford delay. There are only four days before my aunt and uncle arrive.'

'You will take the risk that the reference is a bluff?' He removed his spectacles and polished them briskly on a spotted handkerchief. 'As your legal adviser I should counsel against it.'

'You trust him, too, don't you?' Ellie picked up the holly sprig from the inkwell, twisted it between her fingers and received a painful prick on the thumb for her trouble. 'Ouch.' She sucked the tiny bead of blood.

I only hope that is not a bad omen.

Mr Ague grimaced. 'It is probably enough to have me disbarred from the profession, but, yes, strangely, I do.' He picked up the bell and rang it. 'Langridge, send in the Captain then give Miss Jordan a cup of tea and make sure the waiting room fire is made up before returning here to witness the agreement. You'll be more comfortable outside,' he added as the clerk held the door for her.

I will not be embarrassed by any haggling, you mean, Ellie thought as she followed Langridge.

A cup of tea would be welcome, though. Her mouth felt quite dry. Captain Padgett came to his feet the moment she appeared and she nodded her acknowledgement as coolly as possible. Probably any dashing man in uniform would be enough to make her pulse flutter, she thought as she settled by the fire. There were few enough men in her life, let alone handsome ones.

'You are satisfied with the amount offered?' The solicitor appeared surprised by his easy acceptance.

'Bed and board over Christmas and the amount you suggest seem perfectly acceptable. I have no wish to take advantage of a lady who has a problem.' Drew scrawled his legal, perfectly illegible, signature on the paperwork. 'Miss Jordan does not appear to be accompanied by a maid or a footman.'

'We felt it best not to take her staff into our confidence. There is no reason to distrust any of them, but the fewer people who know this is a charade, the better.'

'In that case I will escort her home.'

'In a hackney carriage?' Mr Ague sounded faintly scandalised.

'I would like to walk and I would be glad of your escort, Captain,' Miss Jordan said from the doorway.

Was it her voice that had decided him to undertake this? There had been passion in her quick defence of her brother, intelligence in the clear way she explained the situation and what she needed and an openness that appealed to him. True, he had not been much in the company of unmarried ladies recently, but this one, Drew was certain, was out of the common. The comment about fortune hunters stung, though, hit a nerve. He needed an advantageous marriage.

He pushed the thought away. That was not what he was considering now. Although there had been the softness of her cheek under his lips, the subtle, elusive, scent of her…

Intriguing.

They said their farewells to Mr Ague and Drew followed her out into the murk of the narrow lanes. A bewigged lawyer, black gown flapping, papers tied with pink tape under his arm, hurried past, the fog swirling in his wake, other figures loomed eerily out of passageways. Miss Jordan took his arm as they emerged on to Fleet Street.

'Where to, ma'am?'

'Hart Street, on the corner of Bloomsbury Square.'

A respectable address and about a mile to walk through the chill and the fog. No shrinking violet, his employer. 'Chancery Lane and across Lincoln's Inn Fields, I would suggest.' She nodded and he realised that she was above medium height, as the little plume on her bonnet brushed his cheek.

They crossed Fleet Street and Miss Jordan laughed when a cart lurched off course and he swung her safely on to the kerb, skirts swinging. They were elegant skirts, simply cut.

Good taste and comfortably off, he diagnosed.

Better to think about clothes rather than how that slender waist had felt under his hands.

Her eyes were green, her brows and lashes dark brown, so he suspected that her hair, concealed by her bonnet, was brown, too.

'Captain—'

'Call me Drew and, if I may, I will call you Eleanor. We should get into the habit, don't you think?'

He glanced down as she looked up, her lower lip caught between her teeth. It was a lovely full lip, far too good to be chewed on. *Nibbled, perhaps...*

'I suppose so, Drew.' She blushed a delicate shade of pink. 'Is that short for Andrew?' When he nodded she said, 'My brother is Theo, my younger twin sisters are Madeleine—Maddie— and Claire. They are seventeen and will have their come-out next year. Do you have any siblings?'

'I have no family at all. I am waiting for the estate of my last relative to be settled, which is why I am both at a loose end and, to be frank, somewhat short of ready cash.' He moved to shield her when another group of lawyers engaged in loud argument swept down Chancery Lane taking up most of the pavement.

'My uncle, the one for whose benefit we are doing this, is Sir Gregory Wilmott. He is a baronet and diplomat and married to my Aunt Dorothea, my father's younger sister,' she explained when they walked on. 'I think Uncle Gregory would have liked to go to sea himself as a young man, but his eyesight is poor. Dr Talbot Jenkins—not a medical doctor—is Theo's godfather. He is a Fellow at Cambridge and is most anxious that Theo takes up the place he has secured. There was no difficulty, despite Theo's age, because he is clearly brilliant. But Dr Jenkins and my uncle do not see eye to eye about most things, which doesn't help.'

'I suppose Dr Jenkins is not a suitable role model for Theo?'

Eleanor's gurgle of laughter was delightful. He hated gigglers. 'I suspect that when Uncle Tal was an undergraduate he took the fustiest, mustiest old don he could observe and has modelled himself on him for forty years.'

'And your companion?'

'Cousin Joan, the widow of the Reverend Henry Nutcombe. She is vague and sweet and not, perhaps, the most intelligent woman in the world, but she is kind to the girls and lends me countenance.'

'And she has failed to notice my courtship of you?' he asked as they turned into Lincoln's Inn Fields. A faint ray of late sunshine penetrated the murk, lighting up the vast green square.

'Goodness, I hadn't thought of that. How foolish of me.'

'You are not used to schemes and deceptions,' Drew suggested, intending to offer comfort.

It earned him an unexpectedly shrewd upwards glance from beneath her bonnet brim. 'And you are?'

'Not of this sort. But army life is all about out-thinking and out-manoeuvring the enemy, so one becomes used to working through the details. Look, the sun is shining on that bench over there. If we sit down, perhaps we can tease out the knots now before we reach your house.'

Drew unbuttoned his greatcoat and spread the skirts on the bench to give Eleanor a dry place to sit. It did bring her rather closer than propriety decreed, but he had no objection to feeling her warmth all down his right side or the occasional bump of her shoulder.

'Where might we have met?' he prompted when she had settled. 'Have you been visiting Mr Ague much recently?'

'The two Mr Agues, father and son, are the trustees for my money, so I do call quite often, especially recently because we have been discussing new investments.'

'I have had a great deal to do with lawyers over this small inheritance of mine. We might easily have met near the Agues' chambers and we can suggest as much without any outright lies. If we imply an acquaintance of at least three weeks, is that plausible? I have been courting you as I walk you home every time and I have just proposed. If I call tomorrow, you can introduce me to your family and invite me to stay over Christmas. Who else knows the truth?'

'My sisters and Theo, that's all. I agree, what you suggest is the best plan.' She turned to smile at him, then froze, clearly finding herself rather closer to his body than she had realised. He could hardly move, not without tipping her off his coat, and he expected her to jump to her feet. But Eleanor stayed where she was, eyes wide, lips slightly parted.

Damnation. He knew he was finding her... tempting, now it seemed the attraction might be mutual.

She had been thinking that Drew Padgett was comfortingly big. It had certainly been a wonderfully novel sensation to be picked up and swung to safety when that cart had lurched towards her in Fleet Street and the way he had stood between her and those lawyers, as though protecting her from marauding French soldiery, had made her heart beat fast.

But now she found herself sitting within inches of that broad chest and getting a very good view of his decided nose and strong jaw and the dark foreshadowing of his evening beard. It was more than she could resist not to lift her gaze to those grey eyes. He was looking at her mouth, she realised, and the tip of her tongue had crept out to run along her lower lip.

Ellie closed her mouth so sharply that she almost bit the end of her tongue.

I must have lost my mind. Surely if I had waited someone else might have applied? Someone stout and rather stolid or plain and worthy and skinny. Now I have to spend days pretending to be in love with a man who makes my toes curl, who is going

to hold my hand and pretend to be in love with me.
A man who might kiss me. Might? Will.

'And tomorrow will be the first day you have
met any of them, so any gaps in your knowledge
can be easily explained,' she said, certain she was
gabbling. She got to her feet rather too quickly,
tangled her legs in his voluminous greatcoat and
found he was on his feet, too, one arm around
her to steady her. 'Thank you.' She stepped away,
made a business of smoothing down her skirts.
'Oh, dear, the sun has gone in. It will soon become quite cold.'

And I sound a complete ninny.

The Captain—*Drew*—helped her over the
knee-high wooden rail that edged the Fields and
led her across the path. It was one of the largest
open spaces in London that was not a park and it
took them several minutes to traverse.

She should not be getting herself into such a
dither. Unlike the other men who had courted
her—and who had all made it clear, with varying
degrees of tact, that they were nobly overlook-
ing her birth for her fortune—this man's motives
were perfectly acceptable. Money, yes, but she
was purchasing his services just as she had bought
Mr Ague's.

Almost home and safe, she thought as they
walked up Little Queen Street and crossed High
Holborn. *What is the matter with me? If I do not
feel safe, then all I have to do is tell him I fear we
should not suit for this enterprise. I would have*

to pay him off, of course, but I can afford it and it would only be fair.

'This house on the corner?' It was smart and expensive, but she wanted to make a good impression when the girls had their come-out.

'It is. You will call tomorrow, then?'

'Yes. Ah, we have an audience,' Drew said. He sounded amused. 'The nearest window. I will pretend I haven't seen them.'

Ellie risked a glance. It was the drawing-room casement and Cousin Joan was watching the street from what she mistakenly thought was the protection of the curtains. Behind her both twins had come to see what had attracted her attention.

Drew halted opposite the window and turned so they were facing each other. For a second Ellie thought he was about to shake hands. Instead he began to peel off her glove.

'What are you *doing*?'

'We don't want to waste an audience.' Drew lifted her bare fingers to his lips. He was going to kiss them? No one except elderly gentlemen kissed hands any longer.

But Drew, it seemed, did. It wasn't even for show, halting a fraction above her hand. Oh, no, the wretch was putting her to the blush in front of her family by lingering over a proper kiss, his lips warm on her slightly chilled skin.

It is only my hand...

Which did not explain why interesting tingles were running up her arm, why she wanted to cup his cheek and lean in so that he kissed her lips.

Drew was clearly a mind-reader. He turned her hand until it was palm up and pressed his lips to that. And not just his lips—she felt the tip of his tongue, moist and impudent, trace a line across the sensitive skin until the sensations made her want to squirm. And grab hold of him.

'Drew.'

He raised his head an inch or so and looked at her wickedly through his lashes. 'I have just proposed and been accepted. You do not want me to appear completely unmoved at having all my hopes confirmed, do you?'

'No, n-not exactly.' Oh, he was reducing her to a stammering ninny now. 'I really must go in.'

'Of course. I will see you tomorrow morning. Would eleven be acceptable? Not the conventional time for a morning call, but we have a lot to discuss.'

'Yes, perfectly acceptable.' Ellie managed to extract her fingers. She had been gripping his hand, she realised. 'Perfectly.' She found she was lifting her bare hand towards his cheek. 'My glove?' she managed to say.

Chapter Three

Ellie was still clutching the glove when the front door closed behind her.

'Miss Jordan?' Peter, their footman, waited patiently while she stood palpitating.

'Oh, yes. Thank you.' Ellie thrust bonnet and gloves at him and unbuttoned her redingote. 'Has tea been taken in?'

'Cook is preparing it now, Miss Jordan.'

Ellie opened the drawing-room door to find her three female relatives staring at her with varying degrees of shock, amazement and, in Maddie's case, poorly suppressed laughter, the wretch.

'Eleanor—who was that man?' Cousin Joan quavered. 'He was *kissing your hand*.'

'He was devouring it,' Maddie corrected.

'And he is delicious,' Claire added. 'Come and sit down and tell us all about him.'

'His name is Captain Andrew Padgett and he is an officer of artillery. And he has just asked me to marry him and I have accepted,' she finished in a rush. 'Oh, Maddie, do catch Cousin Joan, she has swooned.'

Cousin Joan fainted often enough for the reaction to be routine. Their chaperon was inclined to stoutness—and cake—and, as a consequence, favoured severe tight-lacing. Added to her acute sensibility, this meant that she was quite capable of passing out at the slightest provocation. Claire waved the smelling salts under her nose while Maddie lowered her to the sofa.

'Where did you meet?' the twins demanded in chorus as they tucked a rug around their chaperon's feet.

'As you know, I have been calling on our lawyers and Drew—Captain Padgett—has been consulting his own lawyers over an inheritance,' she said for Cousin Joan's benefit. They had discovered the hard way that her hearing was sharp even when she appeared to be unconscious. 'We... er...bumped into each other and he assisted me to cross Fleet Street and then saved me when a wagon almost hit me and it all just escalated from that. A whirlwind romance, you might say.'

Both twins gave her broad grins over the prostrate form of Cousin Joan, who was moaning faintly. When they had discussed what she had been planning to do neither had held out much hope that the right man could be found.

'Captain Padgett is calling tomorrow morning to meet you all.' Ellie sat down and stared rather blankly at her hand. Had she just dreamed that kiss? The little sore prick mark from the holly was still there, so the entire afternoon had not been a fantasy.

'You could invite him for Christmas,' Maddie exclaimed, with the air of having just thought of it.

'Invite who?' Theo came in, followed by the maid with the tea tray. 'I thought we had a houseful.'

'Ellie is betrothed,' Claire announced gleefully.

Theo grinned. 'Congratulations, Ellie.'

'One does not congratulate a lady on her betrothal—one congratulates the gentleman.' Cousin Joan sat up and pushed her lacy cap straight. 'One offers felicitations to a lady, otherwise it implies that the lady is over-anxious to secure a husband.'

If she only knew...

'Then felicitations, Sister dear,' Theo said. 'Do you think Uncle Gregory will approve of him?'

'He is an army officer. Artillery.'

'And *very* manly,' Claire added, fanning herself with her hand and batting her eyelashes. 'Such shoulders. And long legs and—'

'And as an artillery officer he is interested in mathematics, I understand,' Ellie interrupted.

'Clever,' Theo murmured as he took a tea cup from her to give to their cousin.

'He is calling tomorrow morning.'

'Oh, goodness, I had quite forgotten. I had promised the Vicar that I would help decorate the pews with evergreens,' Cousin Joan said. 'I will send a note at once to excuse myself. I must be here to chaperon you.'

'No need,' Ellie said brightly. 'You can meet

Captain Padgett, then go along to the church. The twins and Theo will be all the chaperons I require.'

'Goodness, yes,' Maddie said earnestly. 'We want to find out all about him. It will be a positive interrogation. We will not leave them alone for a second.'

'Well, I suppose that would be acceptable. But I must meet him first. You are an innocent young woman and this man may not be all he seems to you.'

Ellie would have wagered her pin money against a lump of coal that even with her sheltered existence she knew more about rakes than Cousin Joan, but she nodded solemnly. 'Mr Ague has approved him, obviously.'

'Oh, well, in that case...' Both Mr Agues were infallible in Joan's eyes.

'I have invited him for Christmas,' Ellie explained.

'But we have no room, dear. Your uncle and aunt always prefer a bedchamber apiece and I'm sure your Captain Padgett will not wish to share with Dr Jenkins, you know what an insomniac he is.'

'If we put a mattress in my dressing room I'll sleep there and the Captain may have my bed,' Theo offered. 'Anything for a good cause.' He winked at Ellie. 'I can tell you if he snores.'

Drew rattled the knocker with rather more firmness than he was feeling. A hectic few hours buying new shirts and neckcloths and then being fussed over by Jack's manservant until his uniform was approaching respectability had not left a great deal of time for contemplation the day before. Now it was dawning on him just what he had let himself in for and the possible consequences if the ruse was uncovered.

He could see the headlines now—*Vagabond Viscount in Betrothal Charade. Absconding Aristocrat in Amorous Adventure.* Or *Cash-strapped Heir and the Wealthy Miss J— of H— Street...*

Because there was no doubting that Eleanor Jordan had money. She might be born out of wedlock, but if the Agues were managing her inheritance, and she could afford to pay generously for this sort of subterfuge, then she was considerably better off than he was. Far better off than he would be once he had the millstone of his inheritance around his neck, come to that. The coalmerchant grandfather must have been a warm man and her past suitors had obviously hurt her with their passion for her fortune, not her person.

'Good morning, Captain.' The door was opened by a butler who directed a footman to relieve him of shako and gloves, then showed him into a drawing room. 'Captain Padgett, Miss Jordan.'

Drew reminded himself that this was a social occasion and not a court martial and held out his hand as Eleanor advanced to meet him. 'Miss Jordan. Eleanor.' He held her hand for rather longer than was customary, taking in his first sight of her without her bonnet. His fiancée was even more disconcertingly attractive than he re-called, her hair was the dark, glossy brown he had guessed at.

He realised he was probably staring her out of countenance and turned to smile at the plump woman seated on the sofa regarding him with narrow-eyed attention. Presumably she was the chaperon. 'Mrs Nutcombe?'

She inclined her head. 'Indeed I am. And these are my other cousins, Miss Madeleine and Miss Claire Jordan.' A pair of blonde young ladies both bobbed curtsies. 'And Theodore Jordan.'

Theo, the object of this entire enterprise, was a boyish version of Eleanor, still growing into his feet and hands. Despite his years the look he gave Drew from long-lashed hazel eyes was any-thing but boyish.

This is my sister, the look said. *Don't forget it.*

Drew approved of that.

He shook hands all round and discovered, to his relief, that Cousin Joan was off to assist the vicar with decorating the church for Christmas. 'He relies on me very much in such matters,' she confided.

Everyone seemed to be holding their breath for the sound of the front door closing. The three sisters sank down on the sofa in a row and Theo waved to one of a pair of armchairs as he took the other. 'Captain.'

'We promised Cousin Joan that we would stick to Ellie like glue,' one of the twins announced.

'To protect her from your rakish wiles, you understand.'

'*Claire.*' Eleanor's cheeks were flaming.

'No wiles, I assure you, Miss Claire. But I will be showing your sister respectfully affectionate attention, otherwise our betrothal is not going to be very convincing.'

'Like yesterday afternoon? That was *so* romantic,' Maddie sighed.

'Stop harassing Captain Padgett. He is here so we can tell him all the things he might be expected to know about if he has been courting me—and all the things to be wary of with Aunt and Uncle Wilmott.'

'We will need a month,' Claire said. 'And they arrive the day after tomorrow and so does Uncle Tal.'

'And it is Christmas Eve the day after that,' Eleanor said briskly. 'So we had better begin now.'

Drew felt as though he had just sat through a battle briefing with Wellington and without the benefit of notes. After an hour and two cups of tea he sank back in the chair and regarded the four Jordan siblings, all still talking with undiminished enthusiasm. 'My brain is full.'

'I am not surprised.' Eleanor smiled at him and his body reminded him that although he might be mentally fatigued, *it* wasn't and Miss Jordan was looking very fetching in moss-green wool with berry-red ribbons. 'Would it help if you spent a quiet half-hour with Theo? The better you know him the easier it will be to convince Uncle that it is unnecessary to force him into the Navy.'

'Of course.'

Theo was already on his feet. 'We can go into the study.'

Drew followed. This was a very self-confident sixteen-year-old, but Drew's performance with his uncle was perhaps all that stood between him and a miserable life at sea.

Theo opened the door into a pleasant book-lined room holding a desk with neat stacks of paper, a chalkboard covered in scrawled equations and, incongruous in the corner, a muddy pair of riding boots, a cricket bat and a fishing rod.

The youth who was apparently responsible for pin-neat paperwork and chaotic sporting equipment went to stand on the far side of the desk. 'If you hurt my sister, I'll make you wish you had never been born,' he said without preliminaries.

Out of the corner of his eyes Drew could see the tremor in the ink-splattered hand, but he gave no sign of it. He could toss the lad across the room and crack all his limbs without breaking a sweat, even now when he was barely convalescent from his battlefield wounds and fever. Theo was bright enough to recognise the fact, but he would still doggedly protect Eleanor.

'Excellent. I'd think worse of you if you did not feel like that. Now we've got it out of the way, shall we sit down and you can relax?'

Theo nodded, an abrupt jerk of his head, and subsided into his chair. 'Thank you, sir.'

'Call me Drew. So, what is so terrible about the Navy? You need excellent mathematical skills for navigation.'

'I am interested in pure mathematics, not applied.' He waved a hand at the chalkboard and Drew studied it, shook his head and did not even pretend to understand a line of it. 'The artillery or the Ordnance would be just as bad. I do not wish to undervalue your role, sir—Drew, I mean, but I want to be a creative mathematician. I need to work with others in the same field.'

Drew had known someone like that, a daydreamer of an artillery lieutenant who would go off into abstract calculations while shots flew about him. Until the day one took his head off.

'I'm not of that academic world and there's no way I can convince your uncle to look favourably on it. But I could try to persuade him to let you go into the army at some future date. We take subalterns older than the Navy does midshipmen so he won't be expecting anything to happen for at least another year, by which time you'll be at Cambridge. You are going to have to develop a passion for sweeping strategy, battlefield tactics and the latest ordnance in short order. Can you use a sword? Box?'

Theo shook his head, but he looked interested.

'We can find plenty of exceedingly manly things to do that should impress your uncle and I'll work on him, try to convince him that your skills would be wasted on navigation. I'll bring you some texts on artillery.'

He was not at all the kind of lad Drew had expected—pale, solitary, absorbed in his studies. That he worked hard was obvious, but his reaction to Drew's suggestions showed real enthusiasm. There was potential there and it would be a pleasure to get this round peg into a circular hole.

'I had best go and pack up my things,' he said. And there was his dress uniform to collect from the military tailors who, with the inducement of some of Mr Ague's guineas waved under their noses, had promised to do their best to restore it in under twenty-four hours. Then there was the tailor in Clifton Street who might not be up to Weston's standard, but who had also fallen under the spell of ready money and who were adjusting a swallowtail coat left by a defaulting client. They had also produced a pair of pantaloons which, after Jack's valet's utmost endeavours with his Hessians, completed a respectable outfit for day.

Eleanor left the drawing-room door ajar and kept an ear pricked for any sound of raised voices from the study. Theo was grateful for her scheme for his salvation, but he was also the man of the household and he took that role very seriously as far as his sisters were concerned.

It was all worryingly quiet, then she heard the sound of voices in the hall and went out. Theo was laughing, Drew smiling. *Thank goodness.*

'I was just saying that I must leave now if I am to be ready to move here tomorrow,' he said and her heart gave a ridiculous little jump when he transferred that smile to her. Then the amusement faded as he looked around the hallway. 'Do you not decorate for Christmas? I had thought to bring a wreath for the door, but I will not if you do not wish it.'

'Yes, please. That would be delightful.' Ellie looked around, realising for the first time how the days had crept up on her. 'We always decorate with evergreens when we are in the country, but I bought this house in February because I wanted us all to become used to London before the twins made their come-out. Now I do not know where to obtain holly and all the things we need, not at such short notice.'

Drew was disappointed, she thought, although he hid it well. Perhaps after years in the army he had been looking forward to a proper traditional Christmas in an English home. Her imagination conjured up images of snow-swept mountain passes and flickering fires barely warming the men huddled around them with scarce any food for their hungry bellies.

'We will have your wreath and we will decorate a table for presents,' she promised. And the food and wine would be excellent. 'I have been so preoccupied with other things that details have escaped me this Christmas.'

'We usually go out to cut branches,' Maddie said. Her lower lip quivered and for a moment Ellie thought she might cry. 'I never thought it would be different here, which is so foolish—we can hardly go and cut down foliage in the parks.'

'We'd be arrested if we did. Never mind,' Theo said. 'We'll know better next year.'

'I kept all the red ribbons from last Christmas,' Claire said. 'We can use those.' She gave her twin a jab in the ribs and Maddie glanced at Ellie, then fixed a firm smile on her lips.

Bless them, Ellie thought, *they don't want me to feel I have let them down.*

Which she had. She was the adult in the family and it was up to her to make Christmas special for them.

'What time should we expect you tomorrow, Drew?'

'I'm not certain, but certainly by noon. I am glad to have met you.' He gave a slight bow to the girls in the doorway, clapped Theo on the shoulder and then stopped and caught Ellie's hand in his. She expected him to kiss it again and steeled herself not to blush too much.

Impossible. He makes me blush just thinking about him, she thought, and then gave a little gasp as he pulled her gently towards him and kissed her cheek. Then, as he straightened, his lips brushed against hers, just for a fraction of a second.

'Goodbye.'

Drew left in a chorus of farewells from everyone except Ellie, who was discovering that when a certain man's lips touched hers she felt an urgent need for Cousin Joan's smelling salts.

Chapter Four

After almost a year she would have thought she would be used to how noisy London could be. Ellie opened one eye on to grey winter gloom and guessed it must be before seven. There was the very faintest sound of the servants beginning their morning routine far down in the basement, but that was not what had woken her.

Down in the street, three floors below, someone was cursing, there was the sound of metal-shod wheels on the cobbles, laughter. Ellie dragged the pillow over her head and closed her eyes. She could have at least another half-hour of sleep, surely?

But there had been something familiar about that laughter. *Theo?* Ellie threw back the covers, slid out of bed and shivered her way across the room in her nightgown. It was hard to see without throwing open the window and leaning out, but there was an empty flat cart below. A man was holding the reins and talking to someone on the pavement she couldn't see. Then he whistled piercingly and the horse set off, leaving the street empty of all but the milk delivery, one footman jogging along on an errand and a laden wagon unloading coal opposite.

She pulled on her dressing gown, pushed her feet into her slippers and went downstairs, rubbing the sleep from her eyes.

'Shh! You'll wake the household.' The deep voice was surely Drew.

'We're up, they can get up.' That was definitely Theo. 'We need all the help we can get with this lot. The hall's impassable.'

'What on earth is going on?' Ellie demanded as she rounded the newel post. 'Ouch!'

'Mind the holly,' Drew's voice warned, a moment too late.

Ellie jumped back on to the bottom stair and looked round. The hallway was a mass of greenery. She could see berried holly, fir branches, trails of ivy and great bunches of bare willow stems, green and golden. It smelled wonderful and looked chaotic.

Somewhere in there were her brother and her make-believe fiancé, but all she could see were two pairs of boots and two pairs of arms above, both clutching sacks.

'What are you doing?' she demanded.

One sack was lowered to the floor revealing Drew, hatless, his hair tousled, his cheeks red with cold. 'You wanted to decorate.'

'This house, not Carlton House,' she protested.

Theo dropped his sack, spilling pine cones across what could be seen of the tiles. 'We have been up since half-past five. At least I have, Drew must have been up even earlier.'

'No one else is awake. I'm not even dressed.' That fact began to sink in as she realised that Drew was regarding her with unmistakable interest. True, her nightgown was flannel and went from high frilled neck to her toes and her dressing gown was thick wool and might have been a nun's habit, it was so chaste. Even so she felt her nipples harden and the wretched colour come up in her cheeks. But her hair was down and… 'How did you get in?' she demanded, submerging embarrassment in irritation.

'I went to the basement door. The scullery maid was just making up the fire in the range. She told me where Theo's bedchamber is.'

'She let a strange man into the house?'

'She knew exactly who I was—surely you don't think the staff would lose any opportunity to stare at Miss Jordan's betrothed?'

Blast the man, he looked amused—and still interested in her state of *déshabillé*.

Two can play at that game, Captain.

Ellie let her gaze slide down from the top of his disarrayed hair. *So thick…* Past the pine needles clinging to his coat. *Those shoulders…* Down to his battered boots. *Oh, my, such long legs…* And back. At which point she met an amused pair of grey eyes and one quizzical lifted eyebrow. Spontaneous combustion was apparently not a myth.

'We thought the best tactic was to clear paths from the service door and the foot of the stairs to the dining room and deal with the rest after breakfast,' Theo said, apparently impervious to whatever it was simmering between the two of them.

'Yes, do that,' Ellie said, intending to be brisk and managing snappish. 'We do not want the staff's lives made more difficult, do we?' She turned and swept upstairs, the effect spoiled by her tripping over her hem on the middle step and cursing.

'She doesn't sound pleased.' Theo's voice carried clearly as she continued to stomp upstairs.

'Perhaps she doesn't like surprises. Look, you pick up the pine cones and I'll start stacking this lot under the stairs.' Drew sounded calmly practical, not at all like a man who had been sending her smouldering glances seconds ago.

She went into her bedchamber and confronted the long mirror. Those hadn't been smouldering glances at all, she realised as she stared at the woman in the glass. Drew had either been repressing hysterical laughter or wondering just what he had done agreeing to woo such a fright for a week.

On one side of her head the hair was flattened and on the other it was sticking up like a disordered haystack. There was a crease mark from the pillow on one cheek. Her dressing gown had a coffee stain she hadn't noticed before, the braid was trailing off on the bottom edge of the hem and she had pulled it on in such a hurry that the skirts of her nightgown were all bunched up on one side, making a most peculiar bulge.

The knot in her dressing gown cord was so tight that she bent a nail wrenching at it and the pain jerked her out of the state she was working herself into. This was simply a charade, a stratagem to protect Theo. What Drew thought of her was neither here nor there provided he could maintain a good-enough façade of wanting to marry her. And what she thought of him was irrelevant, too, because she was not going to be marrying *anyone*.

That was certainly as good as a splash of cold water for settling her emotions in order. She was not legitimate, which meant that any gentleman with a care for society's opinion would not wed her and she had two young sisters to bring out, which meant she could certainly not lower their status any further by marrying unwisely. Or behaving unwisely, come to that. Their coal-merchant grandfather was enough of a handicap for the twins without their shady sister indulging in scandalous *affaires*. So, even if a hard-up half-pay officer in shabby regimentals made her heart—and other, less mentionable organs—flutter, that was all it could be. Some fluttering.

Ellie thought she had everything well under control when she came downstairs half an hour later. Her hair was smooth and swept up into a practical chignon. Her gown was practical, too, a day dress in dark green. Her temper was even, her smile as she came into the dining room was, she hoped, just warm enough to show her pleasure at the sight of the neatly ordered piles of evergreens.

The twins were already downstairs, buttering toast as they chattered about ribbons and wreaths and how best to decorate the hall. Theo was at the buffet, heaping his plate with the appetite only a sixteen-year-old youth could demonstrate, and Drew was addressing bacon and eggs like a man who had been up since before dawn. He came to his feet as she entered and she made a point of smiling more broadly. His expression warned her that she was probably overdoing it.

'Good morning again. I hope you both make a good breakfast as a reward for your labours. Do forgive me for being so grumpy first thing—you know what a bear I am when I am woken early, Theo. Where did you find such a good selection of evergreens, Drew?'

'I asked the porters at Albany where I have been staying. They suggested the Hay Market and Covent Garden, so I got to Hay Market before dawn, found a carter who had just emptied his wagon and who was ready to earn a few extra shillings. I bought some evergreens there, then came to pick up Theo and we went down to Covent Garden to finish up.' He looked at her, clearly assessing her mood. 'It looks a lot, but the servants will appreciate some decorations below stairs, no doubt.'

'It will look quite wonderful,' Ellie said. 'But we will all have to work exceedingly hard to fin-

ish today. Girls, can you take the guest rooms
first? Don't disturb Cousin Joan, you know how
she likes to read after her breakfast and this is
the last morning she'll be taking it in bed for a
while. Theo and Drew, if you decorate the stairs
and the hallway, then Maddie and Claire can add
ribbons and bows. I'll do this room and the drawing room.'

It was a very long time since he had decorated
a house for Christmas, Drew realised as he hung
over the banisters, coat off, twine clenched in his
teeth, holding the end of ivy sprays in place while
Theo wove them round the spindles. Army officers were more likely to decorate their tents and
lodgings with candles stuck in empty bottles and
the bones of whatever scrawny fowls they had
managed to acquire than worry about artistic pine
cones and ribbon bows. His mother had always
insisted on decorating lavishly but mere menfolk
were relegated to cutting the greenery outside,
lugging it in and then standing up ladders being
ordered about.

'Are we doing it right?' he asked Theo, who
was tucking pine sprigs into the ivy.

'Oh, yes, this will be fine and the girls will
tweak it anyway.'

It wasn't simply the distant memory of decorating a house that was coming back to him, Drew
realised as the twins' laughter echoed down from
the bedchambers. It was being part of a family.
The teasing, the companionship, the occasional

little spats. The warmth. That came from Eleanor, he was certain. Theo and the girls were intelligent, cheerful and friendly but it was Eleanor who worked to make this house a home, who looked after them, worried about them, focused them.

'Twine?'

Drew passed the last strands to Theo. 'I'll get some more.' They had begun at the top of the flight of stairs and were halfway along the banisters. He was already head-down, so Drew simply gripped the bottom of the spindle and rolled over, dropping the six foot or so into the hall. He landed on the balls of his feet, facing into the area under the stairs.

There was a shriek and pine cones rained down around him.

'Eleanor?'

'You scared the living daylights out of me!' The shadowy figure took a shaky step forward and revealed itself as his betrothed, swathed in a vast white pinafore that she'd gathered up in front to carry the cones. 'I swear I've two sixteen-year-old boys on my hands, not one.'

She might be lecturing him, but he had scared her, he realised. Her cheeks were white and her hands trembled as she smoothed down her apron.

'I could have landed on top of you. I'm sorry.' He stepped in under the slope of the staircase and reached for her. It was probably an indication of shock that she let him pull her into his arms.

Soft curves, a flurry of fabric, the scent of buttermilk soap and jasmine water, her breath feathering on his exposed neck. His body was making the straightforward calculation *woman + against me + soft = bed sport* and was springing to attention.

Then something changed as he held her, the simple physical reaction ebbing away to be replaced by that warmth he had been musing about. He felt Eleanor's tense body relax as her hands closed gently over his forearms, holding him as he held her. Drew felt a strange kind of recognition. This was like coming home. This woman was—

Eleanor gave herself a little shake and stepped back out of his embrace, her expression impossible to read. But he could interpret the message that her body had just sent him as clearly as if she had slapped him. She had sensed far more than an apology or an instinct to soothe after a scare. Whatever had just passed unspoken between them was not what she wanted, not what had been in their agreement.

Signs of affection to convince her relatives and the servants, yes. More, no. She was a wealthy woman and the last thing she wanted was a half-pay officer. Or the Vagabond Viscount with his estate in ruins and a shambles of a house waiting for him behind bramble thickets that would have kept out the Sleeping Beauty's suitors.

And the Vagabond Viscount had too much pride to become a fortune hunter. He intended to turn around the house and the estate before he looked for a wife. And when he did, he supposed he needed a lady with impeccable bloodlines and an upbringing that would have trained her to be a viscountess if he were to have any hope of rescuing the family name and giving his children their place in the *ton*.

He and Eleanor were wrong for each other and he should have recognised the dangers in this charade the moment he felt the first stab of desire, the first flicker of liking and attraction.

He couldn't think of any words that would do more good than harm, only the practical.

Let's pretend nothing happened just then.

'Have you seen the twine?'

'It is on the hall table.' Eleanor pointed. 'Both balls of it. I need one to secure these cones to the swags over the fireplace or they will fall off.'

She was talking too much, he thought as he turned away, picked up the twine and handed her the smaller ball. 'Here. Is that enough?'

'Yes. Thank you.' She snatched it from his outstretched hand as though she was frightened she might actually touch him.

Drew climbed the stairs back to Theo, cutting lengths off the string with his pocket knife as he went.

'Ellie is as jumpy as a cat,' Theo remarked, securing one end of the ivy.

'She is anxious about this ruse of ours and your uncle's reaction, I imagine.' Drew made himself consider the banisters. 'Some holly? No, too prickly. It might catch the ladies' skirts.'

'The twins will make bows.'

'You can manage the bottom section by yourself. I'll hang the wreath on the front door.' Getting out in the cold air might clear his head. Drew found the circle of holly and opened the front door.

'Is it snowing yet?' Theo called.

'I sincerely hope not, we don't want your guests held up.'

'Don't we?' Theo said darkly.

'No. We need your uncle here being convinced that the Navy is not for you. The sky looks heavy, but there is no sign of snow.'

'I don't expect snow is as much fun in the town as it is in the country. It will all turn to slush and they wouldn't let you make snowmen in the parks, would they?'

'Probably not.' Drew lashed the wreath firmly to the door knocker. 'This needs a ribbon or two.' He closed the door again, but not before the fog swirled into the hallway. 'You could probably get away with snowball fights, though.'

'Snowball fights?' That was Maddie, Drew thought. He was almost certain he had worked out which twin was which. She came downstairs, hands full of ribbons in crimson and silver and gold.

'If we get snow. Could you make a large bow for the door wreath?'

'Which colour?' She held up the selection.

'Gold,' Drew said at random.

'Excellent choice.' She beamed at him, then pulled out a length of golden satin. 'Hold that in the middle like so…' She soon had him in a tangle of ribbon like a game of giant cat's cradle.

'Are you sure you know what you are doing?'

'Of course. Just hold still, I'll snip it here. And there you are.' She held up a perfect bow with long streamers. 'Let's fix it.'

'I'll do it, it is raw cold out there.'

Maddie took his hands in hers when he shut the door again. 'Ooh, you are frozen. Let me rub them. Is that better? I am so glad you came to rescue us.' She put her head to one side and regarded him, rather like a kitten uncertain which end of a piece of string to pounce on. 'I don't suppose you would really like to marry Ellie, would you? Only I think you would make a most superior brother-in-law.'

Chapter Five

Marry Ellie. The words hung in the air between them. 'I'm just a poor soldier,' Drew said lightly, a fraction of a second late.

'Well, Ellie has lots of money,' Maddie said. 'Papa left her so much because he felt guilty about you know what.' Her expression hardened and she released his hands. 'But perhaps you mind about that.'

'No. It was not her fault, was it?'

Tell that to society. Tell that to Lord Chamberlain when Viscount Ravencroft wants to have his wife presented at Court.

'It makes no matter to me,' he said honestly.

It's the rest of them that's the problem.

'Well, then?'

'One, your sister does not want to marry me. Two, I am her employee. Three, I am not a fortune hunter.'

'Mr Harrington last year was. Ellie got quite fond of him, I think, and then we discovered he had proposed to two other ladies within the previous month and their trustees had turned him down. He was quite desperate, Mr Ague said. I suppose it would wound your pride to be thought such a one.'

'Of course it would, but you forget points one and two.'

Poor Eleanor. No wonder she is so fierce on the subject.

'Two is neither here nor there.' Maddie picked up the ribbon she had dropped and began to fashion another bow, her gaze sliding sideways to watch for his reaction.

'But point one is. And I didn't mention point four, which is that, as charming as she is, I do not wish to wed Eleanor. I have things to be doing come January and they do not include marriage.'

'If this was a Christmas fairy story, you would be a prince in disguise, sent to rescue Ellie from the dragon—or in her case, withering into spinsterhood.'

'Well, I am not a prince.'

Maddie stuck out her lower lip mutinously, then reached up and pinned the bow she had just made on his shirt front.

'Ouch!'

'Oh, did the pin stick in?' she asked, all wide-eyed innocence. 'I'm sorry.'

'Hussy,' Drew said mildly, removing the mass of gold ribbons.

'I don't suppose you are a frog, either, are you?' Maddie said and took herself back upstairs.

'Did I just hear Maddie asking if you are a reptile?' Theo moved down a step and started on a new section.

'Amphibian,' Drew corrected absently. 'I'll put fir branches around the newel post.'

Ellie closed the drawing-room door and leaned against it. She was not sure what she was holding back—a passion-inflamed Drew or her own impulse to rush back and throw herself into his arms again.

Only he wasn't inflamed with passion, was he? she told herself. *He was simply trying to deal calmly with a woman who was overreacting to a fright. It is not his fault that he is making me feel positively...wanton.*

And it had to be desire, nothing more. She knew perfectly well that she had no choice as far as marriage was concerned. With her money she must be constantly alert for fortune hunters and because of her birth she needed to merge into the background so as not to spoil the twins' chances when they made their come-out.

And besides, he is not interested in marriage, so why am I even thinking about it?

Occasionally she caught Drew looking at her with something like warmth in his expression, but that was either typical male assessment of anything female and passable-looking or he was practising playing the betrothed man. She was the foolish one with the daydreams that she should have grown out of long ago. Look what had happened with George Harrington. She hadn't been in love with him, but she had liked him and enjoyed his company and had believed his protestations of affection. His deceit hurt.

Ellie dumped her load of pine cones on the table and tried to focus on the swag she had constructed across the mantelpiece. She must be very careful not to embarrass Drew, who thought he had taken on a purely business proposition. It wasn't his fault that close proximity to a pair of broad shoulders, an easy air of command and a pair of compelling grey eyes were making her... *yearn.*

'When should we expect your guests?' Drew passed Ellie the toast. 'It feels remarkably like the morning before a battle to me, I have to say. We've polished our weapons, we've scouted the battlefield and now all we can do is sit and wait in full battle array.'

He does look rather splendid, she thought wistfully.

Drew's uniform was brushed and pressed, his shave immaculately close. 'They'll be here late afternoon, I expect,' she said, fixing her attention on the marmalade. 'Uncle Tal will have come down from Cambridge on the Mail yesterday, but he stays the night with an old friend. Uncle Gregory's estate is in Hertfordshire and he will have hired a post chaise to bring them.'

'I've got to finish that letter to Tompkins,' Theo said. 'I've completed the theorem we were working on together and I might as well get it off to him today. I don't imagine I'll be able to get anything done once Uncle Gregory is here. I'll be too busy making manly conversation with Drew about trajectories and bare-knuckle fighting, I suppose.'

'I have to finish wrapping presents,' Claire said, getting to her feet. She went out, Theo and Drew settled back in their seats and then got to their feet again as she came back. 'Oh, don't keep standing up—I just wondered where the mistletoe has been put. At home in the country it is always in the hall.'

'Mistletoe? I haven't seen any. Did you forget to buy some, Drew?'

'No, I found a magnificent large spray. Theo?'

'Oh, blast.' Theo looked up from where he was scribbling an equation on his table napkin, a habit Ellie had utterly failed to break him of. 'I put it in the wine cellar to keep cool so the berries didn't fall off.'

'We've got plenty of time,' Drew said. 'I'll hang it after breakfast. Where do you want it?'

'In the hall would be best. But it is a very high ceiling.'

'We'll manage.' He smiled at her, reassuring and competent and not at all flirtatious. So why did her toes curl?

They trooped out half an hour later and stood in the middle of the chequered marble floor, looking up.

Drew pointed 'There's a hook that must once have held a lantern. That will do.'

'It is a good fourteen feet and we only have ladders to lean against the wall, not the A-shaped ones to stand in the middle of the floor.'

'Not a problem. If you get the mistletoe, Theo, and someone can find me the string, we'll have it fixed in no time. Do we want ribbons as well?'

'Of course,' Claire said. 'The silver satin ones.'

Drew made no effort to find something to climb on, Ellie noticed. Instead he removed his uniform jacket, stripped off his stock and rolled up his sleeves.

Theo emerged from the door down to the basement with a large bunch of mistletoe and handed it to the twins who began bickering amicably about how big a bow was needed and what length the streamers should be.

'How are we going to get it up there?' Theo asked.

'Take off your boots and coat, then sit on my shoulders. When I stand you'll be able to reach the hook.' Drew took a sturdy chair and set it beside him and went down on one knee. 'Is the mistletoe ready?'

The twins held up the decorated bunch, their mouths slightly ajar at the sight of two males in the front hall stripped to their shirts. Theo at least had his waistcoat on, but Drew's braces, holding up his tight uniform trousers, were not something a young lady saw every day of the week.

If at all, Ellie thought distractedly, wondering

if she should make the girls go into the drawing room.

Then Theo slung his leg over Drew's shoulders and settled there, feet dangling in front, his hands on his head. 'Are you sure about this? I'm not exactly a lightweight.'

'That is very true. Lord knows what your sister feeds you,' Drew said. 'Just sit still and let go of my ears.'

Ellie could see his ribcage expand as he took a deep breath, and another. And then he stood, levering himself up with one hand on the chair, staggering a little until he got both feet planted. 'Right. Give him the mistletoe.'

Ellie was standing behind him, her back to the front door, her gaze riveted on Drew's back. Broad shoulders were braced under Theo's weight and the drag of her brother's legs pulled the shirt tight so that she could see a hint of the muscles taut beneath, follow the strong masculine taper to his waist. The uniform trousers were snug over his buttocks and clung to the firm horseman's thighs.

Magnificent.

For a second she thought she had said it aloud, revealing to her siblings and the staff who had come crowding into the hall to watch the show that she was ogling a man's backside. But if she had, the whisper had been lost in Theo's breathless instructions.

'Left a bit, can you? A bit more. This confounded hook's bent. If I can just—There!'

As he spoke there was a resounding knock on the front door behind her. Ellie jumped and Hobson hurried forward, sliding himself cautiously around Drew. 'I will say you aren't at home, Miss Jordan,' he murmured as he passed her.

She turned to watch as he eased the door ajar, then stepped back abruptly as it was pushed wide open.

'For goodness sake, man. Is this any way to answer the door? We are catching our deaths of cold out here.'

Uncle Gregory at ten in the morning?

Behind her Drew spoke, sharp and urgent. 'Sit still, you idiot!'

The swinging door and a sudden press of bodies sent Ellie stumbling forward into Drew. Someone swore, then she was in the midst of tumbling, twisting bodies and landed with a shriek on something firm, warm and definitely human.

The back of Drew's head hit the rug with a thump, reminding him, as if he needed to know, that there was solid marble underneath. Somehow he had managed to twist so that they had fallen away from the solid hall chair. Theo's heel had raked down his chest as the lad had fallen and Drew's shirt was ripped completely open. He hoped vaguely that was all that had ripped. The scars from his encounter with the French lancer in June were healed, but there had been a few moments as he was lifting Theo when he could feel the sensation of the spear point pulling out of his flesh all over again.

No one was screaming about blood in all the mayhem that was echoing around his spinning head, so he supposed he was still in one piece. Not all the sensations were unpleasant. There was a soft female form draped over his legs and something tickling his bare stomach. He raised his chin and squinted down at the top of Eleanor's head. His body eagerly pounced on a distraction from pain, as keen as Theo with a mathematical equation to solve.

This one went *bare skin + warm female + lying down = take* all *my clothes off.*

Minus enraged relatives = pull yourself together, he corrected himself at the sound of the male voice above him.

Eleanor scrambled up, her elbow fetching him a sharp blow that, thankfully, dealt with any embarrassing consequences of erotic calculation.

'Drew, are you hurt?' She was staring, aghast, at his torso.

He heaved himself into a sitting position. 'No. Those are a souvenir of Waterloo, that's all.' He looked round. 'Theo?'

The lad was sitting up, too, white in the face and clutching his left wrist. Drew got up, ignoring his thumping head and protesting midriff, and went to crouch down to shield him.

'Let me see. Anything hurt beside your wrist?'

'No.' Theo looked up, past Drew. 'Don't fuss, Ellie.'

'What is going on here? Is this a madhouse?' The enraged male voice was still ranting on, with a counterpoint of female twittering and another man making soothing noises.

'I'm worried that Theo has broken his wrist, Uncle Gregory,' Eleanor said.

Drew was between Theo and the door and he could see his fingers moving. *Perfect.* He leaned close and whispered, 'Follow my lead.' Then louder, 'I think you are right. Claire, pass me your shawl, would you please?'

He flipped it around Theo, made a sling and put his arm inside, then pulled him to his feet by his good arm, pinching the soft skin near his armpit as he did so. Theo's yelp of pain was perfect. 'Bear up, lad. Can't be more than a simple fracture.'

'Hobson, send for the doctor.' Ellie was at their side as he helped Theo towards the stairs.

'No need. I've plenty of experience setting breaks like this, darling.'

She gave him a startled look at the endearment and he winked. Eleanor opened her mouth, closed it, shot her brother a quick glance, then nodded. 'Very well, if you think best, Drew. I will be up in a second.'

He heard her as they climbed the stairs with exaggerated slowness. 'Claire, Maddie, take your aunt and uncles into the drawing room. Hobson, the tea tray at once. I'm so sorry, everyone. What a welcome—but I'll be back shortly...'

'What on earth?' Theo demanded in a furious

undertone as they followed one of the footmen to his bedchamber.

'Wait for your sister.' Drew guided him through the door and turned to the footman. 'Hot water, bandages, something to make a splint, laudanum. Wintergreen ointment if your housekeeper has it.'

Eleanor came through the door as the footman hurried off. 'What is going on? Has Theo broken his wrist or not?'

'Mild sprain, I'd say. Wiggle your fingers, bend it back—that hurts? Side to side, bend it that way. Yes, sprained. Pity, because a broken wrist takes a while to heal. No climbing rigging with a healing break. No climbing rigging at all if it is permanently weak and, unfortunately, they so often are.'

'You… My goodness, that was quick thinking. But I do not like to lie to my uncle,' she added, biting her lip.

'No one need lie to anyone. It will not be our fault if he leaps to the wrong conclusion. Although a broken wrist is neither here nor there alongside the major untruth of our betrothal, is it?'

'Oh, dear. You are quite right.' She looked so downcast that Drew almost put his arm around her.

And who would that comfort? Not Eleanor to whom you are nothing but a means to an end. Only you, his conscience said severely. *You are beginning to wish this was no deception. Pull yourself together.*

'If you go down now, I will follow directly.

Prepare to disagree with what I say, but give way in the face of my superior masculine reasoning.'

Eleanor pulled a face at him, but the footman returned before she could make a retort. 'Peter. Please gather up the Captain's clothing and find him a new shirt. I will see you downstairs. And, Theo, you are to rest.' She did not quite slam the door behind her, but it was a near-run thing.

Drew dismissed the footman and studied Theo's arm. 'You are right-handed, aren't you?'

'Yes. The left being strapped up won't be a problem.'

'Excellent.' Drew slit the shirt sleeve, then began to strap the wrist into a splint. 'It hurts a lot, remember. Your instinct is to allow your sister to mollycoddle you, but you are going to respond to my bracing treatment and act as though it is no more than a sprain. However, when you think you are being watched, see if you can manage a wince or two or an expression of stoical suffering. Play it down, it will be more effective. There. Now, let's get you into your coat—I'll cut the seam up from the cuff buttons a little—and here's a better sling than your sister's shawl. Practise looking pale and interesting and come down in about ten minutes. All right?'

Chapter Six

'And just who is this half-naked man? I would like to know.' Uncle Gregory paced back and forth on the rug before the fireplace while Aunt Dorothea nodded energetically and Uncle Tal made vaguely soothing noises.

'Captain Drew Padgett, of the artillery. We are betrothed. And he is normally perfectly decently clothed,' Ellie said. 'That was just in order for them to hang the mistletoe.'

'*Betrothed?* Since when, might I ask?' her aunt demanded.

'The day before yesterday. Captain Padgett proposed then. I have known him for some time.'

'*Some time?* But who is he? The man may be a complete fortune hunter.'

'Mr Ague has investigated him,' Ellie said, exaggerating somewhat. 'That is where we met, when I was visiting Mr Ague. Captain Padgett was calling on his solicitor in respect of an inheritance.'

'Ah, well. Ague is sound, very sound,' Uncle Gregory conceded.

'And Captain Padgett saved me from a nasty accident when a wagon went out of control as I was crossing Fleet Street,' Ellie added. 'And he is so good with Theo. Being an artillery officer he understands mathematical principles far better than any of us.' She cast an anxious look at the ceiling above. 'I do hope Theo is all right. Captain Padgett does seem to expect him to be as...as...'

'Manly as he is,' Maddie supplied. 'Captain Padgett is very much the gentleman and the officer.'

At which point Drew opened the door and came in. Maddie blushed and Ellie could only hope no one else saw his eyelid drop in the hint of a wink.

'Aunt Dorothea, Uncle Gregory, Uncle Tal, may I present Captain Drew Padgett. Drew, this is Lady Wilmott and Sir Gregory Wilmott and Dr Talbot Jenkins, Fellow of Cambridge University.'

Drew had brushed his hair, resumed his uniform jacket and stock and, she swore, actually clicked his heels together as he bowed to her relatives. 'Lady Wilmott, Sir Gregory, Dr Jenkins. I must apologise for the scene as you arrived. I trust you were not much alarmed, Lady Wilmott? There is no need to concern yourself about Theo, I have fixed and splinted his arm.'

'No, not at all alarmed. Concerned, naturally.' Aunt Dorothea would not admit to alarm if a troop of Cossack horsemen rode through the drawing room in pursuit of a pack of wolves.

'We had not expected you until much later,' Ellie explained as they all resumed their seats, even, she was relieved to see, Uncle Gregory. Drew sat down on the sofa next to her, a respectable six inches away.

'The threat of snow persuaded me to come up to London yesterday. We stayed at Grillon's overnight. You are not with your regiment, Captain?'

'I have been on sick leave since June, Sir Gregory, and since then on general leave. I have a modest inheritance coming to me and when that is settled I will make a decision about selling out.' He turned and took Ellie's hand in his. 'Of course, now that is something Eleanor and I must discuss together.'

'June? Waterloo?' Uncle Gregory demanded.

'Yes, Sir Gregory. An encounter with a French lancer.' He said it as though there had been a mild exchange of fisticuffs.

Ellie thought of the red scars across his chest and stomach and clutched at his hand. It closed around her fingers, warm and calloused and comforting.

'And yet you indulge in acrobatics in the hallway,' Aunt Dorothea said.

'I have been emphasising the importance of keeping fit to young Theo.'

The door opened to admit Theo. He sat down hastily in the nearest chair and produced a brave smile that made Ellie want to giggle. 'Please excuse me, Aunt, if I sit.'

'Theo, why have you come down? You should be resting in bed,' Ellie said, half-rising before Drew pulled her back down beside him.

'No, Eleanor, you really should not mollycoddle the lad,' he said firmly with a patronising smile that removed all desire to giggle and replaced it with the urge to box his ears. *It is simply acting*, she told herself. 'Your brother is perfectly all right, aren't you, Theo? The effort to be sociable will take your mind off the pain.'

Theo nodded. 'Of course,' he said, bravely.

'Your wrist is broken?' Uncle Tal asked. 'Not your right one, I'm glad to see.'

'My left is hurt.'

'A fall like that with the hands put out to save oneself is always the most dangerous for breaking wrists,' Drew said. He seemed to have forgotten that he was holding Ellie's hand and his fingers were idly drawing circles in her palm, his thumb pressing lightly on the swelling below her own. It was most unsettling, although not unpleasant.

Not unpleasant at all.

'I suspected such an injury at once,' he added. 'They respond well to being immobilised immediately. However, there is always the danger that the wrist may be left permanently weakened.'

'Weakened?' her uncle said sharply.

'Ah, yes. There was talk of him joining as midshipman quite soon, I believe? It could be a problem, of course.' He managed to make it sound as though that had only just occurred to him. 'It isn't something that would be a handicap for an army officer, but climbing rigging, keeping one's footing in rough seas—and certainly handling a sextant—those need both hands to be strong.'

'Good grief.' Sir Gregory stared at Theo in alarm. 'You must not worry, my boy. Proper treatment and exercise will soon put it to rights.'

'Yes, I'm sure,' Theo said, looking at Drew. 'I'll try not to fret about it. But you think that even if it is too weakened for the Navy I might still be able to join the Army? It wouldn't affect my riding?' He turned a wistful look towards his uncle. 'That was something I would have missed so much in the Navy.'

Don't overdo it. Ellie signalled frantically with her eyes. 'Uncle Gregory knows best, Theo,' she said placating. 'I'm sure the Navy is safer anyway.'

'Safety is not something that concerns Theo, I'm sure,' Drew said. 'He wants to do his duty.' He turned to look at the older man. 'I understand yours takes you on a diplomatic mission, Sir Gregory. Is it something you are able to talk about?'

By breakfast on Christmas Eve Drew thought he was beginning to make some progress. Theo was playing up well, acting the brave invalid impatient to put his injury behind him. Eleanor was fussing just enough to give point to his own bracing interjections and Dr Jenkins was being tactful and saying nothing about the university.

The two scholars vanished into the study mid-morning when Theo was supposed to be resting, but Sir Gregory did not seem to notice and Drew had managed to brush the chalk dust off the lad when he reappeared.

'Time for some manly sports, I think,' he said, pushing Theo firmly back into the room. He folded the chalkboard, shoved the desk to one side and stacked books on the piles of paperwork.

'"*Calculations for the Elevation of Field Guns*",' Theo said, picking up one. '"*Geometry for Artillery Officers...*" I've already had a look at these. They're interesting. But what the blazes do we want with two broom handles?'

'Singlestick practice. Ever tried it?' Drew swung at Theo's ankles, making him jump. 'Nice and noisy,' he added with a grin. 'Let's get that arm strapped firmly to your side and we'll have some fun.'

It did not take more than a few clashes of the sticks before they attracted an audience. Jumping and dodging were enough to jar Theo's sore wrist and he put on a good show of gritted teeth and bravely suppressed winces. His sisters clustered around the door, applauding both fighters impartially until chased away by Cousin Joan, clucking with disapproval over the shirt sleeves on display, but Eleanor marched straight in, her uncles behind her.

'Drew, how could you be so thoughtless? You'll hurt him!'

'Nonsense, my dear,' Drew said and grinned

at her narrow-eyed response to his patronising tone. She might think he was overdoing it, but they hadn't the time for too much subtlety. 'The lad needs his exercise. Another five minutes will do no harm.'

'I'm enjoying it,' Theo said with a stab at Drew's midriff that won applause from Sir Gregory.

'What's this you're reading?' Dr Jenkins skirted the combatants and picked up the nearest book. 'Artillery tactics, eh? Thought you weren't interested in this practical stuff.'

'There's more scope for development with land-based artillery than there is with naval gunnery,' Theo said, momentarily distracted. *'Ouch.'*

'Indeed? Explain that to me, would you, my boy?' Sir Gregory picked up another of the texts.

Drew edged out of the door and into the empty dining room, taking Eleanor with him. He pushed the door closed on the sound of Theo's fluent, incomprehensible and entirely fictitious lecture on the geometry of cannon fire. 'It really is only a slight sprain.' Somehow he had kept hold of her hand and now she was in his arms, her head against his chest. He was not complaining, even though Eleanor seemed more moved by the need for reassurance than anything else.

'I know,' she said, breath warm through his shirt. 'I'm not overdoing the fussing, am I?'

'No, it is perfect.'

You're perfect. Soft, feminine, intelligent and loyal.

There was a strong shell around Eleanor Jordan, he had come to realise, but she put it on as a knight dons his armour. She was head of her little family and she would fight to a standstill for them—but who was there to fight for her? A sixteen-year-old youth, two young sisters and adult relatives who, fond as they were, found her birth an embarrassment and would like to see her married off. And a canny solicitor who seemed to be all that stood between her and unscrupulous fortune hunters.

And there is me, Drew thought, adjusting his stance so he was holding her steady without either of them having to clutch at the other. *Me for a week,* he reminded himself, even as he lowered his head so he could nuzzle into her hair.

There it was again, that feeling of warmth, of rightness, when he was around Eleanor. Who needed this embrace more? Drew told himself that he was simply unsettled by change, by the loss of the easy army comradeship, by the looming responsibilities ahead of him.

'I'm sorry.' Eleanor was moving back, flustered now, but still within the circle of his arms.

'Don't be. This is difficult, I know.' Drew injected as much confidence and reassurance into his voice as he could, aware he was more used to rallying troops than supporting women. 'You are anxious, on top of entertaining and creating a happy family Christmas.'

'Yes,' she agreed, quite firmly. 'That's what it is.'

Good, all I need to do now is let go.

Apparently he had lost the ability to make his limbs obey. He still embraced her, his hands linked at the small of her back. She leaned against them, looked up into his face as Drew lost his grip on common sense. And kissed her.

He retained enough control to keep his hands where they were and not go roaming across her body, tracing that lovely flare from waist to hip, running up under the swell of her breast. He forced his imagination away from the weight of it in his palm, the way she would gasp when he slid his fingers under the edge of that chaste neckline, the flutter of her eyelashes as he ran his thumb over the point of her nipple. Instead Drew focused everything on the taste of her, the little sigh as she opened her lips to his, moist and warm and welcoming, the deeper sigh as her hands came up to cup his head, hold him still.

As though I have any intention of going anywhere.

Except possibly straight to perdition.

What the hell was he doing? This was not for show, not to add verisimilitude. He was alone with a virgin in a room with the door closed and he was kissing her with every intention of reducing the pair of them to a puddle of lust. Never mind the fact that she was responding. He was the one with experience, he was the one who had to stop this. Now.

'Oh.' It wasn't the most sensible, let alone sophisticated thing to say, but it was apparently all she was capable of. 'Oh,' Ellie said again and sat down with a bump on the nearest dining chair.

'I apologise, that was unconscionable.' Drew reached for the door handle.

'No. Don't. Don't open the door yet and do not apologise. It was not your fault and you would have stopped if I had not responded, wouldn't you?'

'Of course.'

'Then it was no one's fault and, besides, I enjoyed it. Goodness, what a very forward thing to admit.' She eyed him warily, half-expecting Drew to bolt while he still could, after finding himself in a compromising position with a young lady behaving badly.

'We have been playacting the lovers, I suppose it was inevitable if we let down our guard.' He sounded stiff and no wonder.

He didn't agree to this, she thought dismally.

He undertook to take part in a charade, not provide an education in romance for a spinster. That was what some of the respondents to her advertisement had thought, that she was a frustrated woman looking for a lover. It had shocked and embarrassed her then, in Mr Ague's office, and now it appalled her. What if Drew thought that was what she'd had in mind all along, or that she had decided that now he was in the house, in her pay, she could use him like that? But that kiss had been a revelation. George Harrington had kissed her with what she had thought was passion, but she had never once felt like this.

'Eleanor,' Drew said and she braced herself. Then he smiled, the set of his shoulders relaxing as he moved away from the door and took a chair on the other side of the table. 'We should stop blaming ourselves. Your sisters and brother are not the only healthy, unattached, people in this house. It is natural, not shameful, but perhaps we should take more care with closed doors and empty rooms.'

'Yes, of course,' she agreed and got to her feet. 'You are quite right. Goodness, is that the half-hour striking? I must go down to the kitchen and check on the, er, Christmas puddings. Or the goose. Or something.'

She fled, there was no other word for it. Out of the door, along the hall, through the baize door and down to the basement where Cook, more than capable of managing, admirably concealed her irritation at the intrusion.

At least the heat of the kitchen gave some excuse for her pink cheeks when she emerged ten minutes later.

'Eleanor, a word if you please.' Her uncle stood at the study door, his brows drawn together into one of his more imposing frowns.

'Uncle Gregory?' Surely not a lecture on morals, that would be Aunt Dorothea's province. She followed him into the study, wondering where Theo had got to.

'This Captain Padgett of yours.'

'Yes, Uncle?' Now her knees were knocking. Ellie sat down and attempted a confident smile with a touch of doting for good measure.

'I'm very impressed by him, I have to say. Good, upstanding young man, excellent influence on Theo.' He gave her a severe look. 'Counteracts your coddling, young lady.'

'Yes, Uncle Gregory. I am glad you approve of Captain Padgett, your opinion is very important to me.'

'He does fully understand your circumstances?'

'Yes, Uncle.' She was expected to be shamed by her birth, so she cast down her gaze and tried to look regretful. In fact, she saw no reason why she should be ashamed, but there was no denying that it was a confounded nuisance. 'I was very frank with him, I wanted no misunderstanding.'

'Good, good. I can only assume that an army officer with no family to consider can afford to follow his heart in such matters.'

He gives family *a capital letter*, Ellie thought. *And sounds rather disapproving of the idea of listening to one's feelings.*

'He is expecting an inheritance, Uncle. He will sell out then and manage his estate, I believe.'

'A quiet country life. Excellent. Very suitable. You say Ague has investigated him thoroughly? Make sure he negotiates the settlements as I won't be here to do it.'

He got up and paced a little. 'I have to admit that Padgett is shaking my conviction about what is best for young Theo, especially if the lad has weakened that wrist.' He pulled at his lower lip, clearly discomforted by the idea that anyone could unsettle a notion of his. 'Hadn't realised the boy was so horse-mad.'

Neither had I.

'And your young man and that old fusspot Jenkins both seem to feel there is more scope for someone with Theo's talents in the army. Not that I've any influence there.'

'Whatever you think best, Uncle.'

I really am going to burst my corset laces if I have to pretend to be meek and mild much more. I sound a complete dimwit.

'Theo does seem very interested in the artillery and he would exert himself more and rise faster if his interest is engaged, I suppose.'

'A very sensible observation, my dear Eleanor. You have given me something to think about.'

Don't look too relieved, she cautioned herself.

'Is that all, Uncle? I was going to consult Aunt on the best time for dinner this evening if we are all to attend the Midnight service.'

'Yes, run along, dear. And do not worry about your brother.'

Eleanor had ungritted her teeth by the time she found her aunt and Cousin Joan and discussed at tedious length the time for dinner, settling on the hour she had already agreed with Cook. But at least the conversation meant she had told her uncle no more lies.

* * *

'What are you doing standing in the hall with your eyes closed, muttering to yourself?' Drew said, so close that she jumped. 'You aren't under the mistletoe, so you cannot be waiting for me.'

'I am counting to one hundred,' she said, with a reproving look for his teasing. 'And then I will go and tidy myself before luncheon. After that I will wrap presents and think calming thoughts.'

'What has provoked the need to count and be calm?' Drew edged her backwards and she glanced up. *Mistletoe.* 'An excuse to murmur together,' he said as he caught her in his arms and bent his head close.

'I do not think you need many excuses,' Ellie said, low-voiced, and tried not to be so spineless as to melt into his arms. *Again.* 'Uncle is being patronising, but he does appear to approve of you and to be coming round to the idea of the army for Theo.'

'I think we may be almost there. I have assured Sir Gregory that I will do my utmost to get you to accept what will be best for Theo, which is something I can do without lying to the man and—'

The rattle of the door knocker brought Drew's head up and made Ellie jump. 'That front door will be the death of me, what with Uncle and Aunt arriving and sending you and Theo toppling and now this…'

Hobson passed them. 'Doubtless the post, Miss Jordan.' He opened the door to admit a cloud of snowflakes and the blurred form of the postman who handed him a small stack of letters, touched the brim of his tall hat and hurried on.

'Snow,' Ellie said, delighted. 'That makes Christmas perfect.'

'It will take an old soldier a few years of peace before he greets snow with anything other than a scowl,' Drew said. 'Frost is often welcome because it makes marching easier and the guns don't get bogged down in mud. But snow? We all feared snow.' Ellie wondered if he had realised he had shivered in the warmth of the hallway.

'For you, Captain Padgett.' Hobson proffered a salver containing a thick packet. 'I have placed the remainder of the post on your desk, Miss Jordan.'

'The porters at Albany must have forwarded this. Will you excuse me while I look through it? Something may be urgent.'

'Yes, of course. I am sorry, I had forgotten about your inheritance. Does it make you much work?'

'Some.' His smile was rueful. 'Not as much as I fear it will cause me when I finally have my hands on it. Everything has been much neglected.'

One of those inheritances which come with dereliction and debt, I suppose.

She watched the lean figure take the stairs, two at a time. Drew would probably do well to sell whatever he could—perhaps that was what would take the work. He didn't seem anxious to confide in her about it, but it was, after all, none of her business.

Ellie went to sort the post before indulging herself in an orgy of silver paper, ribbon and little boxes. Wrapping presents was one of the things she enjoyed most about Christmas.

Chapter Seven

D rew retreated to his room, checked that Theo was not lurking in the dressing room that had become his bedchamber, and scanned the letters and documents that had arrived in the post. Everything was going well, his lawyers wrote. The delay because of the festive season was unfortunate, but the keys would be his after Christmas. Any cheer that brought was dampened by the report sent by the agent he had hired to inspect what he could of the house and estate without access to keys or legal authority. The man apparently had an imagination. To *appalling* and *overgrown* he added *and more fitting for a Gothick novel*.

There was no point in becoming depressed about it now. This was Christmas and he owed it to Eleanor to join in with the spirit of the season. Drew took the parcel from the bottom of the clothes press and opened it.

He had shopped in a small store run by a charity that sold the work of disabled ex-soldiers.

There he'd found a whole range of simple wooden boxes that had been decorated with split straw, dyed and cut and fashioned into patterns, much like marquetry work. There was enough variety to find unusual presents for men and women and without depleting his resources too far.

Claire had given him paper and scraps of ribbon and he did his best not to make a hideous mess of wrapping them. He carried them downstairs and added them to the decorated tables that were already scattered with labelled parcels, positioning his offerings so the lumpier sides and rather uneven bows were hidden.

'You've bought presents?' Ellie joined him, her arms full of artistically wrapped gifts. 'You shouldn't have.'

'Not bought gifts for my hosts and my betrothed? It would have seemed very strange not to. Here, let me.' He took the topmost from her pile and added them so it further disguised his failures in parcel-tying. 'Considering that when I last wrapped a Christmas present I was probably younger than Theo, I suppose my efforts are not too bad, but I think they are better disguised until people have had several glasses of wine.'

Ellie's gifts were all shapes and sizes, some soft and floppy, others tiny boxes, some clearly books. 'There,' she said, stepping back at last. She linked arms with him and leaned against his shoulder a little as she surveyed the effect. 'Thank you.'

Drew looked down at the top of her head and managed not to give in to the urge to kiss the glossy brown waves. He was becoming too fond of Eleanor for comfort. 'What for?' he asked instead.

'For being here, for joining in as one of the family. For helping make this Christmas even though we aren't in the home we grew up in. For being the older brother Theo needs and for being...' Her voice trailed away into a murmur.

'For being what?' Drew bent down so that her curls brushed his cheek, so that his nostrils were filled with the elusive scent of jasmine and warm woman that he was coming to recognise as *Eleanor.*

'For being you,' she whispered.

He kissed her as something clenched in his chest, even as every sensible instinct in him screamed *No.* He had thought he recognised the dangers inherent in this charade—the embarrassment of being found out at best, a suit for breach of promise at the worst. It had not occurred to him that sensible Miss Jordan might fall for him, that he— *No.* This time it got through to his willpower and he lifted his head. 'Eleanor.'

'I know.' She took her hand from his arm and went to the table, not looking at him as she fussed with labels and bows. 'Don't get fond of you. That was what you were going to say, wasn't it?'

'Something like that,' Drew admitted. She was too perceptive not to tell if he was lying to her. She still had her back to him, her bent head exposing the tender, vulnerable nape of her neck. Drew clasped his hands together.

Don't touch.

'Can we not be friends after this is over?' she asked.

'That would not be—practical.'

'No?' She did turn then, her smile a little forced. 'No, I suppose not. Imagine explaining to your wife when we met. Dearest, this is Miss Jordan, we pretended to be betrothed one Christmas.'

'I have no intention of marrying, not for some time. I was thinking of your relatives.'

'Oh. I see. No doubt you are right. The girls will be disappointed, they have quite fallen for you, but I expect their beaux will distract their minds when they come out.' Her smile seemed normal now. Perhaps he was imagining things, the sweetness in her kiss, the glint of moisture in her eyes, the tension that hummed between them.

He was no longer Captain Stanton, able to marry where the fancy took him, provided that fancy involved a young lady willing to live on army pay, possibly to follow the drum. Now he was a viscount with responsibilities and a mountain to climb before he could seek a suitable bride.

'Will you come to church this evening?' Eleanor asked, pulling him out of thoughts of a cold, empty house filled only with draughts and ghosts and into the warmth of this one. The twins' laughter echoed down from the floor above and he smiled at Eleanor.

'Of course. Which church?' He followed her out into the hallway.

'St George's, just along the street.'

'The lion and the unicorn church?'

'What can you mean?'

'You obviously keep your eyes chastely lowered on your way to services,' Drew teased. 'Have you never seen the etching of 'Gin Lane' by Hogarth?'

'Yes. Horrid thing.'

'You can see the spire of St George's in the background, with the lion and the unicorn at its base.'

'Then Gin Lane is a street near here?' Eleanor shivered.

'In the rookery of Seven Dials. The worlds of poverty and privilege are never far apart in London.'

'No. I must speak to the vicar about what he does to help the poor. I have neglected charity works since we have been in London.'

'You'll not go near Seven Dials.'

Eleanor blinked at his tone. 'Is that an order?'

'Yes, I rather think it is. I do not have to be *fond* to care what happens to you.' He moved towards her as he spoke and she put out a hand. That strange tension seemed to make the air shiver—

'Ellie! Have you seen my velvet muff? The one that goes with my new pelisse? Oh. I'm sorry, am I interrupting?' Claire stopped on the half-landing and looked at them.

'No, not at all.' Eleanor turned to her sister, all brisk reassurance. 'Drew was just warning me about venturing into the area south of the church. Apparently it is where Mr Hogarth drew that awful "Gin Lane" picture. And didn't you put your muff in a hatbox? I'll come and help you look.'

* * *

Ellie found the muff, exactly where Claire had put it. 'There you are.'

'Oh, thank you. Ellie, don't go.'

She turned back. 'Is something wrong?'

'That was what I was going to ask you. Have you and Drew quarrelled? You both seemed so tense just now.'

'Quarrelled? Goodness, no. It is just that...' Ellie sat on the end of the bed and searched for the words. 'It is rather difficult pretending to be in love with someone when you aren't.'

Claire scrambled up and sat with her back against the other bedpost. 'Actually, what you mean is that it is difficult to pretend to be in love for half the people in the house and pretend *not* to be in love for the other half.'

'What?'

'Is my addition wrong? Pretending to be in love for Aunt, the uncles and Cousin Joan. Pretend not for me and Maddie and Theo. Oh, and Drew of course. Yes, half and half.'

'Claire, I am not in love.'

Yes, I am. I'm not just fond of him, I'm not simply tormented by desire for him. I love Drew.

Her sister snorted. 'No?'

'No...yes. He doesn't want to marry me. And Drew is not a fortune hunter.' But not being a fortune hunter was a very good reason why he might not allow himself to think and feel beyond those kisses. Was that a tiny flutter of hope she felt just then?

Claire's lower lip stuck out in a mutinous pout. 'I think you are being idiotic. This is Christmas. Magic happens at Christmas. Tell him you love him.'

'I almost did,' Ellie confessed. 'But he was embarrassed. He certainly made it very clear that this is a business arrangement. He is very honest.'

But I could tell him how I feel, tell him I know that he isn't a fortune hunter, that I think we should let ourselves find each other once this charade is over, give whatever this feeling is a chance to grow.

'Then you are both idiots. I hope I never fall in love because it is obviously bad for the brain. There's the luncheon gong.' Claire began to scramble down, stopped halfway and hugged Ellie. 'But I love you.'

Ellie avoided Drew all afternoon, which was easy enough as the men seemed to gravitate to the study. What the four of them were finding to amuse themselves she could not imagine, but as there were no raised voices she sent in a tea tray. She managed somehow to chat to her aunt and Cousin Joan at the same time as daydreaming about Drew and about a version of herself who was bold enough to tell a man she wanted him to court her.

The ladies went up to change for dinner, leaving Hobson with strict instructions to send the men up in plenty of time, too. Ellie's fantasies about Drew were detailed enough for her to imagine him in his shirt sleeves kissing her passionately under the mistletoe and declaring that he didn't care about her birth or her money, only her. That he had loved her at first sight, that—

'Ellie, that is a divine gown!'

'Um? Oh, sorry, Maddie. Yes, it is, isn't it?' She smoothed down the rose-pink skirts with a smile. It was new and expensive and perfectly simple with a low neckline edged with brilliants and tiny puff sleeves. 'I will have to change before we go to church, I can't go out on to wet streets in this, but it is worth it.'

She went down arm in arm with her sisters, their skirts brushing the decorated spindles on the staircase. There was the mistletoe still hanging in the hallway and there was Drew.

Her imagination had been so full of him, tousled and coatless, his shirt open at the neck, his eyes heavy with smouldering promise, that she almost gasped as the man crossing the hall turned and looked up.

His dress uniform was immaculate, scarlet and black, gold lace and bullion, shining leather and crisp linen. His hair had been trimmed, his shave was close and his eyes… Drew looked at her as if there was no one else on the stairs, as if there were no other women in the world.

And then he smiled and bowed and clicked his heels and Maddie and Claire squealed and ran downstairs to exclaim at his magnificence. Drew looked over their heads and smiled, but the heat was gone and the intensity. Or perhaps she had only imagined it.

Wishful thinking, Ellie told herself as Drew opened the door for them and they all trooped in to dinner.

'This is our special Christmas meal,' Ellie explained to Drew as he sat at her side, Uncle Gregory at the head of the board, her aunt at the foot. 'The servants have Christmas Day off and we will be doing our own cooking tomorrow. Can you cook?'

'Over a campfire,' he admitted. 'That is just about all. Oh, and toast.'

'Then you will be relegated to kitchen boy, I'm afraid. You may have to pretend to be the scullery maid as well.'

He grinned, although she suspected he didn't really believe her. Perhaps he thought the staff would have laid everything out for them to do a little pretend preparation by making the tea. A dose of reality had chased away her daydreams and now, sitting next to him, she wondered how she had ever imagined she would have the courage to risk another approach.

Then the pleasure of the Christmas meal took over and she found her aching heart eased as she looked around the table at the familiar, smiling faces lit by the flicker of candles, the glow of firelight.

The goose was delicious, golden-skinned and flavoursome. There was beef for those who preferred it and pies and savoury tarts and vegetables gleaming under melted butter or rich sauces. The twins were allowed one glass of white wine each and became giggly. Aunt Dorothea's cheeks were pink and Cousin Joan was almost as overcome as the girls. The men ate as though they had been starved for a week, Maddie tactfully cutting up Theo's meat for him so he managed to keep pace with his elders.

A plum pudding, flaming with burning brandy, provoked gasps of delight, but Ellie had room for only a sliver of damson tart.

Finally the last spoon scraped across an empty plate and they all sat back, a little flushed, decidedly full, very happy. 'Please give my compliments to Cook and all the staff, Hobson. You have outdone yourselves this year,' Ellie said. There was a chorus of agreement as the footmen cleared the table.

Aunt Dorothea prepared to rise, but sat again at a gesture from her husband.

'I have an announcement. As you are all aware I had intended accepting Admiral Torrington's offer to find Theo a midshipman's berth in the New Year. However, I have been listening to what Captain Padgett has to say on the matter and also to my good friend Jenkins.'

Uncle Tal, who had kept hold of the dish of sugar plums and was sharing them with Cousin Joan, blinked in surprise.

'The Navy does not seem to me now to be the best use of Theo's talents and the Captain may well be correct that he would do better in the artillery,' Uncle Gregory said. Under the table Ellie groped for Drew's hand and found it already reaching for hers. 'However, given that his advancement in whatever field he enters depends upon his mathematical skills, I have decided he should attend university before deciding his future path.'

Theo had gone so white that Ellie thought he might faint. Uncle Tal's mouth was open, Aunt Dorothea was nodding sagely and Cousin Joan looked confused.

Ellie found that she was speaking. It was that or get up and dance a jig around the room. 'That sounds very sensible, Uncle,' she managed to say staidly. 'I am sure you know best. Theo?'

'Thank you, sir.' Theo said, then turned a beaming smile on Drew. 'I will do my best to make you proud.'

'May I have my hand back?' Drew whispered and she realised she was holding it in a fierce grip.

'Sorry.' She looked at him, embarrassed that she should have reached for him in the first place, but he was smiling.

'Don't be. We have accomplished our mission,' Drew said. 'And see, I still have the use of my hand.' He was smiling as he raised his glass to her.

'Thank you.' She returned the toast.

Magic happens at Christmas, Claire had said. It seemed she was right. Perhaps, just perhaps, more enchantment might follow if she wished hard enough.

Chapter Eight

They walked through the snow to the church, well bundled up. Sir Gregory went first, his wife on his arm. Dr Jenkins escorted Cousin Joan, Theo was flanked by the twins and Eleanor and Drew brought up the rear.

'Just enough snow,' he said, tucking his hand into the crook of her elbow. Like her sisters Eleanor was carrying a muff, both hands snuggly inside. It was a good thing, Drew told himself, because he wanted to hold her hand. She had reached for him at the dinner table without realising it, he knew, just as he had reached for her. He could still feel that fierce grip, the thrum of her pulse.

His reaction told him more than he wanted to accept about his feelings for the woman at his side. He was falling for Eleanor. If he asked her to marry him, would she say *yes*, or would she have thought better of it after the way he had snubbed her before? If he told her he was a viscount, that might weigh with her because it would help her sisters' prospects, although that reaction was not what he wanted. But if he didn't she might think him the hunter he feared he was.

Or I can leave and set about reclaiming the estate, get on an even financial footing and then seek her out. But what if someone snaps her up first? Some confounded vicar, some country squire. Some other fortune hunter.

'Just enough snow?' Eleanor queried and he realised he had been lost in his thoughts.

'Enough to make everything look magical, not enough to be dangerous.'

'Magical,' she echoed. 'You see the magic, too?'

'Of course.' He smiled, although she could not see his face. 'I'm secretly a romantic.' Perhaps he imagined her sigh, but they had arrived at the church and it was too late to query it. 'We can't see the lion and the unicorn now,' Drew said, glancing up. 'Look in daylight.'

After I've gone.

Drew sat beside Eleanor, the rest of the family around them, listened to the familiar words of the Christmas story and joined in the singing. He watched as Claire yawned and was nudged in the ribs by her sister and Theo found the right place in the prayer book for his cousin and blushed when his aunt nodded her approval. When he glanced down at Eleanor he saw she was looking at them herself, dabbing at the corner of her eye with her handkerchief.

'Are you all right?' he whispered.

'Just happy,' she whispered back and leaned against him a little as he held the hymn book for her and the choir launched into the soaring glory of 'Adeste Fidelis'. It wasn't deliberate, he thought. She was not being provocative, simply feeling comfortable with him.

I will ask her. When her aunt and uncles have left, I'll risk it. I won't tell her about the title, I'll be honest about the estate and the finances. And I'll tell her that I am...more than fond.

His mind shied away from the word *love*. If he loved her and she refused him, that was going to hurt more than he thought he could stand.

Years of discipline, of hardship, of fighting his way up the Peninsula, had left no space for dreams. *What if* and *I wish* led to disappointment and unhappiness in his experience. But now, surely, he could let himself fantasise a little? The warmth of family life, companionship, the laughter of the twins, the challenge of Theo and most of all the woman beside him. Warm, loyal, lovely and, he strongly suspected, passionate.

And stop thinking about that here, he chided himself as the congregation began to file out, strangers smiling and greeting each other, the glow of the season melting normal reserve.

He looked down and Eleanor smiled up at him. 'I am so glad I placed that advertisement.'

So am I.

Drew woke to the rattle of fire irons in the grate. That was a very inept housemaid. He rolled over and sat up to find Theo on hands and knees on the hearthrug.

'What the devil are you doing?'

'And Merry Christmas to you.' Theo, who was wearing a banyan and slippers, did not look round. 'I'm on fire-lighting duty. The girls have got the water heating, so if you go down and start bringing up the cans you and I can wash when I've done these.'

'You really meant it when you said the servants had the day off?'

Theo balanced coal on the kindling, then touched a taper to the result. 'Of course. There.' He regarded the flames with satisfaction. 'It will be warm in here by the time you've got the water.'

Drew scrubbed a hand through his hair, got up, found his own robe and slippers and splashed cold water on his face. He had the direst expectations for breakfast.

Maddie and Claire, in woollen chamber robes and with their hair in plaits down their backs, were ladling water out of the copper in the scullery into large cans. 'Good morning, Drew! Merry Christmas.'

'And to you both. Where's Eleanor?'

'Here.' She emerged from the pantry, a basket of eggs under one arm, a jug of milk in her hand. 'Merry Christmas, Drew,' she murmured as she came up on tiptoe to kiss his cheek. 'Can you take cans up to the front bedchamber for Aunt and Uncle, to the one opposite yours for Uncle Tal and the room next to it for Cousin Joan? Then cans for yourself and Theo? We can manage one each for ourselves.'

'Of course,' he said, caught off-balance by that kiss and her smile and the charm of the thick plait of hair lying over the shoulder of her old woollen robe.

I'll ask her tomorrow when her relatives have gone. I won't be able to pretend nothing has happened—good or bad—with them here.

But he was going to slip into the drawing room and add a little extra to his present for her.

By nine o'clock everyone was dressed and downstairs. The sisters had banished the men and the older women to the dining room while they made breakfast alongside the servants who were cooking and eating their own at leisure.

'Phew!' Eleanor put a platter of bacon and eggs on the table and sat down as the twins brought in the coffee and tea pots. 'That is all for now. We can cook more if anyone is hungry when this has gone.'

They could cook, Drew admitted to himself. His forebodings about leathery eggs, burned toast and bitter coffee had been wide of the mark. Perhaps Eleanor wouldn't mind too much being mistress of a tumbledown house with very few servants...

After they had finished breakfast Eleanor announced that clearing up could wait until presents had been opened. 'That will give time for the staff to finish in the kitchen and for more water to heat,' she explained, ushering everyone into the drawing room.

Drew, she noticed, was quiet, almost subdued.

He's retreating into himself because he feels an outsider.

'Drew, will you hand out the presents?' she asked, with sudden inspiration.

He nodded and took up a position by the laden table.

Goodness, how handsome he looks, she thought as she saw her aunt watching him. Aunt Dorothea smiled slightly and nodded. *She approves. But what am I feeling so happy about? She approves of a charade, that is all.*

It was an effort to keep her smile steady as Drew picked up the first parcel. 'Sir Gregory, this is for you.'

Everyone watched as Uncle Gregory, who was one of those infuriating people who had to carefully untie every knot and smooth out the paper, eventually revealed a pair of embroidered slippers. 'Madeleine, my dear, how thoughtful. And so beautifully stitched.'

Maddie, who had muttered and grumbled through weeks of sewing, beamed and took her own gift, one of Drew's endearingly lumpy offerings. 'Oh, how pretty! Thank you, Drew.' She held up a charming little box, decorated in pink and cream and a dark brown pattern. 'This will be perfect for handkerchiefs.'

He explained who had made the box and Aunt

Dorothea, opening her own version of the same thing, remarked, 'I am sorry that I cannot patronise such a worthy cause myself. Let me have the direction of the store, Captain, and I will include it in the letters I am writing to friends before my departure.'

Drew seemed surprised to find there were gifts for him, too. Claire, the best of them with a needle, had embroidered 'D' in the corner of six large linen handkerchiefs, Ellie had wrapped a handsome pair of calfskin riding gloves which he tried on immediately and thanked her warmly for her skill in finding just the right size. Eventually there were only two parcels left, one for Ellie and one for Drew.

She knew what his was: Maddie had framed a small watercolour portrait of her elder sister with cardboard and gilt paper and she held her breath as Drew unwrapped it. Maddie was better at landscapes than people and she hoped he would not show any amusement at her lack of skill.

He was so quiet as he looked at it that Maddie was becoming anxious. Then Drew smiled at her. 'This is wonderful. Almost as lovely as the sitter.'

'You like it?' Maddie was beaming now, used to the teasing with which her siblings normally greeted her artistic efforts.

'You have caught the sweetness of her heart and the intelligence of her mind,' Drew said simply and Ellie had to swallow hard before she disgraced herself with tears.

He handed her the final present and she re-

alised it was from him. Another of those lovely
little boxes by the feel of it. She opened it and saw
it was decorated in green and gold and, as she
moved it in her hands, something shifted inside.
'This will be perfect for ribbons,' she said, lifting the lid. Inside was a small tissue paper parcel
that contained a pendant made of a green stone,
heart-shaped, a little worn and chipped. It looked
very old, very lovely.

'Drew, this is exquisite.'

'It is rather battered, I'm afraid. I found it in the
mud beside a ford in Spain,' he said. 'I've carried
it ever since. It was my good-luck piece.'

'But I cannot take your luck,' she protested. 'It
has kept you safe all this time, even at Waterloo
you survived those horrible wounds—'

'I don't need luck now,' he said quietly, for her
ears only. He seemed almost serious, despite the
smile. 'What I want is more important than something that can be trusted to providence.'

Did he mean her? 'Drew?' Ellie whispered.

'Tomorrow,' he said as he sat beside her. The
others were showing each other their presents,
talking loudly enough across each other for them
not to be heard. 'If I am disappointed, or if I am
joyful, I will not have to hide it from your aunt
and uncle.'

He intended to propose, he could mean nothing else. 'I hope you will not be disappointed,'
she said, carefully, then stood up. 'The clearing
and dishwashing party must assemble. Uncles,
Aunt, Cousin, please make yourselves comfort-

able and try not to be startled at the sound of crashing china.'

'It was only one plate, three years ago,' Theo grumbled on his way to the door.

'And a cracked tureen last year,' Maddie said, following him.

'I'll clear,' Drew said. 'I doubt I'm to be trusted with good china and glass in soapy water.'

He fits in so well, Ellie thought, watching while she dried dishes.

Drew was bringing in fuel for the copper and stoking it up for more hot water and she tried not to stare at the way his arm muscles flexed or the ease with which he lifted the heavy coal bucket. Maddie was elbow-deep in the water, Claire was scraping and stacking, Theo was putting things away and from the servants' hall came the sound of laughter and yelps of pain.

'They are playing snapdragon, I expect,' she said when Drew sent her a questioning look. 'You know, raisins soaked in brandy, set alight and everyone tries to grab as many as possible.'

'Lord, yes, I haven't played that since I was a child. My fingertips still smart at the memory.'

Ellie could imagine him as a child. Curious, intelligent, a bit wild. His hair would be unruly, his pockets full of catapults and shells and probably a pet mouse or a frog or two. For the first time she allowed herself to imagine what his own children would be like.

Our children.

'Ellie!'

'Oh, sorry.' She took the dripping plate from Maddie and told herself that she was allowing her hopes and her imagination to run away with her. She might be building bricks out of straw— an entire house of them. Drew might have meant something else entirely.

And there was luncheon to prepare, now they were in the kitchen, just a light buffet of cold meats and fruit to set out. Then she could relax, knowing that everyone could just help themselves as the fancy took them and she wouldn't have to worry about food again until evening. Speaking of which...

'What can I do now?' Drew asked, coming back in from the yard shaking pump water from his hands.

'Potatoes,' Ellie said, handing him a knife. 'There's a sack over there and a pan there.'

'How many?' he asked, eyeing the size of the sack.

'Until I say *stop*,' Ellie told him with a grin.

'Is the head cook amenable to bribery?' Drew asked and, before she could do more than squeak, she was in the pantry, the door closed, and he was kissing her.

'Drew!' Ellie batted him away. Her hair was coming down, one strap of her apron had slipped from her shoulder and she was panting. 'The girls are out there, you, you, *reprobate*.'

'I'll behave myself,' he promised, with a glint in his eyes that she did not trust one bit. 'Just let me fix your hair.'

It was five minutes before she emerged from the pantry to find her siblings studiously engaged in slicing cold meat and bread, filling water carafes and looking so unconcerned and innocent that she wanted to throw the rolling pin at them, the little wretches.

So that is what Christmas is like, Drew thought at midnight as he stretched his toes out to find the best warm patch left by the warming pan. *I had forgotten. Next year perhaps I will be sharing it with Ellie and Theo and the twins at Ravencroft Manor. Perhaps. Don't hope too much*, he warned himself. *You should ask her to wait until you have the worst of things under control, until the estate is beginning to break even at least, and that won't be by next year.*

The thought that she might believe him a fortune hunter, that he could behave like one, had him tossing and turning until the bedclothes were tangled around his legs. It took the discipline that he'd used before battle to calm the anxiety churning his guts. He made himself think about the past day, about the laughter and the friendship, about the foolish charades and the cut-throat family card games where they played for the little mother of pearl fish tokens and Lady Wilmott had proved herself as dangerous as any card sharp.

The guests were leaving immediately after breakfast, he had learned. Dr Jenkins was travelling back to Cambridge and the Wilmotts were driving down to the docks for their ship heading for Genoa. The weather looked set fine, so he would suggest a walk in Hyde Park. There would be space enough to be private with Eleanor, to hazard his future and his heart with her.

I love her, he realised, finally letting himself accept what he had been avoiding for days. It wasn't simply liking or desire or the pleasure of a ready-made family. It was the knowledge that if he couldn't be with this woman for the rest of his life, then nothing would ever be quite right again.

Chapter Nine

'Bliss! My favourite chair again.' Maddie collapsed into an unladylike sprawl in the armchair closest to the fire and picked up a stack of newspapers. 'Not that I don't love them all dearly, but, oh, the relief of not having to be on one's best behaviour all the time.'

'That was what it was, was it?' Ellie teased.

'It is raining,' Drew said from the window seat. 'I had hoped we could go for a walk in Hyde Park.' He sounded disproportionately disappointed.

'Perhaps it will lift. It looks quite high cloud, don't you think?' She found she was holding her breath.

'Yes, I think it will.' The smile Drew gave her made her knees feel so wobbly that she sat down with a bump next to Cousin Joan.

'And if it doesn't I will put on sensible boots and take an umbrella and go anyway,' Ellie announced.

'Oh, no,' Claire declared. 'I'm not coming in that case.'

'Nor am I,' Maddie declared. 'Look, Uncle left all these newspapers.' She opened one. 'I will read all the Court Circulars and fashion advice.'

'I've got work to do,' Theo said. 'I can't believe I really can go to Cambridge. There's so much reading...'

'Oh, good,' Maddie said. 'This is one of the papers we don't usually get and it has a gossip column. But how provoking—all the names have initials and dashes. I wonder who Lady P. is, who is rumoured to be enamoured of a certain Signor A— L—, the world-famous tenor.'

'Those columns are nothing but nonsense,' Drew said sharply.

'Don't be a spoilsport, Drew,' Claire said. 'Read some more, Maddie.'

'*"The blank Regiment of Foot is reputed to be moving to camp near Brighton as soon as the weather improves... Colonel Y is selling his string of racehorses..."* This sounds more interesting. *"Where has the Vagabond Viscount vanished to for the festive season? Captain A— P— S— has not been sighted at the clubs or at Albany this past week. Can it be that the gallant but cash-tight Captain has been courting among the heiresses over Christmas? And when will we see Viscount R—, his fortunes restored, gracing society?"*'

Behind her she heard Drew move and then go still. Maddie lowered the newspaper. 'Captain A— P— S—, who lives at Albany?' she said slowly. 'Captain Andrew Padgett Something, perhaps? A *viscount*?'

A shiver ran down Ellie's spine as though traced by a cold finger.

No. Coincidence. Drew was not a fortune hunter. Drew was not some impoverished aristocrat hunting for an heiress.

'I am Andrew Padgett Stanton. Viscount Ravencroft as of mid-January,' Drew said behind her. His hand, large and warm, touched her shoulder and she shook it off with a violent twist. She couldn't look at him. 'I was going to ask you to marry me today.'

'A viscount,' Ellie said, staring at the fire. Anywhere as long as it was not at her family. At Drew. 'A viscount only marries an illegitimate granddaughter of a coal merchant for her money.'

'I was going to ask you to wait until I had the estate on its feet, at least.'

At least he has the grace not to make protestations of love.

There was a gasp from the woman beside her. 'Twins, Cousin Joan has fainted.' She stood up then, made herself turn. Drew was white about the mouth, his stance rigid. 'I think you had better go now. Apply to Mr Ague for the balance of your fee. You have, after all, earned that in full.'

She thought he might protest, try and explain, tell her something that she could accept, although goodness knew what that might be.

Drew—*Viscount Ravencroft*—made a small bow, turned on his heel and walked out.

Behind her someone swore. 'Theo, mind your language,' she said automatically, then, 'And stay where you are. I'll not have you brawling in this house.'

When the front door banged closed Ellie put down Cousin Joan's hand that she had been chafing, gently shrugged off Claire's arm that was around her shoulders and stood. 'The charade achieved what was needed,' she said. 'That is the main thing. And I may answer Uncle Gregory honestly when he asks me why the marriage has not gone ahead.'

She went into the study, found pen and ink and wrote a note to Mr Ague, requesting that he investigate Viscount Ravencroft. If there were repercussions from this incident she needed to know what she was dealing with. Then she went slowly upstairs and looked into Theo's bedchamber. The gloves she had given Drew lay neatly in the centre of the bed.

One of the maids came when she rang. 'Change the sheets and move Mr Theo's things back into this room at once, please.'

'The Captain has left his gloves, Miss Jordan.'

Ellie picked them up and put them in the trunk on the landing. They would serve as a reminder not to trust any man, if she was ever so foolish as to listen to her heart over her head again. Then she went downstairs. Hobson was in the hall, his expression rather less neutral than usual.

'Miss Jordan, has—?'

'The Captain has left. For good.' She glanced up. 'And have that mistletoe removed, Hobson.'

The porter at Albany let him into Jack's apartment. One look at Drew's face was apparently enough to silence his usual cheerful chatter.

Drew dropped his valise, kicked it into the corner and poured himself a large brandy. It burned down his throat with no discernible effect on his mood. Emptying the decanter was all too tempting so he jammed the stopper back in and turned his back on it.

Eleanor thought him a fortune hunter, one so predatory that he would answer newspaper advertisements in search of a vulnerable victim, it seemed. Pride and temper and the hideous sensation that his heart was breaking had stopped him trying to defend himself.

He looked round the room, at the unlit fire, the clutter of a bachelor apartment. Hell, if he was going to be uncomfortable, miserable, broke and cold he might as well do it in his own home. It did not take long to pack his few remaining possessions, to write a note to Jack and to sort out sufficient coins to tip the porters. Then he strode out across the front yard into Piccadilly and east towards the City, his lawyer and the Belle Sauvage inn for the stagecoach for Suffolk. Away from London, away from love.

The sky was reflecting pink and mauve with the rising sun on the high, thin cloud. Below, across the rough grass of what had been the lawns and the parkland, frost cast a glittering mantle over the landscape.

Drew took a deep breath and exhaled, melting a circle into the frost patterns on the inside of the widow. *Beauty and peace*, he thought as he turned away from the view and looked at the shadowed room, at its stark emptiness, its perfect proportions.

He had been here two weeks and that first morning, as he walked up the potholed driveway, he had almost turned tail. His agent had been right, it looked like a house of horrors from a sensation novel set in a wasteland of neglect. Then he had looked again, mentally stripping away ivy, hacking back brambles and sapling trees, cleaning window glass, cutting grass and planting flowers. What was revealed would be beautiful, a small gem built in the reign of the second Charles. Not a great house, but a home.

When he forced open the door against the protests of rusting lock and unoiled hinges he found that his cousin, manically devoted to destroying the next Viscount's inheritance, had been too selfish to allow the roof to leak or the glass to be left cracked. He might have retreated to two rooms and have been uncaring about cleanliness, but the house was sound.

Drew advertised the long-untenanted farms, then rolled up his sleeves and set to work. Soon he would have to employ staff from the surrounding villages: that was one of his duties, to employ local labour. But for now hard work kept him sane. He chopped wood, cleaned windows, swept floors, boiled up linen in the copper, stuffed mattress ticks with fresh hay. He had lived in worse conditions in Spain. He had eaten worse as well, he thought, as he bought local bread and eggs, milk and bacon and ale. But not wine or spirits, because the temptation to drink himself into a stupor to get through the evenings, the long, sleepless nights, was too great.

He walked slowly though his clean, warm, empty house. He had finally exorcised the ghost of Cousin Matthew, he thought. Now what? He heard laughter and knew it was his imagination, heard footsteps and the murmur of happy people. He walked slowly down the stairs and imagined Eleanor standing there waiting for him. She would love this house, she would fill it with the sounds and the scents and the comforts of a home. He could give her this and a title and standing. He would not be the Vagabond Viscount for long, not if sheer hard work could prevail. He could lend the twins status when they made their come-out, encourage Theo in his career.

Eleanor might have money, but he could give her these things. And love. If she would give him a second chance. Drew made himself coffee, a strong mugful, and went to write a letter.

Three hours later, after more cups of coffee than he could recall, after pacing and sitting, writing and screwing up the results, he reached a decision. He would go to London, tell her face to face how he felt, risk it all on finding the right words when he looked into her eyes.

He stood to start making ready. Was that the sound of wheels on the drive? He was expecting no deliveries. When he opened the front door there was a chaise standing there and the door was opening and—

'Eleanor? *Eleanor!*'

She climbed down before he had collected himself to go and help her. She said, 'Wait, please,' to the postilions.

Drew had reached her by then. 'Come inside, you must be cold.' Yes, she was real. Fantasies did not have pink noses or breathe puffs of steam into the frigid air.

'For a minute,' she said. He could not read her expression, but her hand as she lifted her skirts to climb the steps was unsteady.

'Come into the parlour, the fire is lit.'

She followed him, drawing off her gloves and looked around. The floor around the table was littered with screwed-up paper.

'I was writing to you,' he said. It was extraordinarily difficult to breathe. 'Then I decided to go to you instead.'

'I tried to write as well.' Ellie looked down at the litter at her feet. 'With about the same success.' She had been telling herself not to hope for all the miles of this journey—now she hardly dared risk letting go of the rigid control. 'I asked

Mr Ague to find out everything about the Vagabond Viscount. I learned how your cousin had
formed a grudge and had let it become an ob-
session, how you were left with this inheritance.
And he spoke to his colleagues and told me how
seriously you took your responsibilities, how
you seemed determined to make this commu-
nity thrive again.

'Eleanor—'

'No, let me finish. I found Lord Burnham, back
in London, and he said that you were one of the
bravest men he knew and the best, loyalist friend
he could hope for.' She took a steadying breath
because she was determined not to cry and the
look on his face made her want to weep. 'And I realised that I had jumped to conclusions, that I had
been unfair and that my experiences had made me
distrust all men, even a decent one.'

'So you came to tell me that?'

'I came to see if I had killed whatever it was
that had made you want to marry me or whether
there was any...' Her voice wavered. 'Any hope.'

'Because?' he asked, his voice very gentle.

'Because I would like it very much if you were
to ask me now.'

'I had meant to ask you to wait for me, until I
had rents coming in and this house in order. Yes,
I would be a liar if I pretended that I could not
afford to marry a woman with no dowry, not for
years. But I do not need a rich wife, Eleanor.'

'You are a viscount now. You need one with
breeding. Certainly one who is legitimate,' she

pointed out. She had to play devil's advocate, she had to be certain.

'No, I don't. I need you,' Drew said and she clutched at the chair-back.

'Why me?'

'Because I love you. Because you make me feel warm and complete. I can offer you this house, all the ghosts chased away. I can give you a title and the girls that status. I can give you my love for all of your years.' He stopped and she realised that he was finding it difficult to speak.

'I brought this with me,' she managed, and pulled the battered twig from her reticule. 'There's one berry left, but it is rather bruised, I'm afraid.'

'Stay right there. Don't move.' He strode out of the room, then she heard the sound of hooves, of turning wheels.

'I sent them away,' Drew said, as he closed the door and took the mistletoe from her. 'Was I wrong? There is no one else here now, only the two of us.'

'That is perfect. I love you, Drew, and I am going to be very happy here with you. And I think I am going to dissolve with desire if you don't kiss me now.'

It was like coming home to be in his arms, to feel his strength around her and the warmth of his lips on hers and the beat of his heart against her breast. When he finally lifted his head Drew asked, 'Has that helped?'

'Not at all,' Ellie confessed. 'I think it has made it worse. Perhaps I should go and lie down.'

'Perhaps we should,' he said with a smile that removed what strength remained in her knees. As she sagged against him he swept her up in his arms. 'The mattresses are all filled with hay, I'm afraid,' he confessed as he began to climb the stairs.

'I don't think I'll notice, my love,' she confessed, nuzzling against his neck.

'As a New Year present to ourselves I am going to buy a feather bed for each chamber in this house and then spend 1816 testing all of them with my wife.' Drew shouldered open a door, then leaned back against it, breathing heavily. She rather suspected it was from desire, because she was panting, too. 'But now I am going to make you mine. And then tomorrow we are going back to London, get a special licence and be married.'

'And I will have a bouquet of mistletoe, because I am quite certain I would never have discovered your kisses without it.' And that was the last coherent thing she found she could say for quite some time.

Except, of course, 'I love you.'

* * * * *

ONE NIGHT
UNDER THE MISTLETOE

Laurie Benson

For my husband.
Little did I know that when I stepped into that rowboat
on our first date my life was about to change.
Thank you for always being my anchor.
Merry Christmas, Mr B. I love you.

Thank you to my editor Linda Fildew for her guidance,
and to my team at Mills & Boon for giving me
the opportunity to take part in this anthology.
I had so much fun writing Monty and Juliet's love story.

Chapter One

Kensington, London—December 1819

For all the trouble Lord Montague Pearce was going through trying to find the Ashcrofts' library, he hoped he was rewarded with one heart-stopping kiss. Miss Catherine Fellsworth had informed him the library was located down this particular corridor, behind the third door on the right. That room, he discovered, was Lord Ashcroft's study. He knew Miss Fellsworth could be hare-brained at times, but one would think if you were going to meet a gentleman in secret at a ball, you would make certain you knew the precise location—especially since this was her idea.

For weeks, she had been flirting with him. For weeks, she had been teasing him that she might permit him to steal a kiss. Now tonight, while they danced, she had suggested they meet at this remote location of the house so he could finally kiss her. And she had directed him to the wrong room. While she might be beautiful and was in possession of a very large dowry, Monty wasn't certain those two things outweighed her flighty nature. But if he was going to consider her for a wife, he had to know if she could stir his soul with a kiss. Kisses like that were possible. He had experienced one once before. And if he were to pledge himself to someone for the rest of his life, he needed to be certain he would feel that again. Monty had kissed a number of women in his twenty-seven years and done much more than that with a few, and yet something always left him wanting—except once.

There was one kiss that had showed him that a simple joining of lips could feel like so much more. That was why he had sampled the lips of so many women in recent years. That was why it was important to kiss Miss Fellsworth. And after all this work trying to find the Ashcrofts' library, he hoped her kiss was worth it.

He turned the handle of the fifth door and had to give the large piece of oak a push to get it to open. As he slipped into the darkened room, he let out a sigh of relief at the sight of large bookcases lining the walls. At last, he had found the library.

It appeared Miss Fellsworth had had no trouble locating the room, since he could make out her silhouette in the moonlight as she sat by the window, waiting for him. With effort, he quietly pushed the stubborn door closed and discovered there was no key in the lock to ensure their privacy. He closed his eyes and vowed this was the last time he would let a woman arrange a clandestine encounter. Thankfully they were far enough away from the public rooms in the house so there was little chance of discovery.

The rug under his feet muffled his footsteps as he walked towards her. 'My dear, this is the fifth door, not the third. In the future, you might want to be more careful with your instructions.'

Was she reading? Miss Fellsworth didn't strike him as the type to open a book, unless it was one that contained fashion plates.

His voice must have startled her, because her head jerked up and she snapped the book closed. As he went to step closer, his legs weighed him down as if they were attached to each other with shackles. This wasn't Miss Fellsworth.

'Whoever you think I am, Lord Montague, I assure you I am not she.'

'Juliet?' he let out on an astonished breath.

Her face was cast in shadows with the moonlight behind her, but Monty knew that velvety voice. In the last few years he had heard it in his dreams, reminding him of the one week he had spent with Lady Juliet Sommersby, the woman with the heart-stopping kiss he had desperately wanted to forget. And now that this woman's sister Charlotte had married his brother Andrew, Juliet had recently become permanently affixed to his life—even if it was in a peripheral way.

'What are you…?' He searched for something coherent to say. Why would an eligible woman as attractive and lively as Juliet not be spending the night surrounded by suitors? His brow furrowed as he gestured towards the leather-bound book. 'Why are you reading in the middle of a ball?'

'I don't see why what I do is any concern of yours.'

'It isn't. I've just never seen anyone read at a ball before.'

'Do you regularly inspect the libraries of the balls you attend? Perhaps it is more common than you think.'

He should keep himself at a far distance from her, but he couldn't help approaching the window seat she was curled up on. She sat up taller, looking like a horse ready to bolt out of the gate. Before she had the chance, he snatched the book from her lap and read the title.

'I'm certain you've no interest in the contents,' she said, raising her chin and narrowing her eyes at him.

After reading the title, he held back a grimace. She was right. He had learned about Galileo from his tutors. He had no desire to relive those lessons now.

'I wasn't aware you were invited or even in London for that matter. Have you been in here all evening?' he asked, handing the book back to her.

'No.'

The notion that she might have noticed him while he was unaware of her presence made him uneasy. He had done nothing wrong. His behaviour this evening had been exemplary—except for the fact he had been planning to meet a woman in this very room to kiss her senseless. He turned and glanced at the closed door, expecting Miss Fellsworth to breeze into the library.

'You might want to wait for your lady friend out in the corridor since this room is already occupied.'

'What makes you believe I was meeting a lady friend?'

A sardonic look crossed her face. 'You referred to me as *"my dear"* when you walked in. I doubt you use that term of endearment with any of your gentlemen friends.'

There was no reason he needed to explain his presence to her. The one week they shared together had passed a long time ago and they'd barely spoken since. Yet he felt guilty about sneaking away to spend time alone with another woman.

He shifted on his feet. 'You seem to want to chastise me for stealing away at a ball, yet here you are in a room far away from the activities of the evening. Not a wise place for an unmarried woman.'

'Yes, but I'm reading. I doubt your intentions for being in this room are as innocent. You lost your right to express concern about my welfare years ago.'

She stood up and the moonlight illuminated her smooth skin and brown hair. He knew in the sunlight there were fine strands of auburn mixed in with the brown. Her cheekbones were more pronounced now than when they were together and her large brown eyes no longer held the warmth and humour for him they once had. But the graceful slope of her nose that he would gently flick while teasing her was still the same.

Recalling their brief time together brought a hollowness to his chest. It was best if he left now. There was no telling if Miss Fellsworth would even locate this room anyway and, if she did, they wouldn't exactly be alone.

'I will leave you to your reading,' he said, executing a shallow bow before turning towards the door.

'What shall I tell your friend, should she arrive looking for you?' she called out after him in an overly sweet tone.

Monty paused, and pressed his lips together. She was enjoying baiting him. He turned back around and caught the challenging arch of her brow.

'Tell her you refused to leave, so I did.'

That superior expression of hers fell and she crossed her arms. It was apparent she was holding herself back from saying something else. He was not looking forward to seeing Juliet at his brother Gabriel's home in Kent in a little over a fortnight. Spending this Christmas with her was going to be torture.

When he reached the door, he turned the handle and gave it a furious tug. The door wouldn't move.

Once more he turned the handle and pulled. Still, the door wouldn't budge. Monty was so in-

tent on getting out that he didn't hear Juliet's footsteps behind him.

'You said you were leaving.'

'I'm trying. The door is stuck.'

'Stuck? What do you mean it's stuck?'

'Stuck means it won't open.'

She nudged him aside with her shoulder. 'Let
me try.' As if her tall but delicate frame would
somehow be able to move the large piece of oak
he hadn't been able to, she pulled on the handle
with what appeared to be all her might.

It still wouldn't open.

'Did you lock us in?' she asked as if he were
a child.

'No, I didn't lock us in. There was no key in
the lock and, since the handle is turning, it must
be the door hinge that is stuck.

She closed her eyes and rubbed her brow.
'What do we do now? We are too high up to climb
out of one of the windows.'

'I can make the jump,' he replied with confidence.

'Well, I doubt I can and if I could, how would I
explain the state of my gown after landing in the
snow? There is just enough of it on the ground to
dampen the hem.' She gestured to her white gown
with embroidered holly running along the bottom.

'I'll go. At least we will not be found together.'

'It is just like you to leave me,' she said, crossing her arms again. 'How am I to get out?'

'Does anyone know you're here?'

'Lizzy said she'd get me when Aunt Clara was ready to leave.'

'Then your problem is solved. Just sit tight until your sister comes looking for you.'

'I doubt she will be able to get that door open.' Her expression fell as she looked towards the blasted piece of oak.

'But I'm certain she will be able to find someone in the household who will,' he replied, trying to offer her some comfort.

He was trapped all alone with Lady Juliet Sommersby. All of his senses were attuned to her and that hum that ran through his body when she was close to him was still there, even after all these years. This wasn't good. He needed to get away. Stalking across the room to the window seat that she had just vacated, he pushed up on the window sash. It didn't move and appeared to be frozen shut. He rapped gently with the side of his fist to break the ice but it did no good.

Juliet had gone to the other window and apparently that one was frozen as well. He came to her side and tried his luck with the sash. When it wouldn't move, Monty let out an exasperated breath. 'It's no use. We're stuck in here…together.'

For one week, four years ago, Juliet had looked forward to the few times she had been able to sneak away to spend time alone with Lord Montague Pearce. Now, she was considering breaking a window to escape being confined with him.

'We could—'

'The panes are too small, Juliet. Even if we managed to break the glass without calling attention to the room, I'd never fit through. It's not an option.'

'How did you know what I was thinking?'

'Are you going to deny that you were considering breaking a windowpane? I could see the intention in your eyes.'

This wasn't happening. Juliet hadn't wanted to attend the Ashcrofts' Winter Ball for fear of running into Monty, but she wasn't left with much of a choice when Aunt Clara insisted. Lady Ashcroft was one of her aunt's oldest friends and staying home at her aunt's town house would be considered an insult. But after two hours of sitting with the chaperons, walking the ballroom with her sister Lizzy and dancing with three unobjectionable gentlemen, she had not seen Monty and assumed the evening would continue to be surprisingly enjoyable. Until the moment she turned from the punch table and saw him walk into the dining room in fine spirits, dressed in well-cut black attire that hugged his athletic frame.

The muscles clenched in her chest as she watched him pause by the doorway to greet another gentleman with that infectious smile of his. It was one of the things she remembered that attracted her to him when they were first introduced. The man possessed the kind of smile that lit up his entire face, making his hazel eyes sparkle and anyone near him want to smile as well. But after the way he had betrayed her, she no longer had use for that smile and the man who it belonged to.

It was bad enough she would be forced to be in his presence soon in Kent when their families converged together at Christmas. Did she really need to see him during her short stay in London as well?

When a perfect and petite young woman approached him with flirtatious smiles, Juliet had had enough. She was not about to stand there and watch him flirt with a diamond-encrusted debutante. The moment he left the dining room with the woman on his arm and headed towards the ballroom, she made her escape to the Ashcrofts' library where she had every intention of hiding away for the remainder of the evening, reading—until this wretch had to ruin everything.

Juliet tugged on the door handle again. Still the door didn't move. 'Oh, it's no use. We'll just have to wait for my sister to find us.'

In the moonlight streaming from the window behind her, she could see the colour drain from Monty's face.

'She will not be finding *us*,' he replied, stepping away from her as if she had the plague. 'She will be finding *you*.'

'And where exactly do you think you will be?'

'Hiding. No one is finding us alone together.'

She scanned the room and made a sweeping gesture with her hand. 'There is nowhere to hide. There are no curtains to stand behind, only wooden shutters. You're too big to hide behind any of the chairs. And someone will see you if you place yourself under the table.'

'I'll think of something. If you can get everyone in and out as quickly as possible, they might not even notice me.'

'That is a rather confident assumption I am not willing to make. This is a disaster.'

'I agree,' he said, with a deliberate nod.

Did he have to agree so readily? There once was a time he would have begged her to stay with him for just five more minutes. 'Very well,' she replied, glaring at him. 'I'll station myself here to listen for Lizzy. You think of somewhere you can go in the room so you will not be seen.'

'We could close the shutters. It will make the room dark.'

'And how would I explain reading in such a room?'

His brows wrinkled and he rubbed the back of his neck. 'I hadn't got to that part of the plan yet.' The agitation he was feeling was evident in his tone.

The room was cool since there was no fire to warm the hearth. The coolness had felt good after being in the overly warm rooms with their fires and the crush of the crowd. Now there was a foreboding chill that ran through her body and she rubbed her sleeves to generate some heat. Monty took to pacing the floor, like one of the lions she had seen in the Tower's menagerie.

How long would Aunt Clara want to stay? When they were home in Bath, her aunt would often stay at balls and assemblies until close to two in the morning. It wasn't possible it was anywhere near two right now. She leaned her back against the door. Monty continued to pace twenty feet from her, outlined in the moonlight. He wasn't as lanky as he had been when they first met. His shoulders were broader now, his chest tapered down to a narrow waist and his features had matured into those of a man.

Juliet softly banged the back of her head against the door, punishing herself for finding anything to admire about the man.

The brass handle of the door moved, startling her so much that she jumped away from it. She stared wide-eyed at Monty, who was staring back at her. Quickly he moved to stand beside the hinges of the door and pushed himself against the wall. When the handle jiggled again, he put his finger to his lips.

'It might be Lizzy,' she mouthed silently to him. She was just about to call out to her sister when a soft female voice came through the door.

'Lord Montague, are you in there?'

His eyebrows rose as he silently stared at the door.

'Lord Montague are you in there? Open the door. It's me. I thought the library was the third door, but then I remembered it's this one.'

Juliet silently mimicked the woman who continued to turn the handle, while Monty glared at her.

'I don't understand why you've locked it,' she

continued. 'I'm not in there yet. Can you hear me?' The woman rapped softly against the door.

'She is going to cause a commotion if she keeps this up. You need to do something,' Juliet whispered in a clipped tone.

While they were deliberating what to do, the handle started to move again.

'I said can you hear me?' the soft voice called through the door.

'Say something,' Juliet whispered back sharply, 'before her voice gets any louder than it already is.'

They went to switch places.

'Miss Fellsworth. Is that you?' It was Lizzy's voice now coming through the door.

Juliet looked at Monty as her heart beat faster in panic. His eyes were shifting as if he were in the process of working out how they should proceed.

'Your Grace,' the woman replied. 'I was just… just…'

'Is there a problem with the door?'

'Yes, I was… I was…'

'Let me try. My sister is inside reading.' The handle moved and it was no surprise when the door did not. 'Juliet, can you hear me?'

'Say something,' Monty whispered to Juliet. 'It's better if you respond. Miss Fellsworth will think I never found the library.'

'Lizzy, is that you?' Juliet asked, trying to sound surprised.

'Open the door, Juliet. Why did you lock it?'

'I didn't. The door is stuck. Can you turn the handle and push hard?'

'I can try.' The handle turned, but the door remained closed. Even though her sister was also tall, she was slim and didn't have much force to push against the door. 'I will go and find one of the footmen and see if they can help.'

'Very well. I'll be here. All alone. Not going anywhere.'

Juliet pushed her ear against the door and listened. There was no sound of her sister's retreating footsteps or that of Miss Fellsworth.

'Can you hear anything?' Monty whispered.

'Not a thing, but this door is so thick that I'm not surprised I can't hear noises unless they are from people close to it. What are you going to do when she comes back with a footman?'

'I'll stay here behind the door. Don't open it all the way. Just slip out. I'll wait a while before I leave to give you time to get everyone out of the corridor.'

'What if he wishes to remain to fix it?'

'You're a smart woman. Think of something to discourage him.'

Being called smart by the likes of Lord Montague Pearce should not make her feel good. It shouldn't make her feel anything at all. For four years she had worked on not feeling anything towards him. And yet, those four little words made her shoulders go back instinctively. How she wished Lizzy would hurry.

Juliet turned away from Monty and put her

ear against the door. She felt him come up behind her and a tingling sensation ran down her
spine. How could he still affect her this way after
all this time?

The sound of her sister's muffled voice pulled
her attention away from Monty.

'It appears to be stuck,' she heard Lizzy say. 'Is
there something you can do to open it?'

'I can try, Your Grace,' came a deep-throated
response. 'If you're near the door, step away. I'm
going to try to get you out,' the same voice called
out.

Juliet stepped to one side as Monty moved and
leaned his back against the wall beside the door.
Hopefully they would get it open and she would
be able to leave without anyone noticing he was
there.

The handle turned, followed by a loud 'thud'.
The large heavy door swung open with such force
it smacked into Monty, eliciting a muffled 'oof'.
Unfortunately, his exclamation was loud enough
for the footman, Lizzy, Miss Fellsworth and another woman she did not recognise to look behind
the door and see that Juliet had been alone in a
room with Lord Montague Pearce.

She was ruined.

Chapter Two

Juliet sat in her sister Charlotte's London drawing room, trying to gain back some control of her life. When she had walked into the room a short while ago and spotted Monty sitting there in his well-fitted bottle-green tailcoat and buckskin breeches, she almost turned around and walked out. She had avoided speaking with him yesterday when he called on her. Couldn't she have just a few more days of pretending she didn't have to face the consequences of Sunday night's ball?

'This is unfair,' she protested to Charlotte, who was beside her on the sofa. 'Nothing inappropriate occurred between Lord Montague and myself. It was all an accident. I'm sure Lizzy will attest to that.'

Across from her, Charlotte's husband, Lord Andrew Pearce, who was also Monty's older brother, eyed Juliet over his teacup. 'It doesn't really matter what Lizzy would say. Other people saw you in that room together. They are the reason the two of you must marry.'

Monty appeared to be attempting to wipe a severe headache from his brow as he sat beside his brother. 'I'm surprised Gabriel wasn't the one to have this discussion with us.'

As the Duke of Winterbourne, one would think Monty's oldest brother, Gabriel, would be the one to dictate decorum.

'Since Andrew and I had to get married, we thought it best if we were the ones to discuss this with you,' Charlotte said.

'But the two of you actually did something to warrant that you wed,' Juliet stated, her voice raising an octave for emphasis. 'We've done nothing.'

'Society doesn't see it that way,' Andrew offered.

He was four years older than Monty and bore a striking resemblance to him, with his light brown hair, chiselled features and hazel eyes. Sitting beside each other, there was no denying the two men were brothers, although Juliet preferred Monty's leaner, athletic frame to Andrew's very tall and broad one. Not that she preferred Monty's frame at all any more. He was an average man…more or less. Less, according to her head. More, according to the way the blasted man could still make her heart race when he smiled. Thankfully, he wouldn't be smiling today. Neither one of them wanted to marry the other.

Juliet turned to Charlotte. 'You know I have no wish to marry. Perhaps if I speak with Aunt Clara she may agree to go away with me again. Perhaps this time we could travel to India.'

Monty suddenly got up and stormed towards the hearth, giving them his back. From the stiffness in his shoulders as he faced the fire, it was evident he was regretting going into the Ashcrofts' library two nights ago just as much as she was.

As her thoughts shifted back to escaping to India, she recalled the last time her aunt had saved her by taking her away. Juliet had been living with Lizzy and her husband, the Duke of Skeffington, since their parents, the Earl and Countess of Crawford, had died. When Monty broke her heart, Aunt Clara had taken her to Paris until the Season was over so she wouldn't have to see him again. When they returned, her aunt invited Juliet to live with her in Bath, far away from London and the man standing fifteen feet from her. How could one man invoke so much change in her life?

'Juliet, think rationally,' Charlotte broke into her thoughts. 'You and Aunt Clara were back in Paris only a few months ago. She has responsibilities in Bath. She cannot keep leaving her investments and her homes. Perhaps if you and Montague spent some time together, you'd discover that you suit each other very well.' Charlotte glanced at her husband, who smiled at her with affection in his eyes.

Juliet stopped herself from rolling her eyes. Just because Charlotte and Andrew eventually grew to love each other didn't mean that was the road Juliet's relationship with Monty would take. She had loved him once. That was enough for one lifetime. She wouldn't be foolish enough to fall for him again.

'How would we even explain this?' she tried again, using another tactic. 'I live in Bath and haven't been in London long enough for Lord Montague to court me. Are we just to say we were caught in a compromising situation and had to marry? How is that any better than going our separate ways? Either way we face a scandal.'

'We will say Montague had been courting you outside the eyes of the *ton*. That it was done in secret.'

With those words, Monty turned his head and their eyes met. She knew he was silently questioning if she had told Charlotte about the secret assignations they had once shared. She gave him a slight shake of her head. There had been no reason to tell anyone about the time they had spent together that ended so horribly. To this day, the only people who knew what happened were Aunt Clara and Lizzy...unless Monty had told someone else. Her gaze shifted to Andrew, who was staring into his teacup as if he were searching for another reason why they should wed. Did he know about the past she shared with his brother? When she arched an enquiring brow at Monty, he gave an imperceptible shake of his head in return.

There had to be another way to avoid marrying him.

'For the past six months, Lord Montague and

I have shared this family connection because of your marriage. Certainly that should give us an excuse to be together at the ball,' Juliet pleaded, looking between Charlotte and Andrew for a glimmer of hope.

Charlotte chewed on her lip as she quickly glanced at Andrew. They knew something they weren't saying.

Monty had gone back to staring at the flames, needing to avoid looking at the woman who would rather leave the country than marry him, when the silence in the room made him turn to look at his brother. He could tell Andrew and Charlotte had heard about what had happened after Juliet was quickly ushered out of the ball by her sister and aunt before he even had a chance to speak with her—and it was obvious that Charlotte was struggling with what to say. He would put her out of her misery.

'Word is already out,' he said, addressing Juliet. 'The ballroom was abuzz with it not long after you left. I tried to explain the innocent mistake to my acquaintances, but the damage had already been done.'

'This is all your fault,' she hissed, pointing her finger at him in an unladylike manner. 'If you would have conducted yourself like a gentleman and not a rake, none of this would be happening.'

'Monty...a rake.' Andrew sputtered into his tea with a laugh before Charlotte kicked him with the tip of her slipper.

'It was a momentary lapse of judgement,' Monty countered to Juliet, choosing to take Andrew to task later. 'A lapse that, at this moment, I regret more than you can comprehend. You make it sound as if I am a debaucher of unmarried women.' His voice rose and he knew he was shouting. She still had a habit of eliciting passionate responses from him—even if this time it was in anger.

'It appears you are quite good at *momentary lapses in judgement.* One would think by now you would have outgrown that affliction.' Her voice was becoming just as loud.

'Well, it appears I continue to have the worst taste in women,' he spat out.

'Then perhaps you should join the monastery and leave all of us alone!'

'If only I could, but I have to marry you!'

He wasn't sure at what point during their exchange they had moved closer to each other, but they were now a few feet apart with just Charlotte and Andrew seated between them, eyeing them as if they were watching a game of battledore and shuttlecock.

The contempt in Juliet's eyes made his chest hurt. This was why he hadn't liked looking at her since she had come back into his life after Charlotte and Andrew announced their engagement. He never wanted to see what she really thought of him reflected in her eyes. She had seen a side of him that he wasn't proud of.

'Perhaps the two of you should sit down and have some tea,' Charlotte offered.

'Tea isn't going to fix this, Charlotte,' Juliet said with annoyance in her voice as she looked down at her sister.

'No, but it will make me feel better.'

'Let them have their row, Charlotte,' Andrew said, sitting back on the sofa and draping his arm along the back. 'It will be better for them to speak their minds now. Then they can move past their anger.'

Was he mad? They needed to get married. There was no moving past this anger. It would be there every day for the rest of their lives. Monty had wanted to get married some day, but being forced to marry someone out of obligation was an entirely different matter. If there was one thing Monty despised more than any other, it was having the decisions of how he would lead his life taken away from him. But he knew that neither he nor Juliet had a choice in the matter if they were to lead respectable lives in England.

It was still infuriating!

Tears were pooling in Juliet's eyes, but she raised her chin. Her outward strength was something he had always admired. He hadn't had the opportunity to speak to her since she had been ushered out of the library by her sister as if he was a viper that would bite them both. They needed to be left alone so they could be less guarded in what they said to one another.

He looked down at his brother's wife. 'I need to speak with your sister alone.'

'Oh, heavens,' Charlotte said, standing up. 'Of course you do. We'll be in your brother's study. Take all the time that you need.'

Andrew clasped him on the shoulder in a silent show of support on his way to the door. Monty waited for it to close before he motioned for Juliet to have a seat and remained standing until she had settled into the sofa across from him.

'I tried to call on you yesterday to talk about what happened, but I was informed by a servant that you weren't accepting callers,' he said, trying to gauge how much she hated him.

'If Aunt Clara or Lizzy had known you were visiting the house, I assure you they would have made a point of showing you into the drawing room themselves.'

'Is it possible they found out I called on you and they sent word to Charlotte? Perhaps that is why we were summoned here?'

'It's possible.'

'We do need to talk.'

'Talking will not change what is wrong between us. Long ago I accepted that you and I have no future together. It is not easy for me now to adjust to the possibility that we might.'

'It is more than just a possibility, Juliet. You and I both know we need to marry.'

'But there are people who have been in our situation that have not.'

'And they have suffered in various ways for

that decision. Avoiding the inevitable will only prolong the gossip and speculation. Just last night I was asked if it were true that we were found playing… That is to say in the middle of…'

She was an unmarried woman. He couldn't exactly tell her his friend had asked if it were true that they were found *'playing at St George'.* Would she even know that meant having sex with her on top? Of course she wouldn't. In all likelihood she didn't even know that was something a woman did. And now he wanted to scrub his brain because he was imagining her riding him as her dark hair caressed his chest—and it was a magnificent image.

'You do not have to choose your words carefully with me,' she said, impatiently. 'I understand what you are trying to say.'

The sharpness of her tone was enough to slice the image into fine ribbons.

'Then you know the longer we wait, the worse the tales will become. By tomorrow, half of London could think you are carrying my child.'

'It is not that easy for me, Monty. It is not easy for me to look into your eyes and tell you I will happily be your wife—and that I am so grateful that you are willing to marry me to preserve your honour.'

'I am willing to marry you to save your reputation. I am willing to do this, so you and your aunt do not find yourselves shunned by Society.'

She pushed the palms of her hands against her eyes and rubbed. When she looked at him again, it was through narrow eyes. 'How could I ever have believed I was in love with you? Skeffington did me the biggest service of any guardian in all the land by refusing to allow me to marry you. I was never grateful for having him appointed as my guardian. He was an odious man. But today... right now... I am thanking the stars he was mine.'

Those sharp words pierced his chest in places he hadn't felt in a very long time. The reminder that the old Duke had refused to allow him to wed Juliet, still to this day, was a blow to his pride. He could still recall the way he had demeaned Monty and all the horrible things that he had said about his family.

'There is nothing left for us to discuss, Monty. I do not want to attach myself to you for the rest of my days.'

'You didn't always feel that way.'

'Do you truly think discussing the past will be to your advantage after what you did? When Skeffington denied your request for my hand, I asked you to go to Gretna Green with me and elope. We could have been together years ago, but you kept me waiting in the back garden of Lizzy's house for hours that night and when you finally arrived, you told me you were mistaken. You didn't love me. You've already told me that you don't want to marry me.'

'This isn't about what either of us wants, Juliet. It is about what is required of people in our station. I will not be responsible for your ruin.'

'What about what I want? What about what

I want for my future? I cannot answer you now, Monty. This decision is too monumental. I will send word to you tomorrow. There is no need for us to speak about it further and, frankly, I have no wish to be in your presence any longer than I have to.'

She walked towards the drawing-room door, indicating their discussion had ended and he should leave. When she came to the threshold, she paused and turned to him. 'Know this—whatever I decide is not an indication of how I feel about you. I have never forgiven you for making me believe you loved me and then breaking my heart. And I never will.' With that she left him alone to find his own way out of the house.

He couldn't blame her for feeling that way, but he *had* cared about Juliet. He assumed he always would in some way. He just hadn't cared enough to throw his future away by eloping with her and causing a scandal.

'I knew I would find you here,' Lizzy said to Juliet as she stood in the doorway of the cutting room that was housed in the ground floor of their Aunt Clara's house.

The air was scented with orange and cloves from the pomanders Juliet was making on the table in the small room that led out into the garden behind the London town house. Bunches of dried herbs and flowers hung from the exposed beams of the ceiling, making it appear as if you were standing under the branches of a tree.

Lizzy adjusted her shawl, bringing it tightly around her shoulders, and stepped further into the room. 'Are you not cold?'

Juliet drew her attention away from pulling cloves out of the bottle in her hand. She doubted the chill that ran through her had anything to do with the temperature of the room and more to do with her conversation with Monty that morning. 'This gown is keeping me warm and I have my gloves,' she replied, holding up her hand and showing Lizzy her brown-wool, fingerless gloves. She resumed taking out the cloves one by one from the glass bottle. It would have been easier to dump them on the table and pick them up that way, but she was finding that removing them one at a time was somehow stopping her mind from racing with thoughts about her future.

Out of the corner of her eye she saw Lizzy walk over to the wall and study the aprons that hung on the pegs. Her sister tilted her head this way and then that. If she was going to be this particular about her apron, Juliet couldn't watch. Finally Lizzy settled on a crisp white apron embroidered with white roses along the hem. After hanging up her shawl, she tied the apron strings around her waist and approached Juliet's side. She glanced at what Juliet was doing before she took out an empty bowl from the open shelf under the table and set it in front of her.

'Where would I find the mint?' she asked, looking around.

Juliet pointed to the corner. 'We have quite a bit still hanging.'

A few minutes later, Lizzy returned with a bunch of dried stems, tied with a thin red ribbon. She surveyed the bottles Juliet had placed on the table. 'Have you taken every bottle off the shelves?'

'There are a few left. I took all the ones that I thought might appeal to me.'

'There are over twenty here.'

'I'm feeling indecisive at the moment.'

Lizzy untied the ribbon that held the mint together and slowly unwound it. 'What are you making?' she asked, her voice light and overly casual.

'A pomander for Charlotte for Christmas.' She held up the orange she had been studding with cloves. 'I know how much she likes them.'

The room remained blissfully quiet as Lizzy went about pinching off the dried mint leaves as Juliet continued to jab cloves into the orange—until Lizzy broke the silence.

'I understand Lord Montague was also at Charlotte's house this morning when you were there. What a convenient coincidence.'

'Why do I have a feeling that you found out he called here yesterday and I refused to see him—and that you then sent word to Charlotte to arrange for us to meet there?' She jabbed two more cloves into the orange.

'I don't believe I was the only one to suggest that. I understand Lord Montague's brother, the

Duke of Winterbourne, was also eager for the two of you to have a discussion about what needs to be done.'

'Do not meddle in my affairs, Lizzy. I am a grown woman and your husband is no longer my guardian.'

'Of course he isn't. Skeffington is dead.'

Juliet looked over at her sister, who continued to keep her attention fixed on carefully pinching off the mint leaves.

'Even if he were not, I am two and twenty, old enough to make my own decisions about how I should conduct my life.'

'Oh, you're quite right.'

'I don't need your help.'

'I understand.'

'Then you will respect my wishes and stay out of my affairs?'

'What would ever make you think I will do that?'

'Lizzy!'

'Juliet, you know it is not in my nature to resist offering my assistance when I feel I can be of use.'

'You mean meddling. You cannot resist meddling.'

'I consider it assisting.'

'Well, I do not need your assistance with Lord Montague.'

Lizzy scooped up the pile of mint from the wooden table and dropped it into the white bowl.

Juliet leaned over to see how much she had pinched off. 'What are you making?'

Lizzy's brow furrowed as if she was just now deciding what she would do with all those leaves. 'I'm making something to place on my bedside table. I believe mint is an excellent scent to wake you up in the morning.' She glanced at Juliet through the corner of her eye and then focused on pinching off more leaves. 'What did Lord Montague have to say?'

Juliet inadvertently pushed a clove into the fragrant skin of the orange with a bit more vigour than necessary. 'He did the honourable thing and offered for my hand in marriage.'

'That's wonderful,' Lizzy exclaimed, looking at Juliet with a relieved smile before turning quickly away, scanning the various bunches of herbs hanging above them. 'I imagine that makes you very happy.'

'Happy? Happy! I am not happy. None of this makes me happy.'

'But you had wanted to marry him once.' She leaned over the table and took down a bunch of herbs. 'Now you can have your wish.'

'I wanted to marry him four years ago when I thought he loved me. He proved that he does not. He should have fought for me. He should not have allowed Skeffington to throw him out of the house for asking for my hand.'

There was a slight sputter of noise from Lizzy's side of the table. 'Juliet. Lord Montague was newly out of Cambridge. Skeffington was one of the most powerful men in Britain and had great influence. Do you honestly believe that there was anything Lord Montague could have done to make him change his mind?'

'He should have at least tried. His brother is a duke.'

'Who was frequently at odds against Skeffington in the House of Lords. And from what Skeffington yelled at me when he found me later that day, being the younger brother of the Duke of Winterbourne was part of the reason he refused Lord Montague's request. He recoiled at the idea of our families joining together. You are lucky Aunt Clara took you away when she did. I know he was thinking of marrying you off to one of his old political cronies after Lord Montague asked for your hand.'

Juliet hadn't told Lizzy about her plan to elope with Monty. She knew if she had, Lizzy would have found a way to prevent it to avoid the scandal that would have ensued. And she saw no sense of informing Lizzy of it now. It would just prove how foolish she was when it came to Monty.

'What did you say to Lord Montague when he asked for your hand?'

'I told him it was not something I could give him an answer to so quickly. I told him that I would send him a letter with my answer tomorrow.'

'Why in heavens are you waiting? You were caught in a compromising position. Just say yes.'

'It's not that simple, Lizzy. I don't want to be married to him. I don't love him any more.' She had hated him for so long, she knew there was no room in her heart for love.

'Don't be foolish. You thought you were in love with him once. That is more than most people who marry can say. Things may change and you might discover you are fond of him again.'

'I could never love him again. He lied about being in love with me. How can I trust him?'

'I'm not asking you to trust him with your heart. I'm saying he may be a pleasant enough husband. You need a husband to ensure your financial security. As a duchess, I am privy to all kinds of information and I've never heard a dishonourable thing about him. In fact, he is one of the most sought-after bachelors at Almack's, which is surprising since he is only a third son. But he is the son of a duke so...'

Lizzy had had a horrible marriage to the Duke of Skeffington. She liked to remind everyone of her wealth and status, but Juliet knew that was because her sister had to find something in her life to be proud of. Without identifying that one benefit of being married to a man old enough to be her grandfather, who could verbally reduce a brawny footman to tears, Lizzy might have sunk into a deep state of melancholy—or become one of those women who escaped inside a haze of laudanum. Aunt Clara had often remarked she thought Lizzy was the most resilient of the three Sommersby sisters. Even if that were true, surely someone who had lived with a husband like that could understand Juliet's reluctance to marry Monty.

'Do you still wish to marry again, Lizzy?'

'Me? No. I thought I wanted to. For years I fantasised about being married to Lord Andrew, but he fell in love with Charlotte and I realised I'm not a person who needs the love of a man in my life. Skeffington most certainly did not love me, but he did leave me wealthy which allows me the freedom to never have to marry again.'

'But you are telling me I should marry Lord Montague?'

'Yes, to avoid ruin. Your life will be easier as his wife. You will not be shunned by Society.'

'I'd rather remain in Bath away from Society.'

'But Society travels, as do words. It will not take much time before your neighbours in Bath hear of how you were compromised at the Ashcrofts' ball. What then?'

'I do not care what people think, Lizzy.'

'What about the men you will meet who will think you are agreeable to lewd encounters? If you do not marry Lord Montague, men will assume you are eager to become a mistress. I have seen it happen, Juliet.'

'Lizzy…'

'I will never force you to marry him. My marriage was forced upon me by our father. I had no false ideas Skeffington would fall in love with me. He was looking for a young wife to bear him an heir. When that didn't happen, he had no further use for me. I did not have a marriage based on love. I had thought I would find happiness with Lord Andrew, but I wasn't the woman who captured his heart. It still hurts when I see him with Charlotte. It reminds me of what I will never have. I've come to realise there are some people who find love and there are those of us who do not. If you do not love Lord Montague, you will survive. It does not mean that our lives are empty. We learn to fill it with other things.'

'You mean like shopping?' Juliet smiled as she reached for another clove.

Lizzy bumped her shoulder against Juliet's. 'Never underestimate the euphoria that comes from wearing a beautiful new dress or a lovely pair of new shoes.'

'I will remember that should I find myself with as large an income as yours.' It was nice to smile. It felt like she never would again after leaving the Ashcrofts' ball.

Lizzy scooped up the new leaves she had pinched off and put them in her bowl. 'Charlotte has made enquiries with Lord Andrew about his brother. Lord Montague is independently financially solvent and does not spend an inordinate amount of time at the gaming tables.' She picked up another dried stem. 'Juliet, you need to think about your future. Lord Montague can guarantee security. You will be able to manage your own home and you may even have children.'

It was hard to look at Lizzy. Juliet didn't want to think about her future. She didn't want to think about what it would be like to spend the rest of her life attached to Monty, knowing he did not love her. The scent of cloves and oranges filled her lungs as she took a deep breath.

'You found something about Lord Montague you liked once,' Lizzy continued. 'Marrying a man you like is infinitely better than marrying a man for love. Do not marry for love. Look what it did to Charlotte when Jonathan was killed. Do you want that much pain in your life? I certainly do not. Marry someone who you can have a cordial relationship with. If you can look at him and not be repulsed with the thought of him touching you, you will be better off than most.'

Lizzy painted a bleak picture of marriage. At one time Juliet expected to marry for love, but Lizzy was right. Love was for the fantasies of the young debutantes with their eyes fixed on the stars. The reality of life was much different. Love caused nothing but pain. When Charlotte's first husband, Jonathan, died during the Battle of Waterloo, her sister had been despondent for years. It was only recently, when she met Lord Andrew, that she had come back to life. Who would want to suffer like that over love?

She glanced into Lizzy's bowl and gave it a sniff. 'What did you put in there?' she asked wrinkling her nose.

'Mint.'

'And what else?'

Lizzy gave a slight shrug. 'Whatever that was,' she replied, motioning to the remainder of the bunch of herbs she had taken down.

'Those are bay leaves.'

'Do they not go well together?'

'Smell them.'

'Oh, bother, you know I'm not very good at this. I don't have the nose for making pleasant combinations that you and Aunt Clara do.' Lizzy pushed the bowl away and wiped her hands on her apron. 'Juliet, I know you. I know how you think. You cannot run away every time you have a problem.'

'I realise that.' Her sister knew her well enough to know she was considering asking Aunt Clara to go away with her again.

Lizzy reached below the table and brought up another bowl. 'Do you think Lord Montague is in love with Miss Fellsworth?'

Juliet pushed a clove too far into the orange again. Now they were not all even. 'Oh, Lud!' She tried to pick it out with her nail. Monty's feelings towards Miss Fellsworth were not something she wanted to consider. It was too painful to think that he had found love with someone else while she had not. She didn't want Monty back in her life and she hated the fact that she didn't want him in Miss Fellsworth's life either. Why should he marry for love, if she wasn't able to?

She would marry him—and she would do it just for spite.

Chapter Three

❦

Juliet might be the first woman in all of Kent, and probably all of Britain, who needed to sit in the middle of her wedding for fear of passing out. Unfortunately, that didn't stop the vicar from continuing with the ceremony and she was still marrying the lying Lord Montague Pearce sixteen days after a stuck door sealed their fate.

'Perhaps if you put your head to your knees,' her sister Charlotte whispered in her ear from where she was crouched next to her.

Juliet glared into her sister's green eyes. She knew Charlotte was trying to be helpful, but she would not make more of a spectacle of herself than she already had. When her legs grew weak as the vicar asked her to take her vows, Andrew quickly slid a nearby chair in the ornate drawing room behind her so she could sit. At least one of the men in the room was concerned she might crack her head open on the parquet floor as she eventually lost consciousness.

'A glass of wine?' Charlotte suggested with growing concern.

'I drank some earlier,' Juliet whispered back. 'And he is still next to me. It didn't make him go away.'

The man in question stood a few feet away beside her, his athletic frame stiff with his hands clasped behind his back. The formal black tail-coat and trousers Monty wore had fitted both their moods perfectly. The only thing missing was a black armband to signal the death of any future happiness either of them might have had if it weren't for this wedding. Neither one wanted to be there, so she shouldn't have been surprised at the lack of concern from the man she was about to marry, who kept his gaze fixed on the portrait across from them of the gentleman that hung over the fireplace—but it still stung.

Once more she was reminded that Monty never really cared for her. He certainly didn't love her and had made that quite clear when he refused to run away and elope with her.

There was a time she would have given any-thing to stand beside him with both their families in attendance as they exchanged vows to bond them to each other for the rest of their lives. Now, she wondered if she might welcome her groom dying prematurely from an accident, like tripping on someone's gown at a ball and falling face first into the punch bowl to drown. It would save them both from a lifetime of misery.

She suspected at that very moment he was once

again regretting his attendance at the ball a fortnight ago. At least she knew she was. If she had known that retiring to the library that night to avoid seeing Monty flirt with the beautiful diminutive heiress would have led to this forced marriage, she would have continued to endure the gossip freely given to her about them and the speculation that he was considering offering for Miss Fellsworth's hand.

Even the threat of losing consciousness in the middle of her wedding ceremony had not changed the fact that she still was going to have to marry him. And at Christmas! Not only had he ruined her life, he had the nerve to ruin her favourite holiday, as well!

With one more deep breath, Juliet stood and looked over at Andrew. 'I am feeling better,' she lied, considering her legs still felt a bit like jelly. 'You may take the chair away now.'

'You're certain?' he asked with true concern etched on his brow.

Her request finally drew Monty's attention away from the portrait and he shot his brother a pointed look. 'She said you can take the chair away.'

Ignoring his brother, Andrew looked once more at Juliet as if gauging her stamina before he removed the chair, its delicate construction appearing more so in the hands of his imposing form.

Father Vincent cleared his throat and scanned the prayer book over the wire frame of his glasses. 'Now, where were we?'

'The ring,' a chorus of voices said in unison from their various family members who stood around them in Winter Hall, Montague's ancestral home in Kent that belonged to his brother Gabriel, the Duke of Winterbourne, and his wife, Olivia.

'Yes, yes, of course.' Father Vincent turned to Monty and raised his grey bushy brows expectantly.

What if he truly had wanted to marry Miss Fellsworth? What if they would live the rest of their lives together with him hating her for preventing him from marrying the woman he really loved? What if he planned to continue to meet with Miss Fellsworth in secret even after they were married?

She should not have relinquished the chair!

Monty must have placed the gold band near the first knuckle of his pointer finger when Juliet's world had begun to spin. Now he was rubbing her wedding band with this thumb and appeared hesitant to relinquish it, which she was beginning to think was fine with her. He could keep it if he liked it that much.

'The ring, my lord,' Father Vincent said, gesturing towards it with his prayer book.

Monty looked down at the ring and wondered what would happen if it magically got stuck on his finger. Would they have to go through with the ceremony? If they needed to fetch a new ring, he might have time to escape and put this all behind him.

It was time for her to recite her vows to be his wife. He had dreamed of hearing her say those words once—however, today he would be overjoyed if divine providence struck her mute. There was little luck of that happening. He stared down at the ring on his finger. He had eagerly purchased it at Rundell & Bridge the first time he proposed—even before she had accepted and thrown her arms around him in her excitement. Once they had parted ways, he should have sold it back to the jeweller. It was one of those tasks you know you need to do, but always find excuses not to. Who could have imagined that some day he would be placing it upon her finger?

Monty met the expectant eyes of the vicar before looking at his bride, who probably should still be sitting in the chair that Andrew had taken away. She was as pale as the soft white-muslin gown she was wearing. He prayed he wouldn't be the first man whose bride fainted in the middle of their wedding ceremony. Even though they were standing with just their family around them, he was certain word would somehow get out through the servants or during a night when the vicar imbibed in too much altar wine.

Turning to face Juliet, he removed the ring from his finger and pushed aside his thoughts of it rolling across the drawing-room floor. Suddenly, she shoved her hand behind her back and leaned close to his ear.

'We need to talk,' she whispered to him.

'Now?'

'Yes, now,' she whispered back impatiently. 'Before you put that ring on my finger, there is something we need to discuss.'

He stepped back and shifted his glance between her and the expectant vicar. 'Lady Juliet and I will be but a moment,' he said to the man. Ignoring the questioning looks from those around them, he took Juliet by the hand and led her out into the corridor, closing the door behind him.

She wrapped her arms around her waist and began pacing in front of him. He waited for her to stop, wondering what she could possibly have to say to him now that she couldn't have said to him in the last few days. Finally she stopped in front of him.

'I can't do this to you. I thought I could, but I can't.'

'What are you doing exactly?'

'Marrying you, of course.'

'Of course.' He rubbed his lips to prevent himself from uttering the curse that was about to come out. 'Juliet, you were the one who said in your letter to me that aside from arranging where we would live and your financial settlement, there was nothing we could say to one another that we had not already said. I respected your wishes. And now…now you want to talk?'

'Do you love her?'

It took a moment for his brain to process her question. 'Love who?'

'Miss Fellsworth.'

'Miss Fellsworth? Why do you think I love Miss Fellsworth?'

'There had been talk about the two of you at the ball.'

'Do you always believe the gossip you hear?'

'You were going to meet with her in the library. You were having an assignation with her.'

'For a kiss. I was to meet her that night for a kiss. Just because I wanted to kiss her does not mean I am in love with her.'

She pushed him.

'What was that for?'

'I am well aware you kiss women you do not love. You do not have to remind me of that!'

Would there ever be a time that Juliet would let his actions of the past remain there? Her mere presence was a constant reminder of how much he had hurt her. It wasn't something he was proud of. It wasn't something he had ever wanted to do. While he had fancied himself in love with her for a few days, he had come to realise it was just heated passion for a woman he was very fond of. Nothing more. Logic told him that he barely knew her.

'Juliet, what is it you are trying to say to me that couldn't wait until after we recited our vows?'

'I can't marry you. I won't be responsible for coming between you and Miss Fellsworth. I know Society dictates that we marry, but I won't do it if you are in love with her.' She put her hand on her stomach and seemed to be trying to steady her breathing.

'Do you need to sit? We could find another chair for you,' he said, looking around the corridor.

'I do not need to sit down. I need *you* to go in there and tell the vicar we will not be getting married while *I* go and lie down…in my room… if I can find it in this massive house your family calls a cottage.'

Rubbing her brow, she turned to leave him, but he pulled her back gently by the arm. 'I am not in love with Miss Fellsworth,' he said in a reassuring tone.

Her amber-coloured eyes searched his. It was evident when she realised that he was telling her the truth because her expression softened. 'Are you certain you have no wish to marry Miss Fellsworth?'

'I'm certain.'

They stared at one another, both unsure what to do next. They were alone in the corridor, standing close enough to one another that he could smell her faint lavender scent. He had always wanted to get her into bed to find out if that scent originated from her skin or her clothes.

Thinking of her in bed caused his gaze to drop to her lips and he remembered that time he had kissed her…the only time.

They had crept away at the Tinsleys' party to meet in the walled garden. That entire day he'd had a strong yearning to touch her, to feel her skin and breathe her in. Propriety kept them apart. He had managed to brush his hand against hers while they stood beside one another and listened to Lady Humphrey discuss the benefits of spending time in the country with the cleaner air, when he let his fingers gently caress hers which were hidden in the folds of her cerulean-blue dress. That one small touch was enough to inflame his entire body and he was able to quietly convince her to meet him in the walled garden one hour later.

No other kiss had compared to the one they shared that day. And he had made it his quest to kiss as many women as it took to find someone who could give him that same experience. Not one of those other kisses ever came close.

Just as he considered kissing her once more, she took a step back. The rise and fall of her chest let him know she had felt that pull that had always been between them, as well. She knew he had wanted to kiss her and, for the briefest of moments, he thought she might have wanted him to.

'I still do not like you or forgive you for what you did.' She crossed her arms and narrowed her eyes.

'I know.'

'Oh, very well, come along, Monty, if we have to get married, we might as well do it now.'

There was a time that he thought the beautiful creature before him, in the white-muslin gown with the blue-satin ribbon under her breasts, was the most romantic person he knew.

He didn't think that any more.

* * *

When they returned to the drawing room, Juliet repeated her vows clearly and without hesitation. Within minutes after that they were married and Monty knew his life would never be the same.

His brothers shook his hand. His mother kissed his cheek. And his new wife accepted hugs from her two sisters, her aunt and Olivia. His nephew Nicholas ran from the room as only a six-year-old could, Monty wishing he could do the same.

How was he to spend the rest of his life with a woman who did not like him? How could he think of consummating this marriage knowing how she felt about him?

'I don't believe I've ever seen a bride look so ill,' Gabriel said in a low voice, as the three brothers watched the women chatting together on the other side of the room.

'Who could blame her?' Andrew joined in. 'She is being forced to marry him.' His lips rose into a teasing smile.

Gabriel tilted his head and Monty knew he was watching Juliet. 'If you had to be forced to wed, Lady Juliet is an ideal choice, if you want my opinion.'

Monty hadn't asked for his opinion years ago when he planned to marry Juliet. As a young man, and the youngest brother, he was eager to exert his independence away from his family, especially Gabriel, who as a duke was accustomed to having people do what he wanted. Monty had come to believe he had proposed to Juliet because part of him wanted to prove he would lead the life he wanted, not the one his family thought he should. But it wasn't until he had become partners with John Temple in his shipping company that he truly felt independent from his family's influence.

'If you'd like any pointers on wedding-night etiquette, I'm sure Gabriel and I can offer you some suggestions,' Andrew said, openly amused with his own statement.

Monty could usually take his brothers' playful teasing. Not today.

'Excuse me. I believe I need to escort my wife into breakfast.' Not waiting for a response, he walked towards Juliet.

She took the arm he offered without a word and allowed him to lead her into the formal dining room where they spent the next two hours surrounded by their family and barely spoke to one another.

Chapter Four

Monty sat in the drawing room where he had pledged himself to Juliet before God that morning and nursed a glass of brandy. The house was dark and quiet now. From what he could tell, everyone had gone to bed, which was where he should have been—with his wife. But he just couldn't bring himself to enter their bedchamber.

He'd had sex with a few women in his life. Each one was very willing to be a participant in the act. Juliet, he was certain, would not be. He would never force himself on her. Just the idea of going upstairs and taking her, knowing how she felt about him, was making his stomach turn. It didn't matter if it was their wedding night. He couldn't do it.

But if they didn't have sex now, would they ever?

He needed the brandy to help him alleviate some of his agitation and try to forget what a mess his life had become in such a short time. At this late hour, it was a strong possibility he was going to spend the entire night in this wingback chair near the warm fire burning in the hearth. The sun had gone down hours ago and Monty was content to sit there with just the dim light from the fireplace casting flickering shadows about the room. It was less complicated down here than it was upstairs with his wife.

Swirling the brandy in his glass, he watched the light play through the amber liquid that matched the colour of Juliet's eyes. He recalled the sadness he saw in them as he slid the wedding band upon her finger. He had put that sadness there with his indiscretion and quest to find another kiss that would affect him the way her kiss had.

What would today have felt like if they had never met four years earlier at the Earl of Haslington's ball when her thick brown hair and fine features caught his eye? What if he had never felt that jolt of excitement course through his body when he touched her gloved hand as they went to dance for the first time together? And what if they hadn't been so drawn to one another that they found ways to sneak off together at the various entertainments that week so they could enjoy each other's company without the eyes of the *ton* on them?

Would Juliet still be sad about being forced to marry him now? Would Monty have pursued her had his brother introduced them six months ago when Andrew became engaged to Charlotte?

He was a different man now from the one who had impulsively proposed to Juliet after knowing her for only a week. Since that time, he had established a life for himself away from his family's work protecting the Crown and found success with his investments in shipping. Now he no longer needed his family's financial assistance and could support himself, a wife and some children.

And more importantly, Juliet no longer had a guardian who needed to approve of the man she married. She was able to make that decision for herself.

If only time had been on their side.

Monty's thoughts were interrupted by the sound of the door opening. He peered around the edge of the high-backed chair and found Andrew standing in the door in his banyan with a startled expression.

'What are you doing here?' his brother asked, stepping into the room.

'I could ask the same of you. Were you planning on meeting someone? I do not think Charlotte would approve.'

'Don't be daft. Charlotte left her book in here earlier and she's having trouble sleeping. She thought a bit of reading might help and here I am.' He shoved his hands in his pockets. 'I'm surprised to see you. I saw the light under the door and wondered who was in here.'

'Well, now you know. Now you can rest easy with the knowledge that no thief was trying to steal the Meissen from the mantel.' Monty turned back around and returned to studying his glass.

The sound of Andrew's muffled footsteps retreated and the click of the door closing was a welcome relief. He just wanted to be left in peace. However, the peace did not last long because, a short while later, Andrew returned with another glass and a bottle of brandy. He flopped into the wingback chair next to Monty.

'There is no need to stay with me,' Monty offered not too subtly. 'You are free to find your wife's book and return it to her.'

'Thank you for your permission to do so.'

Monty took a sip of his brandy and the warm liquid slid down his throat. 'I am simply saying I prefer to be alone at the moment.'

'Wedding nights can be difficult, especially when you are not very well acquainted with your bride.' Andrew poured himself a glass of brandy, lowered the bottle to the floor beside his chair and stretched out his legs, crossing his ankles. 'Would you like to talk about anything?'

'No, I believe I can manage my wedding night. I know what should occur. I'm aware how it's done.'

Andrew dropped his head back. 'Well, I should damned well hope so. I assume you and Juliet have already accomplished that.' He looked over at Monty. 'Why are you down here and not upstairs, asleep in your wife's arms at this late hour?'

'Like your wife, I find I can't sleep.' It was easier saying that than confessing that Juliet despised him so much he couldn't bring himself to touch her.

But even though he tried to hide it, his brother

was always too perceptive. 'You need to fix whatever is broken between you and your wife. Do not make the mistakes Gabriel and I have with our wives and let things fester too long. The longer the strife goes on, the harder it becomes to try and sort out the problem.'

'What makes you think Juliet and I have a problem?'

'You are down here drinking alone on your wedding night and not asleep beside your bride.' He arched a superior brow. 'And I noticed you barely spoke to each other today.'

'We don't have that much in common.' Which was the furthest thing from the truth or at least that had been the case years ago, but perhaps they no longer did have anything in common. He didn't know and felt his brow wrinkle.

Andrew took a sip from his glass. 'You don't need to have much in common to be able to be cordial with one another and discuss things over a meal—which did not occur during breakfast. I know there is discord between the two of you. I noticed it the night I introduced you. I don't know what it is and I do not know what has caused it, but you need to find a way to address it.'

After all this time, Monty still couldn't talk about the humiliating things Skeffington had said to him and how the man had refused to allow him to marry Juliet. And his sense of honour and protectiveness over Juliet would always prevent him from telling anyone that she had then proposed that they run away and elope.

'Juliet and I just don't like each other. Haven't you ever met someone and, for some unknown reason, you just don't like them?'

Andrew did not look convinced. 'May I make a suggestion?'

'Please go right ahead. I know I will not be able to stop you.' Monty took a fortifying sip.

'Tomorrow…rather, today is Christmas Eve. We each have our own responsibilities to provide decorations for this house. After the sun has come up and you've eaten your lion's share of breakfast you will leave, as you always do, to gather the mistletoe. This year take Juliet with you.'

'Why? Why, after I told you we just don't like each other, would you suggest I take her with me?'

'Because the two of you need time alone… away from everyone in this house. You and your wife might find the physical exertion of traipsing through the crisp cold air does wonders for airing grievances. Use the time wisely.'

'You have no notion what it takes to gather mistletoe in this park. It doesn't grow near the house. We will be gone for a long time.'

'All the better. Just advise Juliet to take a scarf and have an enjoyable time,' Andrew said while not even trying to hide his smile in his glass.

'An enjoyable time? That will not be enjoyable. Dragging Juliet through the woods is not how I want to spend my Christmas Eve.'

'Here's another suggestion. Don't drag her. And you should have thought of the consequences before you arranged your tryst with Miss Fellsworth.'

'*You* are going to lecture me on propriety? You must be joking. I am a grown man, not a young boy. I don't need you lecturing me on how I should conduct my life or manage my wife.'

As the youngest brother, Monty always felt the need to prove he was just as smart and capable as his older brothers. Setting himself apart and proving he could succeed without their help was something he had always felt he needed to do since a very young age. He always wanted to feel like their equal, not like the little brother who just followed them around.

Andrew took a long drink. It was obvious to Monty he was trying to choose his words carefully.

'You are right. I am not one to be lecturing you on propriety, however, I hadn't realised my intention of having a discussion had turned into a lecture. Please forgive me.' Those last three words were delivered with more sarcasm than true regret. 'I was merely making a suggestion that spending more time with Juliet now may help ease the two of you into a better relationship in the future.'

Monty let out a long breath and rubbed his hands over his eyes. 'I know you mean well.'

'I'm only trying to help you by showing you the mistakes I have made. For as much as we antagonise each other, Monty, you are my brother and I want you to be happy.'

A look passed between them. It was a look that said all the things Andrew had not.

'I don't think a walk in the woods will change anything, Andrew. You don't know Juliet.'

'And you suddenly do? Juliet is a lovely, sensible young woman.'

Juliet had no idea how long she had been lying in bed waiting for Monty, but if he didn't arrive in the next few minutes, she was getting dressed, going down to the barn and stealing one of the Duke's horses to ride back to London. It didn't matter that it was the middle of the night. And it didn't matter that she had no way of knowing which road led north. She would figure it out or she'd spend Christmas walking along the beach in some seaside town that was far enough away from her thoughtless husband, who had left her alone on their wedding night.

If only she wasn't so tired...

She blinked a few times and tried to see the time. The mantel clock was too far away to see in the dim light of the fire no matter how much she squinted. It had to be after midnight.

Their families had spent the evening after dinner in quiet pursuits in the drawing room. Monty's mother had been nothing but kind towards her since she arrived yesterday. She seemed to sense how nervous Juliet was about tonight and suggested a game of whist to keep her occupied until it was time to retire for the night. Playing cards helped to keep her mind off of the idea of allowing Monty to kiss and touch her later that night. Just the thought of it made her pulse pound and she didn't want to think too much if that sensation was from anticipation or terror.

During dinner he had sat beside her and they had barely said two words to one other. Yet it was impossible to ignore him because she could feel the warmth from his thigh, where it rested close beside hers under the table. That heat sent an unexpected tingly sensation up and down her leg. Silently, she chided herself for having any sort of pleasant physical reaction to his mere presence.

Juliet plumped her pillow and snuggled further under the warm blankets. Even with the fire burning there was a slight cool breeze that blew across her exposed face, neck and hands. Under the blankets she felt warm and secure, which was a surprise, considering it was his bed that she was lying in.

When their various family members began to leave the drawing room and turn in for the night, Monty had escorted her up to this room. It appeared to everyone that they'd be spending the rest of the night together. Except after he opened the door, he told her there was no reason for them to hurry things along and he would join her later. That was hours ago. He had once told her all he could think about was kissing her. Apparently, he didn't feel that way any longer.

Should she go and try to find him? Where would she even look? What would she say?

The bed was so cosy that it was quickly becoming impossible to toss the covers aside and leave. Right now, she just wanted to close her eyes and sleep. The faint scent of cinnamon that seemed to follow him was on the soft white pillowcases. She closed her eyes and buried her face in the squishy cotton as she took a slow steadying breath. This really was a perfect bed for taking long winter naps.

The call of a good night's sleep was too strong and she didn't hear when Monty walked in the room ten minutes later. When he softly called her name from beside the bed, it was as if she were hearing him in her dream. And when the bed dipped with his weight as he slid beside her, the only response she gave was to instinctively roll closer to his warmth.

Chapter Five

When Juliet woke up the next morning, rays of sunshine streamed into the room from the two casement windows, brightening the deep red walls and bed hangings. There was an indent in the pillow beside her that let her know at some point during the night Monty had slept in their bed. She had no memory of him coming in to the room and no recollection of him settling in next to her.

She sat up in bed and rubbed her eyes. Looking around the silent room, she saw that she was alone. The fire had been recently stoked and the room was warm, even though frost had formed overnight on the windows. A note addressed to her was propped against the oil lamp on her bedside table. Breaking the seal, she scanned the short missive from Monty. He informed her that he had not wanted to wake her from her deep sleep last night when he came to bed. The past sixteen days had been difficult for both of them and they needed a good night's rest. He closed the note asking if she would join him in the entrance hall of the house at eleven that morning and advised her to dress warmly. Juliet's curiosity had been piqued and she suspected he had purposely crafted the note to do that.

At eleven o'clock, she sat waiting for him on the wooden bench at the foot of the stone staircase of the entrance hall, wearing her scarlet-wool pelisse trimmed with white fur and her matching hat. Someone must have recently opened the front door because the faint scent of fresh air on a cold winter's day filled the large space.

Monty's approaching footsteps echoed in the hall from the back of the house. He cut a dashing figure with his open navy-blue Garrick coat billowing behind him as he came into view. Juliet's gaze travelled from his polished black Hessians, up his buckskin breeches that showed off his muscular thighs, to the front of his brown tailcoat and landed on the bemused expression on his handsome face. She hoped that expression wasn't an indication he'd caught her admiring his form.

'I wasn't sure if you would be here,' he called out, tossing a linen drawstring bag over his shoulder as he walked.

'I'm curious about what you have planned and why I needed to dress warmly. That is the only reason I am here.'

He placed his hat on his head and adjusted the brim. 'You will see, all in good time.' He glanced down at her matching fur-trimmed boots and gave an approving nod. 'Do you have gloves?'

She picked up her pair of black gloves and dangled them from her hand. 'Are we going on a sleigh ride?'

'No, where we are going a sleigh is not fit to travel.'

He turned towards the door and she hurried after him.

'Why do you have that bag with you? Where are we going?'

Pausing at the door, he turned to her. 'We are going on an adventure.' He leaned closer and dropped his voice to a whisper. 'I remember how much you liked them.'

Memories of sneaking away at the Tinsleys' to meet Monty in the walled herb garden came flooding back to her. Her heartbeat quickened as she recalled the excitement of possibly getting caught with him and of their kiss. All these years later, she could still recall vividly the feel of his lips and the way it awoke a desire in her that she had never experienced before. He had told her that nothing compared to kissing her. He said that he would always remember it.

He had been lying. He must have been since it was apparent he wasn't eager to kiss or touch her now. Lying was what Monty did. She needed to remember that to protect her heart from being hurt by him again.

'I do like adventures—however, I prefer to

know what is planned, in advance,' she stated, not wanting to show her excitement.

He buttoned up his coat and indicated with a nod of his head that she should do the same. 'We are on a quest for mistletoe.'

'Mistletoe? Why do we need mistletoe?'

As they stepped out in to the cold air, a brisk breeze hit her warm cheeks and she pulled up her soft fur collar. There was a dusting of snow on the ground and their boots crunched into the frozen covering as they walked.

'You never did answer me,' she said, trailing after him as he strode down the drive towards the side of the house. 'Why the sudden need for mistletoe?'

He looked at her with both brows raised. 'Because it's Christmas Eve.'

That told her nothing and she almost felt foolish asking again. 'What does Christmas Eve have to do with mistletoe?'

The ground was hard beneath her boots, making it easy to keep up with his long strides as they walked across the snow-covered lawn towards a thick cluster of trees, waving their bare branches in the wind.

'Haven't you ever hung mistletoe in your house on Christmas Eve?' he asked.

When she shook her head, he made a *tsk*ing sound. 'We've always spent Christmas Eve gathering the necessary bits of nature to decorate the house. It's been done here for centuries. Everyone in my family has a specific task. Gabriel goes out with his steward and supervises the hauling in of the Yule log. Andrew cuts the greens that decorate the frames and fireplace mantels, and I am responsible for gathering mistletoe to hang in the house. For years after my father died, I believe the only ones who enjoyed having mistletoe in the house were the servants, but that never deterred us from hanging it. Now, this year, I'm certain Gabriel and Andrew will take full advantage of it.' He looked at her with an arched brow. 'You do know what happens if you stand under a sprig of mistletoe, don't you?'

'Of course I know about kissing under the mistletoe. Simply because it never hung in my house, doesn't mean I haven't been to house parties or visited friends around Christmas.' The fact that Monty hadn't included them in the short list of people who would be enjoying the mistletoe this year stung, even though his statement was true. He wasn't interested in kissing her. Or doing anything else with her for that matter.

'You've kissed other gentlemen?' he asked in a casual tone, keeping his attention on the path in front of them.

The last thing she wanted to talk to Monty about was the two kisses she'd had that didn't come close to stirring the feelings inside her that Monty's had. His kiss had made the earth drop away and time stand still. 'I don't see why I should tell you if I've kissed other men.'

'I'm your husband.'

'Not by choice.'

'But I still am.' He gave her a satisfied smile.

'I don't believe it is wise for us to discuss kissing other people.'

For Juliet, no other kiss would compare to his. Obviously with the tryst he had planned to have with Miss Fellsworth and with the other women he had been mentioned with over the years, he did not feel the same. How could he stir such longing in her, when he didn't feel the same?

He stopped suddenly, but she decided to keep moving without him. 'How many men *have* you kissed, Juliet?'

'Not nearly as many as the number of women you have,' she said over her shoulder.

'How do you know how many women I've kissed?'

'I'm speculating.'

Within minutes he was by her side, with his hand shoved into his pocket. The wind howled through the trees, making the branches sway above them. It was not an ideal day to be out in the park. She was just grateful she had dressed as warmly as she had.

'How much further do we have to go until you find the mistletoe?' she asked.

'Another half-mile or so.'

'Half a mile? Can't you simply cut some closer to the house?'

'No, it only grows in one place in the park.'

Some adventure this was becoming.

It was cold. The grey clouds were thick and the scent of an impending snowstorm was in the air.

And they were just in search of some greenery to decorate the house. Why did she ever agree to accompany him? She could be back at the house right now, drinking warm tea and visiting with Charlotte, or taking a nap in his very cosy bed. Instead she was traipsing through the woods with a man who had made a polite excuse not to bed her on their wedding night.

They walked in silence side by side for quite a long time, as the path curved a number of times, before stopping at a lake with patches of ice close to the shoreline. It was large enough to contain an island in the centre, which appeared dense with trees and shrubs.

When Monty walked off towards a weeping willow tree that stood close to the water, Juliet assumed it was to gather mistletoe. Instead, he dragged a rowboat out from under the thick curtain of branches covered in snow to the water's edge.

'What are you doing?' She knew he could hear the excitement in her voice that was stirred by the prospect of taking a boat out in the winter.

His infectious grin still had the power to make her heart stop.

'I did tell you we were going on an adventure, did I not?'

'Yes, but you didn't tell me that adventure would be out at sea.'

'Would you prefer not to travel to distant shores with me? I do see some ice on the lake. Perhaps it is too treacherous a journey for a delicate flower such as yourself.' His left eyebrow lifted a fraction.

'Roses have thorns, Monty. It's best to remember that.'

He let out a full masculine laugh as he gestured to the boat with his gloved hand. 'Will you join me on this adventure?'

She had always imagined being married to him would not be dull. 'Did you bring me along so I could row for you?' she asked, approaching his side.

'You don't know where we are going. I do. Therefore, it's probably best if I am the one to row.' He gave a gentle flick to her nose with his finger. It was a gesture he used to do with her when he was in a particularly playful mood and it made her heart jump.

He helped her into the boat and when his gloved hand held hers, a tingling heat ran from the palm of his hand, up her arm and across her breasts. She could see her breath and yet that small touch brought such heat. To her disappointment, he dropped her hand quickly and looked completely unaffected by it.

The boat rocked as she shifted into a comfortable position on the bench. 'It doesn't seem very stable.'

'It is. I assure you, we're safe.' He pushed the boat into the water and climbed in.

'Why don't you have a servant get the mistletoe?' she asked, as snowflakes began to drift down from the thick grey clouds.

He looked appalled at her suggestion. 'I could never do that. The location is a secret. I am the only one who knows where it grows.'

'Surely you jest.'

'It's true. The location has been kept a secret for generations in the Pearce family and is passed down from youngest son to youngest son.'

The rhythmic movements of his strong arms as he rowed them through the lake, and the lapping of the water against the boat, was relaxing and Juliet felt her muscles soften. 'If it's such a secret, why bring me along?'

'Because last night I decided that if we don't begin to share things with each other and try to create new and better memories, we will never be able to put the past behind us.'

Juliet didn't know if she was capable of forgetting the heartache she had experienced when he told her he realised he wasn't really in love with her. She had believed his feelings were just as strong and genuine as hers. To find out he didn't care about her with the same depth of emotion had been devastating. She understood what he was trying to do. She just didn't know if it was possible.

It began to snow harder and large flakes were settling inside the boat. As they approached the island, Monty seemed to know instinctively when to turn the boat around and where there was a break in the shrubs and trees. The boat glided to a stop in what appeared to be an inch of water covered with a layer of ice.

'I'll help you out,' he said, while using the oars to adjust the boat so it was floating sideways to the shoreline.

'That's not necessary. I can climb out on my own.'

Before he had a chance to respond, she moved her right leg over the side of the boat. It sank into the muddy bottom of the shoreline lower than she expected, tilting her off balance. He moved quickly to stop her from falling, but the boat tipped and they staggered together in four inches of frozen water.

'This is not the adventure I wanted,' she mumbled, trying to move her once-beautiful boots through the silt of the lake without getting them stuck.

Monty was wearing a pair of Hessians, making it easier for him to navigate through the mud since his boots were up to his knees and water wasn't getting inside them, creating a kind of suction with the mud. Holding her hand, he helped pull her out of the water while the snow started to fall much faster now, creating a fine curtain of white.

The cold air was hurting her wet legs and her feet were freezing in her boots. She wrapped her arms tightly around her body in an attempt to stop herself from shivering. 'The water didn't appear that deep from inside the boat.' If she weren't so cold, Juliet was certain her cheeks would be flushed with embarrassment.

He placed his hand on her shoulder and gave a gentle comforting squeeze. 'It's too cold and now you're too wet. I can return for the mistletoe later. I need to get you home so you can warm up.'

'I'll be fine. Just gather the mistletoe quickly,' she replied, rubbing her arms. She didn't like to complain and had no desire to appear weak in front of him.

'Nonsense. You are beginning to shiver. We will go back to the house.'

They turned in unison for the boat—and noticed it had drifted over twenty feet away from them. It now was floating towards the other shoreline, too far for Monty to wade out to.

'You cannot swim to it. Your muscles will surely lock up if that much of you gets submerged in the icy water,' she stated while bouncing slightly on her feet, trying to keep her body moving in the frigid cold.

Even though they were out of the lake, her boots were soaked through with the icy cold water. Instead of keeping her feet warm, the fur inside her boots acted as a sponge and it felt as if they were hardening with ice.

Their only way off the island and back to Gabriel and Olivia's warm home was that boat. No one knew where they were and, even if they did, by the time they realised they were stranded, she would be frozen to death. It was taking considerable effort not to panic.

'What do we do now?' she asked, trying her best not to sound as if she was about to cry as snowflakes clung to her eyelashes.

Monty looked around and then his body went still, as if he were considering some thought that had suddenly popped into his head. 'Come on. I know where we can go.'

Chapter Six

Monty pulled his freezing wife on to the well-worn path that, thankfully, had not become over-grown. The buckskin of his breeches had kept his legs dry and the way he landed, no water had got into his boots. His wife, on the other hand, had boots that were so wet he could hear them squishing when they began walking. The bottom of her pelisse and, he assumed, the gown underneath were drenched and hardening with clumps of snowy ice the further they walked. He needed to get her warm—and fast. He just prayed Laurel Cottage was still standing.

'Where are we going?' she asked, skidding on an ice patch in the path.

The small thatched cottage with large trees arching their bare branches over it came into view. Monty had never been happier to see the small cottage he had played in as a boy.

'You'll be able to warm up inside.'

'Now *this* is a cottage,' she exclaimed. 'Not that

behemoth house your family refers to as such. I just want to take off these boots. I think they're turning to ice around my feet.'

Monty said a silent prayer of thanks that it wasn't locked as he let her inside. The cottage had changed very little from what he remembered. It had one central room with an inglenook on one wall with a wingback chair, a bed was tucked into the corner, and a small square table with four Windsor chairs completed the furnishings. Green curtains now hung on the three small mullioned windows and a new rug was on the floor in front of the empty hearth. It appeared Gabriel must now be taking Monty's nephew Nicholas here in the summer to fish, just like their father had done with his sons.

Juliet sat in the wingback chair, took off her gloves and struggled with untying the lacing of her boots. 'These ribbons have turned to ice.'

There was a large stack of dry logs in the alcove of the inglenook and Monty threw his hat down and immediately went to work arranging them in the hearth. 'I should have a fire going shortly. It will help melt the ice.'

'I don't know if I can wait that long.'

She continued to work on the ribbons while he stuffed some kindling under the logs and reached for the tinderbox. Once the fire was blazing he turned to Juliet, who had just finished removing her boots. He opened them up and placed them by the fire to dry. Snowy chunks of ice had formed along the bottom of her pelisse and Juliet stood to

unbutton it. Monty got one of the Windsor chairs
and put it by the fire so Juliet could drape the scarlet garment over it.

'This fire feels heavenly,' she said, standing
in front of it.

Nothing, absolutely nothing prepared Monty
for the sight of Juliet bending over, raising the
bottom of her dress and sliding her wet stockings off. He stood there, less than ten feet away,
transfixed at the sensual sight of her slowly revealing her shapely bare legs. The poor woman
was freezing. Her delicate feet were bright red
from her cold boots—and yet he couldn't stop
imagining her legs wrapped around him. Monty
scrubbed his hand over his eyes. He was an ass.

Turning away from the tempting sight of his
wife, he shrugged out of his Garrick coat and
tossed it on the floor. 'Are your feet warming up?'

'Not yet, but standing on this dry rug feels
much better than being in those boots.'

'Here, allow me.' He knelt in front of her and
placed his right foot on the floor. Looking up at
her, he motioned for one of her feet.

Juliet raised her skirt and placed her right foot
softly on his knee. The experience was made even
more intimate when she held on to his shoulders
to keep from falling. To first warm his hands,
Monty briskly rubbed them together before running them over her foot to warm it up. Her foot
was just as cold as the snow outside. It was a good
thing this cottage was close to where he had tried
to land the boat. He didn't want to think about

what would have happened if she was forced to wear those wet boots outside in the cold for very much longer.

Once her foot was room temperature, he motioned for her other one. Her skin was so soft and the arch to her foot was high and graceful. Soon rubbing her foot turned to caressing and their eyes met. The grip on her skirt slipped and the cold wet hem hit his wrist.

'You should take off that dress. Your legs will never warm up with that cold wet fabric lying against them.'

She chewed her bottom lip before she replied to his suggestion. 'I will need you to unbutton my dress. I cannot reach the buttons.'

This. Would. Be. Torture.

He nodded and she put her foot down on the rug and gave him her back. The prolonged anticipation of revealing what was underneath her gown was almost unbearable. His breath was stirring some of the strands of her hair and she smelled like lavender mixed with snowy air. Slowly, he undid the buttons. His mouth went dry and he was forced to swallow hard as he pushed the white cambric gown slowly over the curves of her shoulders, grazing his knuckles gently over her smooth skin. She let the dress slide to the floor and stepped out of it, leaving her in a white knee-length chemise and her stays.

How he wished she would turn around.

Even though the fire was still blazing, the room hadn't warmed up enough yet for her to be comfortable in just some thin cotton. He grabbed his Garrick coat and draped it over her shoulders. She looked back at him with a warm gratified smile. How he wanted to wrap her in his arms…

'I'm going to go out and get the mistletoe while you continue to warm yourself by the fire.'

'Mistletoe? We have no way off this island. I think gathering mistletoe should be the least of our concerns.'

'I won't be long and I'll think of a way off.'

'But you'll need your coat.'

She looked as if she was about to take it off, until he shook his head.

'You need it more than I do and I have my tailcoat and hat. They will offer some protection from the elements.'

The cold outside air and snow were just what he needed to cool the desire that was inflaming his body at the sight and feel of Juliet. When she had leaned forward to step out of her dress, her bottom came very close to brushing up against his growing erection. How he had wanted to put his arms on her waist, press his body against hers and let her feel how much he wanted her.

Andrew was right. They needed time away from the house to make peace with each other and find a way to have a real marriage. And the sooner they did that, the better.

Now that they had shelter from the weather, Monty wasn't overly concerned about getting off the island. When they didn't return to the house, Gabriel would eventually send some of

the servants out to find them. The smoke from
the chimney would lead them here. He just had
to make sure there was enough wood to keep the
fire going. In the meantime, he would spend some
time away from his wife and out in the cold to
calm his body down.

Mistletoe grew all over the small island. There
had to be some growing near the cottage. Without
his coat, he didn't want to venture too far away. It
was still bitterly cold and the snow hadn't stopped
coming down. He walked around the stone structure and spied some mistletoe growing on the
oak trees that arched over the cottage. Taking his
knife out of his boot, he sliced away at the vine,
taking enough to hang in a number of the rooms
in Gabriel's house.

As he was making his way around the cottage, he noticed movement to his left and spied
a rabbit dart out of some bushes and run down a
path that led to the other end of the small island.
It made him pause as he recalled what had been
down that path when he was a boy, something he
had forgotten all about, until now.

Pulling up the collar of his coat, he followed
the path as it curved along the island and stopped
at the very small three-sided structure made of
wood and stacked stone. Just like years ago, inside were two rowboats with oars. Now they had
a faster way off the island. They could return to
Gabriel's house where they would spend the rest
of the holiday with their families gathered around

them before they started their life together in their
new house in London.

But Juliet had not been agreeable to talking
to him much before their wedding. It would be
much easier to avoid each other with their family members around.

He looked back at the path he had just walked
down. Over the tops of the trees he could see the
smoke curling from the cottage chimney. Someone would find them, eventually.

The temperature was dropping and he rubbed
his gloved hands together to try to generate some
heat. With a nod of determination, he walked back
to the house and to Juliet.

The fire Monty had made was a piece of
heaven. Now Juliet was finally able to feel the
rug under her feet and wiggle her toes. Her cheeks
were no longer stinging and her lower legs were
not burning from the ice-covered pelisse and
gown that had been wrapped around them.

She buried her nose in the collar of Monty's
coat and filled her lungs with that slight cinnamon scent. She was finding it rather comforting.
And his calm reassurance that he would find a
way for them to get off the island had done much
to alleviate her sense of panic. She knew it was
dangerous to trust him at his word. He had lied
to her before and it had cost her her heart. But if
believing that he knew a way off the island kept
her calm, then she would choose to believe him.

However, she knew not to open her heart to him again. He would only devastate her with his lies.

She couldn't simply wait by the fire for Monty to come back. Staring at the flames was reminding her of the love letters that he had written to her the one week they were together that she had burned. She shoved her arms into the too-long sleeves of his coat and poked around the cottage. There was a bottle of brandy and some glasses in the wooden cabinet near the table, along with extra blankets, a jar of what looked like some sort of jam, a tea caddy and some cups and plates. She took the iron pot that Monty had taken down from where it hung in the inglenook and placed it outside the door to catch snow. If she collected enough, they could melt it and make tea—if there was, in fact, tea in the locked wooden box. She would leave it up to Monty to figure out how to unlock it.

The cottage was warm now and there was no need to wear his coat, so she hung it on a peg by the door, and wrapped one of the blankets around her shoulders. She took the bottle of brandy and glasses with her to the large wingback chair and snuggled in to keep an eye on the fire as she waited for Monty to return.

She didn't have to wait too long before the door opened and the wind brought in snowflakes along with the cold air. He tossed a small bunch of greenery on the floor and hung his hat on another peg by the door. Walking towards her, Monty combed his fingers through his hair and placed his snow-covered tailcoat by the fire to dry. She had never seen him in just his shirtsleeves and waistcoat before and found she rather liked looking at his wide shoulders and his bicep muscles that were visible through the linen of his shirt.

He smiled as he approached her chair and she handed him the blanket she had taken out for him.

'I thought you might need this since you went out without your coat.'

He shook out the blanket and covered up those shoulders and arm muscles. 'What do you have there?' he asked, eyeing the bottle next to her while he leaned his hip against her chair.

'The label says it's brandy.'

'And where did you find that treasure?'

'It was in the cabinet along with some blankets, a tea caddy, a jar of what might be jam and some glasses and cups. Do you think your brother would mind if we opened it?'

'I don't see why we would even need to tell him.' He gave her an irresistibly devastating grin. 'However, given these circumstances I'm sure he would understand.'

Juliet handed him the bottle and he poured two fingers' worth of brandy in both of the glasses she held. She had never tasted brandy before, but if there was a day to try it, that day was today. He put the bottle down beside her chair and took the glass she offered.

'Have you been able to warm up?' he asked, eyeing the blanket she was wrapped up in.

'I have, thank you.'

'You appear remarkably calm for a woman trapped on an island.'

'You're smart. I remember how you were adept at handling difficult situations. Except, of course, when it came to the situation in the Ashcrofts' library. I'm certain you have a way for us to get off this island. I do not trust you with much, but I trust that you are capable and will keep us safe.'

He stood a bit taller and pushed his shoulders back.

'So, what is your plan?' She eyed the amount of brandy in her glass and missed the slight hesitation before he answered her.

'I know a way off the island.' He took a long sip of his drink. 'Eventually someone at the house will notice we have not returned with the mistletoe. Gabriel will send out a search party. Once they spy the smoke from this fire, they will come here to get us.'

'But what if they do not see the smoke? What will we do then?'

'They will come, Juliet. Maybe not until tonight, but they will come. I will tend to the fire until they do.' He walked closer to the hearth and stared at the flames. 'Might I propose we share that chair?' he asked, turning his head to look at her.

He had been outside in the cold and was doing his best to try to make her as comfortable as possible. How could she make him sit on the floor, or on one of those wooden chairs that were around the table?

'If you can find room for yourself on here, I am willing to share it.'

He held his hand out to help her up. 'I need to sit down first, you can go on my lap.'

'I didn't agree to that.' Sitting on his lap would involve too much touching. His arms might go around her. She hated that she still wanted to feel the warmth from his skin and that had nothing to do with how cold it was outside.

'Well, I'm not going to sit on the arm. I'm tired and want to sit in a comfortable chair.' He tilted his chin down and looked at her through his lashes. 'And, body heat is the best way to stay warm.' He was peering at her intently now.

Something intense flared through her. She could relinquish the chair to him and sit somewhere else. As she glanced around the room, her gaze landed on the bed. The chair was definitely the preferable option. 'Oh, very well,' she said, standing up.

He sat down and moved his glass of brandy to the side so she could sit on his lap without spilling it. It was impossible to sit upright and stiff on his lap. The feel of the muscles in his legs and the firmness of his chest had her softening into him. His arm slid around her waist to hold her and tingling sensations ran through her body.

Juliet stared at her brandy a bit dubiously. Monty clinked his glass to hers and took a drink. Juliet swallowed before taking her first sip. The warmth ran along her tongue, down her throat and spread out in her body. It didn't taste as bad as she expected.

'Do you know why we clink glasses?' she asked, taking another sip.

There was a bemused expression on Monty's face as he shook his head.

'Hundreds of years ago, to prove that you weren't trying to poison your guest, you would pour a small amount of your guest's wine into your glass and drink it first. If someone trusted that their host was not trying to poison them, they would clink glasses with their host to let him know that it wasn't necessary to have him drink their wine.'

'Does that mean I trust you, since I clinked my glass to yours?' he asked.

'I don't know. Do you?'

'I do.'

'I wish I could say I trusted you as well, but I don't.'

'What is it you don't trust about me?'

'You lied to me when you said you loved me and that hurt. I can't allow myself to trust you again.'

He looked down and appeared to give her words some thought. 'Juliet. I don't want to lie to you. I won't. We are different people now. Our lives aren't what they were back then. I want to start over with you.'

They were married now. Had that changed anything for him? If she didn't give him a chance to make things right, would she live to regret it years from now?

'I want to believe that you will be true with me. I want to believe that more than you know, but it scares me. What if I put my trust in you and you lie to me again?'

'That won't happen, Juliet. I care too much for you. I always have.'

He cared for her. He didn't love her, but that was more than Lizzy had had with Skeffington. And love could be dangerous. It had almost crushed Charlotte. Caring for someone seemed nice and safe. But she was already feeling something beyond simply caring for him.

'I wish I could believe that,' she said.

'Then believe it.'

He caressed her cheek and tilted her chin. Slowly, almost hesitantly, he leaned in and brushed his lips gently against hers. Her senses reeled and her breath filled his parted lips. The soft kisses that followed had her remembering why she had thought no one's kisses would ever compare to Monty's.

It didn't matter that they were stuck on an island in a tiny cottage with no way off. It didn't matter that they didn't know when they would be rescued. All that mattered was the man who had slid one of his hands to cup the back of her neck and was feasting on her lips as if he loved the taste of them.

She curled her fingers around the curve of his bicep to ground her from floating away. The blanket that had been keeping her warm was no longer necessary and it slipped off her shoulders. She didn't feel self-conscious about sitting on his lap in just her chemise and stays. He was too occupied kissing her to even notice.

The heat that flared in all the places their bodies were touching made her wish that she could feel his bare skin against hers. When his fingertips trailed up her calf, it brought butterflies to her stomach. Feeling emboldened, she placed their glasses on the floor and undid the knot of his cravat while their kisses became more urgent and exploratory. His mouth tasted hot from the brandy as his tongue glided over hers. She had wanted to touch more of his skin and was rewarded when his cravat fell to the floor and she could place her hand through the opening of his soft linen shirt on to his firm male chest. It felt like nothing she had ever touched before, with its light dusting of hair and the outline of the corded muscles over his flat stomach.

He continued to run his fingertips along her leg, edging upwards. Something hard was poking her bottom and she shifted on his lap. A faint guttural groan escaped his lips through the kiss. His hand slid slowly down her neck and made its way to the curve of her breast. Pulling on the laces of her stays, he trailed kisses along her jaw and then in the hollow of her neck. She hadn't thought much of her neck until now. But now Monty had discovered one spot that made her tingle between her legs. She wiggled against his hardness, thinking it would alleviate some of that feeling and it made her feel a bit better.

The heat from his breath scorched her neck as he let out another faint groan. His warm hand cupped her breast as he crushed his lips to hers once more. The gentle message of his hand and the taste of his kisses sent waves of desire flooding through her.

'I want you, Juliet. I want you as a husband wants his wife. But I will not take you unless you want me as well. Do you…want me, that is?'

Her heart jumped and her pulse pounded. She did. In her head she wished she didn't. It would be much easier to guard her heart from him if she didn't. But every part of her was straining for a way to get closer to him. She wanted to feel his skin. She wanted to continue their kisses. And she wanted, in that moment, to be his wife in every way.

'I want this, Monty. I want you.'

He searched her eyes, as if he was gauging the sincerity of her statement. Then he smiled as his lips met hers once more. He picked her up and laid her gently on the rug, their lips still locked together.

Her stays came off easily as did his waistcoat and shirt. She wasn't prepared for her reaction to seeing Monty in just his breeches and boots. The firelight cast his smooth muscular torso in a warm glow that begged her to skim her fingertips along his skin, discovering him through her touch. He lay there on the rug, watching her growing fascination at the feel of him, with his hand caressing her bare arm and the other propped behind his head with his bicep bulging.

In the past when she imagined making love for the first time to her husband, she never thought it would feel this comfortable and natural. She always believed she would be nervous and feel like she wanted to hide. But Monty was not rushing her. He was giving her the time she needed to move things along at her own pace. She leaned over, and kissed his chest, right over his heart.

The feel of Juliet's lips on his chest was making Monty so hard, he had to take a deep breath to steady his need to roll her over and thrust himself inside her. He didn't want to frighten her with the intensity of his desire and watching her find delight in his body was making his heart pound. She was everything he ever wanted for a wife. Why had it taken him this long to realise it?

He had been searching for someone who could kiss him like Juliet. He had been trying to reassure himself that when he refused to elope with her, he was correct in believing he didn't love her. What they had between them was just an intense passion that was heightened by the fact they were sneaking around to spend time together. He could have asked for her hand the day after they met, but they both had enjoyed the element of danger brought on by their clandestine meetings. When he was faced with the choice of eloping with her and creating a scandal, or walking away with his

head held high because no one would have to
know the Duke of Skeffington had rejected his
suit, he convinced himself the depth of his feelings for Juliet were exaggerated due to the excitement of their secret trysts. It wasn't until he
heard she had left London that he realised there
was a hole in his life when she was no longer in it.

He tried over the years to fill that hole. He tried
to find someone else who could make him forget
about the world with the touch of her lips—who
touched something inside him that no one else
had before or since. It wasn't Juliet's kiss that he
had missed. It was her.

It felt as if they were the only two people in
the world and nothing existed outside the cottage.
He could deny it all he wanted, but the truth was
plain to see. He loved her. And he always had.

He removed the pins from her hair as she
trailed kisses along his neck and when he was
through, he cupped her cheeks for a soul-searing
kiss. Her chestnut hair cascaded around them and
brushed against his chest. It was just as he had
imagined…only with a bit more clothing.

He broke the kiss and helped her slip her arms
out of her chemise. Her small firm breasts were
perfect and his hands explored her soft curves.
Laying her down, he lowered his mouth and
sucked on one of the peaks, flicking his tongue
around her nipple. Her fingers were threaded
through his hair and her back was arching up
from the rug. With his other hand, he trailed his
fingers up her thigh until he touched her in her

most intimate place and rubbed his fingers along her skin to make her wet.

'I need you, Juliet. I need you now.'

It wasn't a question, but she gave him a nod anyway. That was the consent he needed to remove his boots and breeches before he lowered his body over hers. The heat from the fire was nothing compared to the hot passion happening between them. When he finally thrust himself inside her, they were sharing one of those kisses that touched his soul. He went slowly at first, so she could get accustomed to the feel of him. But once she wrapped her shapely legs around him, he knew he could increase the rhythm. He caged her in with his arms on either side of her and ground his hips.

The sounds of her soft moans were the most erotic thing he had ever heard and her laboured breathing was brushing against his ear. If Juliet didn't come soon, he was going to have to start silently reciting the names of the monarchs in order to try and calm his body down until she found fulfilment.

How could he have thought there was someone else in the world that could make him feel this way? How had it taken him until now to realise it?

A lock of her hair had fallen down her forehead and along the side of her nose. He brushed it back and placed his lips against her temple. 'I'm so glad you married me,' he whispered.

Her loud guttural moan filled the cottage and her muscles clenched around him. He pushed him-

self up, resting on his palms and thrust harder…
and deeper. And clenching his jaw, he came inside of her.

For the first time in his life, everything felt
perfect.

Chapter Seven

The sun was hanging low in the afternoon sky when Juliet stepped out of the cottage in her newly dried boots and pelisse. She had just left Monty's side where he was still napping on the bed that they hadn't even considered using when they made love on the floor in front of the fire. If that was what making love to Monty was like, it was distinctly possible their relatives would not be seeing them until Twelfth Night.

His consideration in trying to make her relaxed in what could be a very frightening and awkward time for a woman had opened her heart up to him a bit more. If this continued, she knew she'd fall in love with him all over again. She wanted to trust him. What happened between them occurred years ago. His life was different now. He was a responsible man with a successful business. Certainly someone like that would be honourable. Someone like that would be a man of his word.

There was no telling what kind of life they

would have led if they had followed their passions, as she had wanted to do, and run off to elope after knowing each other for only a week. Maybe they needed this time to grow into the people they were meant to become.

She walked down to the shoreline to see if she could spot anyone on the opposite bank who might be looking for them. It would be a shame to have to leave the cosy cottage and be surrounded by their families again, but she would welcome a nice warm meal. Scanning the bank, she heard her stomach growl and saw there was no one there.

How long would it take for anyone to notice they had not returned? By evening, her maid would surely take notice of her absence. Would Gabriel send a search party out in the dark? Would they even be able to see the smoke curling out of the chimney once the sun went down?

She turned towards the house with the idea of crawling back into bed and snuggling up with her warm naked husband, when she took note of his footprints in the snow. There were tracks of his that led to a large old tree with branches hanging over the cottage and there were other tracks that led to a path near the shoreline. Monty had said the mistletoe grew on the trees around the house. Why would he have ventured down the other path?

The snow had stopped and the temperature wasn't as frigid as it had been earlier. The idea of exploring the island was appealing so she followed his footprints into the woods. Exposed tree roots were visible in the trail, covered with freshly fallen snow, and a light wind blew through the trees that lined the path shaking snow from the branches. If she followed his footsteps she would have a way back to the cottage and wouldn't risk getting lost. In the distance she could make out the water of the lake and realised this trail was taking her to another edge of the island. Why would Monty bother to go this way?

When she stepped out of the woods at the end of the trail, she had her answer.

The sight of the rowboats in the small open structure made her want to be sick. He had lied to her again. They could have taken one of the rowboats and been off this island hours ago. Did he find some sick twisted enjoyment in playing her for a fool?

She couldn't go back to the cottage. She couldn't go back to Monty.

As soon as Monty woke up and realised he was alone in the cottage, he threw on his clothes and went in search of Juliet. Outside, the snow had stopped and the air was still and silent.

It was easy to see her footprints and he tracked them to the water's edge where they had come ashore and then saw that she had turned back towards the cottage. He followed her footprints a few more feet until he realised they veered towards the thicket of trees that led to the path he had taken earlier—the path that led to the boats.

A sense of dread gripped him. How would he explain this to her?

He took off after her at a run and by the time he reached the end of the footpath his deep quick breaths were visible through puffs of air. It was obvious from the condition of the snow that she had dragged one of the boats to the water's edge and left. Icy fear for her safety twisted around his heart.

What if her boat had capsized while she was rowing across the lake? She wouldn't have been able to swim to shore in water this cold. And if she had made it to shore she didn't know the grounds and would never find her way back to the house. The sun would be setting soon. She would be out alone in the dark and the freezing night-time temperatures.

As fast as he could, he dragged the other boat to the water's edge and took off after her, trying desperately to remain calm and think clearly. Water lapped hard against the boat as he rowed across the lake, afraid he would find her upturned boat or see an oar float by. The muscles in his arms strained with the speed with which he was cutting through the water.

Scanning the shoreline ahead of him, he prayed he would see her boat. He had to slow down as he approached land and rowed the boat parallel to the shoreline, searching for any open space large enough for her to come ashore. Fear like he had never known welled up in his throat and he periodically called out her name.

A large shrub had grown far enough out into the water that Monty had to manoeuvre around it. Once he did, he felt his body go weak with relief. Floating within a thicket of branches was the boat Juliet must have taken. He rowed quickly with all his might to get his boat on ground and jumped out, not caring about pulling it fully on to shore.

Once more he was grateful for the snow that helped him track her footprints. He needed to get his bearings as to where they were in relation to the house so, before taking off after her, he turned and looked back at the island. If they travelled to his right, they should be able to get to the house. He called out to her, hoping she wasn't too far ahead of him and could hear him.

The wind whistling through the trees was his only response. Taking off at a sprint, he followed her trail. He had no notion if she had left the island fifteen minutes before he did or an hour. He only hoped she wasn't too far ahead of him.

Eventually, he spotted something red through the trees and knew he had found her. His lungs burned with the cold air and he closed his eyes in relief. It would be impossible to steady his erratic pulse even though he now knew she was safe.

Finding his voice, he called out her name and ran towards her.

Juliet was crushed when she discovered Monty had lied to her yet again. She knew leaving the island without him was foolish. She had no idea how to get back to the house, but she couldn't face him. She needed time apart to try to bury the hurt enough that he wouldn't see her cry. And she did cry—during the entire time she rowed across the lake.

When she was able to row the boat on to the shore, she almost sank to her knees in exhaustion and relief. The muscles in her arms were burning, but she couldn't stop. She was determined to find her way back to the house by nightfall. Let Monty wonder what had happened to her.

She hadn't anticipated that it would be so easy to get disorientated in the woods. Now she was alone and lost. If she found her way back to the house this was what her future would hold. For the rest of her life she would always be alone—being married to a man she could not trust and someone she could not share her fears with.

Chills ran through her and she could feel her body tremble. It might have been from the cold—or it might have been from the fear of being out unaccompanied on a cold December day with night approaching. Were there wild animals in these woods? Were they hungry? How would anyone ever find her in this enormous park?

When she heard Monty call her name, after what felt like hours of wandering alone, tears of relief pooled in her eyes. How he had found her, she didn't know. But she thanked heaven he had.

There was no time to react when he charged down the path and threw his arm around her waist, squeezing her so tightly it was almost impossible to breathe. She held on to him, afraid he was just a figment of her imagination. When she realised he was real, she rubbed her face on his shoulder to wipe away the tears.

And then she broke out of his arms and pushed him back.

'Juliet, thank God you are safe.' He took a step towards her.

She took a step back. 'No thanks to you.'

'Me? I wasn't the one who told you to go off on your own in a two-thousand-acre park that you do not know.'

'No, but you lied to me—again. I couldn't stand to be near you, so I left. If you hadn't lied to me about those boats, I wouldn't have felt the need to leave you.'

'I didn't exactly lie about the boats.'

'You didn't tell me about them. It's the same thing! Do you even know how to tell the truth? Why do you even bother to say sweet words to me? Is it because you feel obligated to do that?'

'Sweet words?'

'You told me you were so glad I married you. Was that a lie, too? Did you feel you needed to say something lovely because I agreed to allow you to touch me?'

'No, of course not. I meant that. I am glad you married me. I should have married you years ago.'

'Argh!' She fisted her hands at her sides and it was taking great control not to push him in the snow. 'I wanted to marry you. *You* were the one who said we shouldn't.'

'We weren't ready then. It would have caused

a scandal, but I should have told you we should wait. I shouldn't have walked away and ended it the way I did.'

'You said we couldn't elope because you didn't love me.'

'And because it would have caused a scandal. I told you that, too. And, truth be told, I didn't want the world to know that Skeffington had turned down my request for your hand. He told me I was a worthless third son and because I had no political aspirations I was a parasite on my family. That I was no better than the beggars on the street asking for money. He didn't believe me when I said I loved you. He told me the only reason I was asking for your hand was because I needed your dowry. He said if I married you, everyone would believe that was why I wanted you. No one would believe we were in love. When I told him I didn't care what the *ton* thought, he then told me he would have to be cold in his grave before I could marry you. That he would never consent to it. He would never tie his family to that of the Duke of Winterbourne's.'

'You told me you loved me. You even said it to him. And yet when we had the chance to run off and be together, you couldn't do it. You didn't love me enough and your pride overruled any feelings you had for me.' She took a breath to steady the hurt squeezing her chest. 'I loved you. I was willing to leave everything to be with you.'

'I couldn't do it. I have two brothers that excel in everything they do. All my life I felt as if I was not quite as good as they were. All my life I have felt as if I am in a race to catch up to their accomplishments.' He shoved his hands in his pockets and looked away. 'Some of the things Skeffington said to me were true. Don't you see? He was right. I had no direction. My family wanted me to enter a career I had no interest in. I was living with their disappointment and yet had no notion of what I wanted to do. I had no idea how I would make my way in the world and was living off the money Gabriel gave me. If I had caused a scandal and eloped with you, there was a chance that well of money would have dried up. What would we have done? How would we have survived?'

'Do you think your family would have really turned their back on you?'

'That was a chance I was not willing to take. Not with your welfare.'

'Why didn't you tell me any of this that night?'

'Because I knew it would be easy for you to sway me into leaving with you. I knew how much I wanted you and I thought if I couldn't find a way for us to be secure, then I must not really be in love with you.'

She looked away from the anguish in his eyes. 'You still lied to me about the boats.' It was the one thing she knew was true.

'Because I wanted to spend more time alone with you—away from everyone at the house. I was afraid if you knew about the boats you would want to leave. Ever since the Ashcrofts' ball you have found ways to avoid being with me. I just wanted us to have some time together to find a way to co-exist.'

Juliet was cold, hungry, and mentally and physically exhausted. She was not in a proper state to process any of this. At this very moment, she just wanted to find a way back to the house. 'The sun will be setting soon,' she said, looking up at the sky. 'Do you know your way back to the house from here?'

'That is all you have to say to me?'

'Monty, I cannot discuss any of this with you now. I am cold and tired and just want some food.'

He nodded. 'Of course.' There was a catch in his voice. His breath was visible as he looked around and then up at the sky. 'If we go east, we should make it to the end of the wood and then we will be able to see the house across the Great Lawn.' He scrubbed his hand across his eyes. 'Unfortunately it is too cloudy to see the sun so I cannot determine which way is east.'

The thick old tree next to the one she was leaning on had moss growing on it. She tilted her head to get a better view.

'If I had to guess,' Monty said. 'I think that way is east.' He pointed to his right.

'No. It's this way,' Juliet countered, pointing in the opposite direction.

Monty narrowed his eyes at her. 'Are you simply being contrary?'

'No, here look.' She gestured towards the moss on the tree. 'Moss usually grows on the north side of a tree. Therefore, that is east.'

'How do you know that?'

'I read about it in a book.'

'Of course you did.' He let out a deep breath and seemed to be considering if he should trust her memory. 'Very well. We will follow your direction. The minute you see anything that resembles a well-worn path, let me know. It should lead us to the house.'

They were able to make their way for quite a while following a fairly straight line. The thick clouds were getting darker, indicating the sun was going down. The clouds would block any light from the moon and the idea of being outside in complete darkness was giving her a prickling sensation under her skin. She glanced over at Monty, who was walking beside her with an appearance of confidence that she found reassuring.

He stopped at a break in the shrubbery and glanced in both directions. 'Here, this is the way.'

He held out his hand to her and she took it. Giving it a reassuring squeeze, he smiled at her. She squeezed his hand back.

'How do you know which way to go, Monty?'

'See that X carved into the tree? That tells me we are on a path that will lead us back to the house.'

'But suppose we should have turned in the opposite direction on the path?'

'The markings down to the lake are an L, the markings to the house are an X.'

'Who did that?'

'I did. When I was about ten. I never wanted to get lost in the wood.'

'That was very smart of you.'

Even though he gave her a careless shrug, she could see the pleased look on his face at her comment.

It was getting darker and all around them the trees were looking more and more like shadows.

Juliet tightened her grip on his hand. 'What should we do when we are on the path after the sun sets and we can't see the markings?'

'We won't be.'

'How can you be so sure?'

He stopped walking and pointed ahead of them at the break in the trees. 'Because we have reached the Great Lawn.'

Stepping out of the wood on to the snow-covered expanse of lawn that led to Winter Hall in the distance, Juliet covered her mouth to hold in the sob that was ready to burst from her lips. They had made it. They were safe. Soon she would be inside the warm house and would be able to have something to eat and drink, and lie down. This emotional day would be over.

She stood there, looking out at the bluish-black silhouette of the enormous stately home with its ninety-degree angles, and watched as lights started to flare up in a row in the front and back of the house.

'They are lighting the torches for us. So now we have light to lead us to the door,' he said from beside her.

Their eyes held and she put her arms around him and gave him a hug.

'Thank you for going after me.'

His arms gripped her a bit tighter. 'I will never leave you again.'

Her heart flipped over in her chest. How she wanted to believe him.

'I might not have made it through the wood before nightfall if it weren't for you,' he continued. 'Who would have imagined that all those little facts your brain likes to collect would one day save us.'

He lowered his arms and their eyes met. It was growing darker and it was becoming hard to see his expression.

'Are you ready to rejoin the world?' he asked, shoving his hands in his pockets.

She threaded her arm through his. 'I am now.'

They walked across the Great Lawn in silence. The snow beneath their boots crunched underfoot. With every step they took, they could see lights being lit in many of the windows inside the large house. By the time they made it to the front drive, Juliet felt as if she could collapse in bed and stay there for the next two days.

Monty had paused and turned to her when they were a few feet from the front door. 'This wasn't what I had planned when I invited you out this morning. I thought we would be gone for a few hours and it would give us a chance to create some pleasant memories. I am sorry.'

'For everything?'

He held both her hands in his. 'I don't regret the time we spent together in the cottage. I'll think of our time in front of the fire for many years to come. And when I said I was glad you married me, I was wrong. Glad is too soft a word for what I feel about having been given this second chance with you. I want to be a good husband to you. I want you to be glad you married me.'

He took a tendril of her hair that had come loose from the pins and was blowing across her face, and tucked it over her ear. She leaned up to kiss him, when suddenly the front door opened and Charlotte came running out.

'Oh, thank God. I've been so worried. Come inside. Come inside. You must be freezing.'

She should have been, but instead Juliet was filled with warmth. He hadn't said he loved her, but she understood him better now. She understood why he had left her years ago and had not wanted to run away. He had been the sensible one. She had been too impulsive. Maybe they could start over. After all, he had wanted to be stranded with her on an island.

The inside of Winter Hall was aglow with candlelight and the flames of warm fires danced in the hearths. Sprigs of holly rested above the gilded mirrors and framed portraits. So much had happened today that Juliet had forgotten it was Christmas Eve.

Monty had been so relieved to see Gabriel's house that all he wanted to do was take Juliet in his arms and hold her. When she put her arms around him, his heart flipped in his chest. Maybe there was a chance for them to work through their past and find a way to a happy marriage. Maybe he could find a way to get Juliet to forgive him.

Juliet took his hand and put her head on his shoulder. 'I just love Christmas, Monty. Isn't it beautiful in here?'

It was now that they were touching.

'The family is in the blue drawing room,' Charlotte said, 'and dinner will be served soon. I imagine you both want to take some time to change and attend to your needs.'

Andrew came striding into the entrance hall with a smile on his face. 'There you are. I thought I heard voices.' He eyed Monty up and down and gave him a slight knowing nod.

'I see you've been busy gathering the greenery,' Monty said to his brother.

'I have. Nicholas was a big help. We found if he sat on my shoulders, we could get the sprigs from the top of the holly bushes.' His brother shifted his gaze between Monty and Juliet. 'You've been gone all day.'

'We have.'

'But you don't appear to have any mistletoe.'

The mistletoe he had gathered was still inside Laurel Cottage. He didn't think he could convince Juliet to go back with him to retrieve it any time soon.

'It's a long story.'

'We have time.' Andrew crossed his arms. The

slight cock of his head and raised brow let Monty know his brother was enjoying himself.

'You'll have to wait for another day. My wife and I are tired from our outing. Please inform Olivia we'd like to dine in our rooms tonight, if she would be agreeable.'

'It's Christmas Eve,' Andrew replied, placing his arm around Charlotte.

'We are newly married. I think we could be excused this year from spending the evening with all of you.' He tugged on Juliet's hand and pulled her towards the staircase.

'Did you find the bottle of brandy I left in Laurel Cottage?' Andrew called after them.

Monty froze on the staircase and turned around. 'How did you know—?'

'I went riding this afternoon and saw smoke coming from the area of the lake and remembered the cottage. I left a bottle of brandy there a few months ago when I stayed on the island, fishing with Nicholas.'

Monty continued to walk up the stairs with Juliet. 'Goodnight, Andrew.'

A deep-throated laugh filled the entrance hall. 'Goodnight, Montague. Goodnight, Juliet.'

They hadn't been in their room long when a maid arrived with two cups of wassail for them from Olivia. The smell of apples and cloves always reminded Monty of Christmases spent in this house. He handed a cup to Juliet, who was sitting on their bed in her dressing gown, waiting for the footmen to bring up buckets of hot water for her bath.

Just as he began to raise his glass to his lips, she reached out and clinked her cup against his. He froze.

'Does that mean…?'

'I trust you. I understand why you did not tell me about the boats, even though I wish you had. And I know now why you couldn't elope with me. We were foolish children to think that we could have fallen in love with each other in a week. I know that now.'

'I love you.'

The heavy lashes that had shadowed her cheeks flew up as she stared at him.

'I do,' he continued. 'I don't know if you will believe me. But I do. I think I always have. For the last four years I've been searching for someone who could make me feel the way you did. I have kissed my fair share of ladies, looking for anyone who could make me feel a fraction of what I felt kissing you, but none of them ever did. I thought I could find someone else to take your place. But there is no one else who can. Not for me.'

He took the cup of wassail out of her hand and placed it along with his on the writing desk by the window. When he went back to the bed, he knelt down in front of her and took both her hands in his.

'You are everything I have ever wanted. With you, my heart feels full and I find I have true contentment in my life. I am not asking you to love me. I know that I hurt you and for a long time you hated me for that. What I am asking is for you to please give us another chance to find happiness with each other. That one day…maybe…you will find you love me again.'

Tears were in her eyes. He didn't know if that was good or bad. But when the first tear slid down her cheek and she leaned in and kissed him, he knew it was a good thing.

'My love for you is still there. I tried to convince myself I no longer cared about you, but that was to protect my heart. I don't know if we are able to stop loving someone completely. I think the love is always there in some form. I am happy with you. I think there was a strange part of me that was even happy while we were walking in the wood, because we were doing it together.'

'I feel as if I've been given the finest Christmas gift I could ever ask for,' he said, brushing her tears away gently with his thumb.

'There isn't anything else you might want?' She had lowered her head and was looking at him seductively through her lashes.

'There might be one other thing.'

Laying her back on the bed, he breathed lightly between her parted lips. 'Merry Christmas, my love.'

* * * * *

COMING SOON!

We really hope you enjoyed reading this book. If you're looking for more romance, be sure to head to the shops when new books are available on

Thursday 29th November

MILLS & BOON

Coming next month

A SCANDALOUS WINTER WEDDING
Marguerite Kaye

'Kirstin.'

He blinked, but she was still there, not a ghost from his past but a real woman, flesh and blood and even more beautiful than he remembered.

'Kirstin,' Cameron repeated, his shock apparent in his voice. 'What on earth are you doing here?'

'I wondered if you'd recognise me after all this time. May I come in?'

Her tone was cool. She was not at all surprised to see him. As she stepped past him into the room, and a servant appeared behind her with a tea tray, he realised that *she* must be the woman sent to him by The Procurer. Stunned, Cameron watched in silence as the tea tray was set down, reaching automatically into his pocket to tip the servant as Kirstin busied herself, warming the pot and setting out the cups. He tried to reconcile the dazzling vision before him with Mrs Collins, but the vicar's wife of his imagination had already vanished, never to be seen again.

Still quite dazed, he sat down opposite her. She had opened the tea caddy, was taking a delicate sniff of the leaves, her finely arched brows rising in what seemed to be surprised approval. Her face, framed by her bonnet, was breathtaking in its flawlessness. Alabaster skin.

Blue-black hair. Heavy-lidded eyes that were a smoky, blue-grey. A generous mouth with a full bottom lip, the colour of almost ripe raspberries.

Yet, he remembered, it had not been the perfection of her face which had drawn him to her all those years ago, it had been the intelligence slumbering beneath those heavy lids, the ironic twist to her smile when their eyes met in that crowded carriage, and that air she still exuded, of aloofness, almost haughtiness, that was both intimidating and alluring. He had suspected fire lay beneath that cool exterior, and he hadn't been disappointed.

A vision of that extraordinary night over six years ago flooded his mind. There had been other women since, though none of late, and never another night like that one. He had come to think of it as a half-remembered dream, a fantasy, the product of extreme circumstances that he would never experience again.

Continue reading
A SCANDALOUS WINTER WEDDING
Marguerite Kaye

www.millsandboon.co.uk

LET'S TALK
Romance

For exclusive extracts, competitions
and special offers, find us online:

- facebook.com/millsandboon
- @MillsandBoon
- @MillsandBoonUK

Get in touch on 01413 063232

For all the latest titles coming soon, visit
millsandboon.co.uk/nextmonth